Also by Vivian Conroy

Stationery Shop Mysteries
For Letter or Worse
Last Pen Standing

Cornish Castle Mysteries
Rubies in the Roses
Death Plays a Part

Country Gift Shop Mysteries
Written into the Grave
Grand Prize: Murder!
Dead to Begin With

Lady Alkmene Callender Mysteries
Fatal Masquerade
Deadly Treasures
Diamonds of Death
A Proposal to Die For

Merriweather and Royston Mysteries
Death Comes to Dartmoor
The Butterfly Conspiracy

Murder Will Follow Mysteries
An Exhibition of Murder
Under the Guise of Death
Honeymoon with Death
A Testament to Murder

The Glitter End

A Stationery Shop Mystery

VIVIAN CONROY

Poisoned Pen
PRESS

Published by Poisoned Pen Press, an imprint of Sourcebooks
P.O. Box 4410, Naperville, Illinois 60567-4410
(630) 961-3900
sourcebooks.com

Library of Congress Cataloging-in-Publication Data

Names: Conroy, Vivian, author.
Title: The glitter end : a stationery shop mystery / Vivian Conroy.
Description: Naperville, Illinois : Poisoned Pen Press, [2021] | Series:
    Stationery shop mysteries ; book 3
Identifiers: LCCN 2021003837 (print) | LCCN 2021003838 (ebook) | (paperback) | (epub)
Subjects: GSAFD: Mystery fiction.
Classification: LCC PS3601.V64 G55 2021 (print) | LCC PS3601.V64 (ebook)
    | DDC 813/.6--dc23
LC record available at https://lccn.loc.gov/2021003837
LC ebook record available at https://lccn.loc.gov/2021003838

Printed and bound in the United States of America.
LSC 10 9 8 7 6 5 4 3 2 1

Chapter One

"WATCH OUT FOR THE TOP OF THE DOOR!" DELTA DOUGLAS'S voice rose in pitch on the final word, and she shut her eyes so she wouldn't have to see the moment when the corner of the large wooden structure would chafe the lintel as it entered her shop.

Holding her breath, she listened for the screech of wood chipping paint, but there was nothing but the hum of the traffic behind her back on Mattock Street and the distant song of a bird in the oaks near the parking lot.

Carefully, she opened one eye and scanned the door. Everything looked pristine. She released her breath with an audible sigh of relief, but then her gaze fell to the structure now being maneuvered around *inside* her shop. When it had been initially unloaded, it had already looked huge, but now, among her precious stationery products, it seemed enormous. She wasn't sure what it was; she had merely expected the deliverymen to bring a display case for a miniature art installation. Miniature meant tiny, right? So why was this thing they carried, resembling a shallow sandbox on tall table legs, so big?

"Look out for the…" She rushed inside, stretching her arms out in a vain attempt to shield the counter's glass top from impact.

One of the men in blue overalls turned to her with a grin. "Don't worry, lady, we know what we're doing."

I'm glad at least one of us does.

Delta raised her hands and raked back her hair from her sweaty face. *This might not have been such a good idea, after all.*

When she had read in the newspaper about the famous Montana artist Tilly Tay, who had spent her entire life re-creating Montana scenery in incredibly lifelike miniature worlds, she had known it would be perfect for their shop, Wanted. The store already reflected their small town's gold rush past, and a miniature world full of prospectors and outlaws would be the perfect addition. After all, Wanted was housed inside Tundish's former sheriff's office with many original features of those Old West days. They had gold-mining scales, an old map with possible gold deposit sites marked on it, and information about the outlaw gangs that inevitably came after the precious finds. It made total sense to add a temporary exhibition to help bring in customers this rainy, and therefore quiet, November.

She and her college roommate Hazel had joined forces earlier that year to run Hazel's stationery shop together. Delta had left the city where she had spent many years working as a graphic designer to finally chase her childhood dream of creating her own line of paper products. Since moving into small-town Tundish, "the town with a heart of gold," Delta had experienced both the thrills and the challenges of managing your own business. There was so much more to running a store than just drawing new designs, and Hazel, with her business acumen and experience, was way ahead of her. Delta was glad she could trust her friend to lead them to the right decisions and keep the administrative side of the business on track, while she hoped her own efforts with Tilly Tay would prove worthwhile in attracting more clientele.

With the leaf-peeping season over and the year slowly winding down, the tourist stream was drying up. Outdoor activities on water and in the mountains could still take place if the weather was good. But, unfortunately, with such a wet November, the canoe rentals had already packed it in, and several of the weekend trail activities were canceled. Tour buses still swept into town every few days, unleashing groups of middle-aged women who took a quick look down wet Mattock Street, ducked into their coats, and rushed into Mine Forever for coffee and pancakes before being shepherded to the gold-mining museum. The shop obviously needed a little more than a deal on notebooks to draw the crowds inside. After seeing Tilly Tay's display proposal, Delta had been pleased with her excellent business idea, but, right now, as she watched one of the overall-clad men shoving aside a table with his hip to make way for his monstrous construction, she wondered why she had ever agreed to a miniature display.

Because it's supposed to be tiny.

Only it wasn't. This shallow sandbox the men were trying to set up was at least twelve feet long and wide, and it dominated the shop completely.

"Wow." Hazel, in a corduroy jacket and purple shawl wrapped around her head, stepped through the door and inched back at once, throwing Delta a bewildered look. "What is this?" Hazel had just returned to the shop from getting some caramel twists at the bakery across the street.

Run by their Paper Posse friend Jane, it offered them an endless supply of treats. Jane had a deft hand at finding perfect combinations for her pastries and sweets and also lent a sympathetic ear when things weren't going too well for Wanted. With her positive outlook on life, she managed to convince her friends that the rainy days wouldn't last forever.

Avoiding collision with one of the men, Hazel slipped over to stand beside Delta and whispered, "Is this it?"

"The start of it." Delta grimaced at her friend. "They are just building the outer housing, as they call it. Judging by the way they put up that wooden base, it serves as a display table where they will build the rest. But I have no idea what else will follow." She gestured through their shop window at a huge truck parked in front. "That is big enough to hold who knows what. In the pictures Tilly sent me, I only saw close-ups of cute little houses, saloons, and horsemen."

Unwrapping her rain-splattered shawl, Hazel gnawed her lip. "We should have considered this more. Oh…" She rushed forward and barely saved a stack of notebooks from a crash to the floor. Throwing a look at Delta, she called, "Can you help me move this?"

Together, they moved the table into one of the old cells

used for displaying washi tape and crafting kits. It was a bit crowded with another display, but they could just wring themselves past the notebooks to get out again.

"This barely leaves our customers space to move. It feels more like a storeroom than a store." Hazel sighed. "I had no idea that Tilly's display would be so domineering. People will take one look inside Wanted and decide it's too full to come inside."

"I assure you it will look great once it's all set up. You won't notice the size of the base anymore, just the sweet little town on top. Customers will flock to see all the details up close," Delta said cheerfully, more to silence her own doubts than Hazel's. Her courage was waning, and she wished she hadn't been quite so impulsive.

The men had finished putting the large wooden base in place. One of them checked if it was solid by leaning on it while the other went back outside. Delta and Hazel watched anxiously through the window, waiting to see what he was going to come back with. It looked like...

"Is that a sandbag?" Hazel asked Delta.

She shrugged, unsure.

He came back in with the large jute bag slung over his shoulder as if it weighed nothing. He lowered it to the floor with a thud that made some sand seep through the bag's fabric and dot the floorboards.

Hazel pointed at it. "Shall I get a dustpan and clean that away?"

"Don't bother, lady. It will get sandier than this pretty soon." The man opened the bag and began pouring sand into the display. The other used his hands to divide it across the surface in a more or less even layer. Some got shoveled over the edge and drifted down.

"We need to vacuum as soon as they're done," Hazel whispered to Delta. "Sand gets carried everywhere if you walk through it. With it being so wet outside, it will get really messy. I don't want people to think it's not clean in here."

While the one man was still working with the sand, the other went outside again. He disappeared into the back of the truck. Hazel poked Delta with an elbow. "Now he will appear with plants." She sounded half joking, half desperate.

"No way," Delta countered, but she held her breath as she waited for him to show himself again. What could he be bringing inside? She wondered if that wooden base with the thin legs could hold the weight of everything they intended to pile in. What if it gave way in the middle of the night and covered their entire business with sand and greenery?

Or worse: what if it gave way with customers in the shop? She could already hear the panicky cries or see the headline in the *Tundish Trader*: *Customers almost buried under shop display.*

She should have thought this through better.

"What's going on here?" a cheerful male voice called as Ray Taylor walked through the door, casually dressed in a leather jacket and stonewashed jeans. Despite the rainy weather, he hadn't bothered to zip up his jacket showing the crisp white shirt underneath.

A former quarterback who had left the team with an injury, he had come back home to Tundish to help with his family's age-old hotel, the Lodge. The hotel lay beautifully against a hillside overlooking the crystal-clear lake near the town. Consequently, the Lodge was booked year-round, often by people whose families had come here for generations, knowing the Lodge and the Taylor family from the very start of their business, when leisure time had still been a privilege of the rich and famous. Old, yellowing photographs displayed at the Lodge's iconic fireside showed the visitors of old, their clothes and fancy automobiles, testifying to the hotel's glorious past.

"Isn't it a bit late in the year for a beachside theme?" Ray queried with a puzzled frown, nodding at the sand-filled display filling up all space.

"That's not a beach." Hazel gestured widely. "It is supposed to become a representation of Tundish in the gold-mining heyday."

"Really?" Ray cast a doubtful look across the empty sand. "I don't see how yet."

"Coming through." The man in overalls pushed himself past Ray, bumping him against the shoulder with an armful of rocks.

"More weight," Hazel hissed to Delta, but the man overheard and commented, "Papier-mâché, lady. Lightweight. Running a paper store, you should know, eh."

Ray frowned at the man's tone but didn't comment. He asked Delta, "So this is a permanent addition to the store? Like a sort of model to show what Tundish was like? I guess it would have been more at home in the museum. Or did Mrs. Cassidy convince you to take it off her hands?"

Mrs. Cassidy was another member of the Paper Posse crafting group and a tireless volunteer at Tundish's gold-mining museum. She could be found regularly, in nineteenth-century clothing, staffing the reception desk or gift booth or taking tourists around the museum's many rooms retelling the rich history of their little hometown.

"Actually, it was my idea," Delta said. She felt obliged to clear Mrs. Cassidy of Ray's suggestion that the display had somehow been forced on them. It wasn't. It had been invited in. *By me.*

Ray focused on her with his deep brown eyes. He gave her a lopsided smile. "To bring in more business? It's not exactly booming right now."

"I thought you wouldn't notice at the Lodge," Hazel said. "You have so many regular guests coming."

Ray kept his eyes on Delta. "Rosalyn managed to pull in executives who have their meetings at the hotel."

Rosalyn was Ray's older sister and manager of the Lodge Hotel. She constantly came up with ideas to pull in new clientele.

Ray continued, "Lunch included and all. That is doing really well. I was more thinking of the town, the diner." He pointed through the window at Mine Forever, sitting on the other side of the street. The diner was completely styled in the town's Old West theme with a huge mattock and sieve on top of the roof and a gold nugget for a door handle.

In summertime, waitresses popped in and out to serve all the customers sitting at the outside tables, watching the busy traffic and authentic fronts of Mattock Street. But, in deep fall, the tables sat empty, every now and then pounded by rain. Customers did step inside for a coffee or hot chocolate, but the busy comings and goings of summer were long past, and the touch of melancholy that hung across everything even seemed to turn Mine Forever's shiny doorknob dull.

"Are they struggling?" Hazel asked with worry in her voice. "I mean, Mine Forever is an institution in this town. They've always been there."

Ray shrugged. "I can't tell you much about it—only that the owner was at the Lodge last week playing cards with friends, and he looked pretty grim and said something along the lines of selling the whole place."

"I can't imagine he'd say that," Hazel said, looking shocked. She nervously wrapped her shawl around her hand and unwrapped it again. "If he can't survive…"

Delta swallowed. Would they be next to discover that their costs began to run higher than their income and that they wouldn't be able to continue much longer? And just when she was considering moving out of the cottage she shared with Hazel and finding her own place to live. Her hopes were to share a new home with her gran, who was in town temporarily, preparing for the sale of her beloved house that she was forced to leave after some unfortunate rezoning. For Gran's sake, Delta wanted a nice place for the both of them where they could live together, but, if money was tight, that could become harder. Gran got money off the sale of her home, of course, but Delta wanted to move in with her to give her company, not live out of her pocket. She hoped Hazel was also still supporting that step away. It had been discussed at the start, but they had grown comfortable with sharing the cottage, the rent, the chores, and meal preparations. It was so much fun and felt just like college where they had roomed together, but, with Gran's arrival, it seemed logical to find her own place quickly.

Ray brought his attention back to the display being set up. The papier-mâché rocks were put in place, and he grinned. "Looks like a kid's terrarium. For frogs or turtles."

"Turtles need water," Hazel retorted.

As if on cue, one of the men pulled a shimmery substance from a container and began to thread something waterlike through the landscape. Ray winked at Hazel. "Your wish is their command."

Hazel flushed. "I'll go make them coffee." She inched past the display and disappeared through the door leading into their small pantry.

Ray rolled his eyes. "Did I say something wrong?"

Delta shook her head. "We're just a bit concerned about this whole display thing." After a moment's pause, she added, "*I* am a bit concerned about it. It was my idea. I thought we needed something to draw tourists now that the main season is over and Christmas not yet in town. Just a bit of excitement. I arranged for the mayor's wife to unveil it tomorrow, with half the town present. But..." She nodded at the truck outside. "I had no idea it would be this massive."

Ray seemed to suppress a smile. "You could think of it as a massive excitement."

Delta had to smile as well, despite her anxiety. "I had imagined them carrying in a glass case holding a few houses and mini people with horses. You know."

The man working on the water stepped back and studied the result of his efforts through narrowed eyes.

"Don't bother with the details," the other said. "Tilly is going to change it again, anyway." He sounded a bit cynical. "We never made anything she liked."

Delta froze, wondering if Tilly was difficult to work with. On top of the huge display, that could mean additional trouble.

Hazel popped up, smiling. "Can I pour you some coffee? And how about a caramel twist from the local bakery? I got them fresh."

The man closest to the door checked his watch. "Thanks, but we have to get going. We have another appointment."

The other seemed to want to protest, but his colleague was already on his way out. "Good luck with it," he called over his shoulder. The reluctant workman followed, muttering a vague goodbye.

Ray said to Hazel, "I'd love a cup of coffee, and a caramel twist wouldn't go amiss either."

"I didn't buy them for you," Hazel snapped and vanished into the kitchen.

Ray hitched a brow. "Touchy." He glanced outside and stiffened. "Hey, look."

Delta followed the direction of his pointed finger. The two men who had left their shop to go to their "next appointment" had merely moved their truck out of sight and were crossing the street to step into Mine Forever.

"Looks like they didn't trust your coffee to be any good," Ray said with a smirk.

"Very funny." Delta looked at the display. "I'm more worried they vanished before we could ask more questions about how all of this is supposed to work."

"Or to avoid having to meet this Tilly they mentioned. The critical one?"

So Ray had also sensed the workmen's desire to evade the artist. "I'm sure Tilly will be perfectly nice. She's a real celebrity. You must have heard of her or have seen some snapshots of her work. Tilly Tay."

Delta gave Ray an expectant look, but his expression was, and stayed, blank. "Never heard of her."

Delta's heart sank. This whole business idea was turning into a big flop. Still she kept smiling. "You'll know who she is soon enough. Her displays are amazing."

Hazel appeared, carrying a tray with three mugs of coffee and a brown paper bag from the bakery.

Ray sniffed the air. "Ah, mocha. Delicious. They don't know what they turned down."

Delta cast him a look, shaking her head slightly to indicate that he shouldn't tell Hazel that the workers had gone to the other side of the street for coffee and treats.

Hazel handed Ray a mug and shivered as she ducked deeper into her thick knit cardigan. A lively pink, it contrasted with her chocolate-brown corduroy pants. "It's chilly."

"More rain to come, I'd say," Ray commented and sipped his coffee.

It was suddenly very quiet. Delta took a bite of the caramel twist and wished Hazel would try to say something nice to Ray. So she was a little in love with him and didn't want to be, but that didn't mean she had to give him the cold shoulder like that.

Outside, a rattling, old baby-blue VW van pulled up and halted. Behind the windows in the back were crocheted curtains in lively yellow and purple. Rust dotted the hubcaps. The exhaust let out a cloud of gray smoke before the van banged to a halt.

The door opened, and a slender middle-aged woman crawled out. A red felt hat with a mangy brown feather stood askew on her gray curls. Her gray knitted vest had known better days and trailed in the back. Her feet were stuck into well-worn hiking boots with bright-orange laces. A chihuahua jumped from the van and circled the woman's feet. With only short fur, he shivered in the chilly breeze. The woman looked down with a smile and scooped the dog into her arms, cuddling him against her. She stood a moment, watching the surroundings with a lively interest in her round, birdlike eyes. Then she came for their door.

"A customer for paper products?" Ray asked softly. "Doesn't look like she has a dime to spend," he added to Hazel. "Don't you take pity on her and start giving her stuff for free."

"Hush," Hazel hissed to him as the customer reached the door. She walked in briskly, and her eyes lit up when she surveyed the monstrous, empty sand-and-rock desert on display. "It's here already. Good. Good." She glanced at Hazel, Delta, and Ray. "Are the boys still around? I don't like the way the water is laid out."

"I have no idea where they went," Ray said. Delta wanted to protest, but he shook his head at her ever so slightly.

The woman sighed. "Oh, well, have to do it all on my own again." She rounded the display with an appraising look on her face.

Hazel said, "I'm sorry, but you are?"

"Tilly Tay. I thought you were expecting me?" Gesturing across the display, she threw Delta a questioning look.

Delta's jaw sagged. The article she had seen in the paper had been accompanied by a picture of a woman with dark curls in an evening dress, looking thirty-ish and very refined. This lady was closer to fifty and, well, a bit eccentric.

Tilly smiled, snuggled the chihuahua against her shoulder so she could hold him with one hand, and reached out the other. "How do you do? Thanks for having me here. I can see it work. Really work. This town has a lot of heart."

"A heart of gold," Ray quoted the Tundish sign welcoming

visitors. He stepped up and shook her hand. The chihuahua eyed him and barked, wagging his tail.

"Ray Taylor. My family owns the Lodge Hotel. Are you by any chance staying there?"

"Oh, no, I sleep in my van." Tilly gestured to the old VW outside. "I really don't have the funds to pay for luxury hotels." She looked him over with her clear, inquisitive eyes. "Judging by that fine leather jacket, I take it it is a luxury hotel."

Ray flushed under his collar, and Delta had to laugh. "Spot on." She shook the woman's hand. "Delta Douglas. We emailed about the exhibition. Welcome to town. Lovely to have you here. And what is the dog's name?"

"Buddy." Tilly's eyes lit up. "How kind of you to ask. Most people overlook him. I guess it's because he's so small. But he likes attention. Don't you, Buddy?" She nuzzled the chihuahua's fur, and he licked her nose.

Delta pointed at her friend. "This is Hazel. We co-own Wanted."

"Oh, yes." Tilly smiled at Hazel. "How nice to meet you. The way Delta described your partnership in the emails, I got the impression you are true friends."

"We definitely are. Since college." Hazel looked mollified

and offered, "Shall I get you some coffee? And some water for Buddy, maybe?"

"That would be nice. We did have a long drive."

Ray gestured at the paper bag with the bakery logo. "There are also caramel twists here, if you care for those."

"Oh, yes. But Buddy only gets dog treats." Tilly picked one from her cardigan's pocket and offered it to the dog. The treat cracked under his sharp teeth. "I'd love a caramel twist, though."

"There you go." Before Ray could offer her one straight from the bag, Hazel said, "I'll get a plate from the pantry." She gave Ray a scorching look and took off.

Tilly laughed. "I'm not one to stand on decorum." She pulled at her cardigan and then began to walk around the display again. "I really don't like the water. I told them before, but they never listen."

Delta looked at Ray and nodded across the street to say they're still there.

Ray shook his head, narrowing his eyes as if it would only lead to trouble if the workers returned to a testy artist.

Hazel brought coffee and a plate for the caramel twist. "Do sit down," she invited Tilly, pointing at an antique chair in which the old Tundish sheriff once sat while he was waiting for news of bank robbers to come in.

Tilly sat down with a sigh. Buddy lay in her lap, curling up into a ball. "It was a long drive," she repeated slowly. Her tone was pensive, and it seemed she was speaking more to herself than the others when she added, "Who would have guessed I'd come back to Tundish?"

Chapter Two

"BACK?" RAY QUERIED AT ONCE. "YOU'VE BEEN HERE before?"

Tilly started as if she became suddenly aware she wasn't alone. Her expression seemed to change from friendly and open to guarded. But she spoke in a normal, clear voice, "Yes, a long time ago." She bit into her caramel twist and complimented them on the bake. "Homemade?"

"No, that is the work of our friend Jane," Hazel explained. She pointed out the bakery and explained that they always got their treats there. Tilly nodded while she chewed on the caramel twist and sipped her coffee. Putting aside the cup, she gathered up the sleeping dog and put him on the chair where she had sat. Then she turned around in a jerk, startling them into backing up a step. "Enough chatter. I have to get to work. You," she pointed at Ray, "can lend me a hand with the boxes."

"What boxes?" Ray asked as he dutifully trotted after her to the old van outside.

Tilly reached in and began to pull out cardboard boxes of various sizes, which she piled into Ray's arms.

"Careful," Delta could hear her say. "It's all very breakable."

Ray came inside, balancing the boxes with a pained expression as if he didn't dare breathe for fear of dropping them. Hazel rushed up to lend a hand, putting them carefully on the floor. As Delta watched them, Hazel leaning over to Ray, she wished her friend was more open to starting a relationship with him. After all, despite Ray's casual attitude at times, he was a good guy inside, with a serious outlook on life. He could do with someone who managed to get close to him and chip away at his armor.

"There." Tilly followed with more boxes. "That's the first load."

"First?" Delta queried anxiously. "How much are you actually going to set up?"

"Why, an entire village, of course. But it's all tiny. Don't worry." Tilly rounded the display, looking at all the boxes. "Oh, yes, this is number one."

There were no markings on the boxes, and Ray raised a brow at Delta. She pursed her lips to indicate she wasn't sure either. But Tilly confidently folded open the flaps and exhaled in satisfaction, extracting something with both hands. It was a tiny welcome sign. She put it in the display on the far left. Delta leaned over to read aloud what it said: "The town with a heart of gold. It's Tundish's sign," she exclaimed in wonder, looking over the exact replica.

Tilly grinned at her. "Of course. You don't want just any town on display here."

Delta held her breath. She almost didn't dare ask. "But... You only knew I wanted you to come here a few weeks ago. You can't have made..."

"A replica of the entire town on such short notice? Of course not. I do admit I have buildings I reuse in displays. But I do try to personalize. I've looked online for the iconic features here, and I re-created them. I want this to be totally realistic."

Tilly reached inside the box and pulled out something between her fingernails. She put it on her palm and held out her hand to Delta. "Have a look at this."

Delta came over and leaned down to study the tiny object. "It's a mattock."

Ray came to stand by her side. "How can you create that at such a small scale?"

"Feel it," Tilly encouraged him.

Ray picked up the minuscule object and touched it to his finger. "It's actually sharp," he said. "I feel a little prick."

"That is because it's not plastic but real metal. I try to stick to lifelike details as much as I can. Over time I got better at it." Tilly held up her hand so Ray could put the mattock back into it. "I try to improve even now. You know, the disadvantage of doing something for decades is that you get complacent and think you know it all. I like to give myself new challenges. And this display here should be better than ever before." She frowned hard. "Which is why the water annoys me."

Delta gave Ray one more look, but he kept signaling her not to reveal that the men were on the other side of the street.

Tilly began to unbox items and build her tiny town. Hazel looked on with evident fascination, and Ray smiled tenderly as he watched her. Under Tilly's nimble fingers, an Old West town took shape: houses, shops, a church with a tiny weathercock on the tower. Tiny people were going about their business, entering the general store, going to the blacksmith with their horse by the bridle, or talking on the sidewalk. The sheriff and his posse seemed to have just left town to follow up on news of a wanted gang nearby.

One house had a tiny chihuahua sitting on the porch, and, when Delta commented on this cute detail, Tilly revealed, "That's Buddy. I put him in all my displays. It's sort of a running gag. People who come to see my work and know about it always try to spot him and take photos of it. You can see it online under 'hashtag BuddyIsHere.'" She straightened up and looked at her work with a happy smile. "I like to put little clues into my work. Things people can pick up on if they look closer than just the casual observer would."

"How fascinating."

Tilly used small stands or rails secured to the wood of the display base to put the tiny humans and animals in so they didn't fall over when the customers' footsteps made the floorboards tremble. The sand obscured the stands.

"I could watch this for hours, but, unfortunately, I gotta go," Ray announced. He waved at Delta and got a curt hand-up from Hazel, who was apparently too busy to see him off properly.

Just as he stepped outside, the workmen appeared from Mine Forever. When they saw Tilly's van in front of Wanted, they froze and glanced about them, looking ready to run away before rushing off to get to their truck and avoid Tilly altogether. *But why? Tilly seems like such a friendly person. Surely, she'll be very easy to work with?*

Wanted's doorbell jangled, and a man in uniform stepped in. Delta recognized him as one of Sheriff West's deputies. As soon as she saw him and the ticket book in his hand, she realized their mistake. They should have told Tilly right off the bat to park her van elsewhere. It wasn't allowed to sit in front of the shop.

"Good morning," the deputy intoned with an expression as if it were anything but a good morning. "Who is the owner of the blue VW van outside?"

"That would be me," Tilly said, rising to her feet. She didn't reach to the deputy's shoulder, and he looked down on her as he said sternly, "You're not allowed to park in front, ma'am."

"It's not parking, Sheriff." She gave him a winning smile. "It's unloading my boxes for the display here. I'm just an old woman, and you can't expect me to walk from the parking lot at the church over here time and time again."

The deputy cast a doubtful look across all the boxes put around her. "Looks like you took them inside and are unpacking them now, ma'am." He cleared his throat. "That means you stopped unpacking from the van and are parked. Which isn't allowed."

Buddy had woken up at the male voice and sat up in the chair looking at the deputy. He seemed uncertain whether he should jump out of the chair and come to his human's aid or hide where he was.

Tilly clasped her hands together. "No, I'm not done unpacking. I still have more inside the van. Please follow me, Sheriff, so you can see for yourself." She walked outside. The deputy followed her, and there was an animated conversation Delta couldn't quite overhear as Tilly showed the man inside her van. He popped his head in and had a look, then resurfaced rather flushed. He waved off her words, nodded, and went on his way.

Tilly came back inside. "Those boxes are all full of other projects," she confided, "and I'm not using them here. But he doesn't need to know that."

Hazel laughed. "You flattered him calling him sheriff."

"Oh, wasn't he the sheriff?" Tilly batted her eyelashes innocently. "He did cut an imposing figure. Someone with real, natural-born authority."

Delta grinned. "I do think you should park the van elsewhere as soon as you can. He might come back later, and I don't want you to have another skirmish. Sheriff West doesn't like violations around town and has drilled his deputies to be totally strict, whether it be with locals or out-of-towners."

"I'll do it in ten minutes. After all, I just convinced him that I'm still unloading." Tilly winked at Delta and resumed work on her display.

Delta kept an anxious eye on the van to see if the deputy would return, but nothing stirred in the street. From the gray clouds above, a drizzly rain was pattering on the pavement, and the few pedestrians out and about rushed indoors again as quickly as they could.

A figure holding a big red umbrella over her head came down the street with a Yorkshire terrier by her side. Delta smiled when she recognized her. "Mrs. Cassidy approaching," she announced. "She is a real fan of yours, Ms. Tay."

"Please call me Tilly. A real fan, you say? She shouldn't see it while it's still unfinished. It looks horrible. Can't you keep her outside?"

Delta thought it looked far from horrible, and the whole assembly process was fascinating, just the thing Mrs. Cassidy would enjoy. But, at Tilly's insistent look, she stepped out into the rain and met Mrs. Cassidy before she could reach the shop's door and get a peek inside. "Hello. Are you headed to us?"

"Yes, indeed. I need a few notebooks as gifts for friends and family." Mrs. Cassidy glanced down to her feet, where Nugget tried to huddle against her shoes. "Vile weather. But it's November, I guess. Can't be helped." She held her umbrella so that it also covered Delta.

"Could you come back some other time? We're setting something up, and we want it to be a big surprise for everyone. Tomorrow morning we'll do a big reveal in the store. For the moment, we're sort of closed." It sounded a bit unconvincing as she was making this up on the spot for Tilly's sake. "Sorry that you came out here for nothing."

"Oh, no, I'm also going to Bessie's Boutique for a new skirt. So it's no trouble." Mrs. Cassidy looked her over. "You look quite excited about this big surprise. In that case, I will come back tomorrow for those notebooks. There's no rush." She glanced past Delta, watching as Tilly exited the shop and headed toward her van. "I'm very curious now."

"Yes, but you do have to wait. We'll let you know via the group message."

The Paper Posse had a message group where they chatted about anything from craft ideas and recipes for a quick dinner to clues in the murder cases Delta and Hazel had been involved in. The Posse had shown themselves to be extremely useful in helping out with information as they worked all over town and knew all the local gossip.

Mrs. Cassidy leaned down to pat Nugget. "Poor little one. I think we've earned us a warm half hour at Mine Forever before going to get my skirt." Straightening up, she added to Delta, "They can do with the business too."

"Yes, Ray mentioned that they are not doing well, and the owner is even contemplating selling. Is he serious?"

"Ray or the owner?" Mrs. Cassidy lowered her voice as she added, "I guess the owner is serious. He is getting older, and he's just not up to thinking up new strategies to bring in customers during the lesser months. It's sad, you know. I can imagine what will happen as soon as he puts the property up for sale. A big chain will swoop in and take over, changing all the individual charm. Imagine the mattock and sieve going in exchange for some large plastic chicken advertising a quick burger meal." She shuddered. "But what can you do about it? I certainly don't have the expertise to help him boost business. Or money to support him during these hard times." She sighed. "Oh, well, it can't be helped, I suppose. See you later." And she crossed the street with Nugget in tow, the little dog wagging her tail as she saw where they were headed.

Delta turned round and watched as Tilly moved the van.

She was grateful that the feisty lady didn't push her luck with the local law. The deputy might not be in sight, but he could appear any moment from a side street and have another look at the situation.

Tilly parked at the church and got out of her vehicle. Just as she was about to walk back to Wanted, a man approached her, standing in her way. He was a head taller than Tilly, with broad shoulders and an insistent expression on his face.

Delta stood ready to step inside and get out of the cold drizzle, but something about the way the man approached Tilly gave her pause. He blocked her path, refusing to let her pass. Tilly had turned red in the face and pulled her cardigan closer around her as if she felt unprotected. Worried about their guest, Delta decided to intervene. She wanted Tilly to feel welcome in Tundish, and at ease, not harassed by some unsavory type.

As she neared them, Delta heard the man's ringing voice: "You're only hurting your own interest by not cooperating. You should reconsider. There's too much at stake." He pointed at Tilly with his left arm, the sleeve of his raincoat pulling up to reveal an ostentatiously large watch. It partially hid something on his wrist—a greenish smudge that could be a tattoo.

"I've made up my mind," Tilly retorted.

"Are you being bothered?" Delta asked.

Tilly started at Delta's voice, glancing around as if seeking the nearest escape route.

The man looked Delta over with his deep-set green eyes. His grizzled hair was damp from the rain splattering on the shoulders of his worn raincoat. "And you are? Family?" He sounded almost hopeful. *Why?*

"Ms. Tay's hostess here in Tundish," Delta said. "And you are?"

"This man is selling products I'm not interested in," Tilly said, still very red in the face. "He was just about to leave."

The man seemed to want to protest, but then he shrugged. "Have it your way. But I warned you." He walked away, the slips of his raincoat fluttering in the breeze.

Delta asked Tilly, "Did he threaten you into buying something off him? Maybe we should see if the deputy is still around and let him have a word with the guy."

"Trying to sell something is not forbidden." Tilly said with force, but her voice was shaky.

"Putting pressure on people to buy is," Delta retorted, leaning over encouragingly. "You should report this. He sounded decidedly unpleasant, even threatening. We don't want such individuals hanging around our town."

"Insurance people usually are insistent." Tilly pulled back her shoulders.

Delta frowned. It had been more than that. The words "there's too much at stake," struck her as strange. At stake for whom?

Tilly continued to explain, "He said that my old van will cause an accident someday, and all my livelihood will go into paying the claims. He is not the first to say so, nor will he be the last."

"I do hope you're not completely uninsured." Delta walked beside her, back to the stationery shop. Her heart beat fast, remembering her earlier fear of the display collapsing. If there was an accident and there was damage—or, even worse, personal injury—who would have to pay for that?

"That's my decision," Tilly said in a kind tone that didn't allow space for discussion.

Delta felt awkward asking any more, even if Wanted was involved in the exhibition. Of course, she should have asked about insurance, liability, and all beforehand. It proved she wasn't business-minded enough, and that hurt. It seemed her plan to boost Wanted's profile was only backfiring on her.

Nothing happened so far, she tried to assure herself. *And, with a little luck, nothing will. Keep smiling and make the most of it.*

She invited Tilly back into the store with a generous sweep of her arm. She stared down the street one more time where she could just see the figure of the pushy insurance man in his oversized raincoat disappearing around a corner. Did he know Tilly from the other time she had been to Tundish? The miniature artist had mentioned it'd been unlikely she'd ever come back. Because something unpleasant had happened then?

Odd.

Very odd.

Chapter Three

TILLY TAY DECLARED HERSELF SATISFIED WITH THE DISPLAY around closing time, and Delta and Hazel said their good-byes. Hazel left for their cottage while Delta settled into her own car to drive to the holiday resort north of town. It had several quite comfortable vacation homes for rent, and Delta had—with some kind mediation from Ray, who knew the resort owners—gotten a vacation home there for six weeks for her grandmother. After Gran had been displaced due to rezoning, Delta had immediately thought up a plan to have Gran move to Tundish and be more involved with her life and the shop. After all, Gran's generous birthday gift when Delta had turned thirty had enabled her to buy into Wanted in the first place. Gran had offered her the chance to make her dream come true, and now she wanted to give back. By renting the vacation home, Gran could explore the town and see if she liked it before looking into opportunities to buy or rent a house.

Delta grinned thinking of Gran and her temporary home. She had made the rental completely her own with small touches—a pillow here and a little lamp found in a secondhand store there. She also cooked every day or baked cake, and Delta couldn't wait to find out what inviting scent would curl into her nostrils the moment she set foot in the cottage. She parked her car, waved to a raincoat-clad family of four who were holidaying next door, and stepped up to the cottage's front door. She knocked briskly and already tried to catch a whiff of something—Gran's chocolate swirl cake was amazing, and she had mentioned wanting to bake it again just the other day.

But there didn't seem to be any smells in the air, save the dampness of the nearby soaked trees.

She walked around the house and, at the back, peeked into the kitchen. The sink sat nice and clean, no dirty bowls from mixing batter or anything in sight. Delta frowned. There were flowers on the table, fresh ones, it seemed. Gran had to have been out shopping earlier. Where could she be now? She had known Delta would come. But she hadn't messaged to say she'd be out.

Let's have a look around. Gran might be on the phone and didn't hear me knock.

But, after she had rounded the cottage and looked in all windows, she was nowhere closer to locating her grandmother.

It's just my fault, Delta tried to tell herself. *I'm expecting her to sit around her waiting for me to stop by. She has a life of her own.*

Well, she had one at home. But here in Tundish? She knew a few people, of course, mainly from the Paper Posse...

Delta pulled up her phone and asked in the Posse's message group who had seen her gran that day.

Calamity Jane replied at once that she had been in the bakery and they had chatted for a few minutes. Wild Bunch Bessie, who ran a boutique in town, offered that she had seen her on Mattock Street, with a grocery bag in her hand, and Mrs. Cassidy chimed in to report she had been at the gold-mining museum to drop off freshly baked scones for the volunteers.

"Is something the matter?" Mrs. Cassidy ended her message.

Before the entire Posse went hunting for Gran, Delta sent: "Am at her cottage and she's not here. I told her I'd drop by for dinner, and she didn't let me know she'd be out."

"She should join our message group," Wild Bunch Bessie declared. "We can think up a fun name for her. She can be the gang's grandmother figure, the one whom you think is quite innocent but carries a poker in her boot."

Delta had to laugh out loud at the suggestion of her polite, petite gran carrying a poker around. But, as she stood and listened to the silence of the resort with its tall trees and views of the deserted lake, she did wonder if maybe this hadn't been a smart location to place an elderly woman on her own. In summer, the resort's vacation homes were all booked, but now most of them sat empty. Would a house in town, with watchful nearby neighbors, have been better?

"Let us know when she turns up," Mrs. Cassidy wrote.

"I will, thanks." Delta lowered her phone and stood, deep in thought.

Then a car horn honked. A dark-green Mercedes rolled toward the cottage. It stopped, and the driver's door opened. A tall gentleman unfolded, with hat and walking cane. He rounded his vehicle and opened the passenger door. Gran climbed out, her cheeks rosy and her eyes sparkling. "Hello, Delta," she called, waving her hand. "So sorry I'm late."

To the man she said, "That's my granddaughter, Delta, who owns the stationery store in town."

"How do you do?" The man took off his hat, uncovering a head full of white hair, and bowed in her direction. Then he said to Gran, "I must be off now. Card club tonight. But I'll call you for that dinner appointment. Don't forget."

"I won't." Gran stood watching as he got into the Mercedes, honked anew, and drove off.

"Who is that?" Delta asked.

"Major George Buckmore. He only lives here in the winter season. In the summer, he's in Europe. Monte Carlo, Biarritz, those sort of places. A real old-school gentleman. He showed up on my doorstep around three with gorgeous flowers. He had heard in town that a fellow fan of everything history had arrived. He invited me on a tour to see some historic sites around town, and I took the invitation." Gran released a happy sigh. "I haven't had such a good time in ages. It was rainy, but that didn't bother us at all. He can tell such interesting stories about everything. History as if you were there."

Delta felt a little piqued that, apparently, the trouble she had taken to give her gran a good time in town and relate some important events had paled by comparison, but immediately rebuked herself. It was wonderful that Gran was making friends here. It would encourage her to come live in Tundish, and that was just what Delta wanted, right?

"How wonderful." She hugged her gran. "Let's go inside so you can tell me all about it. I can cook dinner, if you want."

"That's very sweet of you, darling." They walked around the cottage together and went in through the back door. Gran immediately headed for the flowers on the kitchen table and studied them from all sides with a sweet smile. "Aren't they beautiful? And those colors, just what I like. I wonder how he guessed it."

"Maybe he's seen you in town and looked at your clothes?" Delta supplied. She had opened the fridge and was studying the contents to think up an easy-to-cook but delicious meal.

"That would be very thoughtful. I do like to wear lilac and pink. But for a man to be so observant..."

"He's been in the army. At least, I assume he has been. Major means army major, right?"

"I assume so. We didn't talk about his career at all. We were far too busy going into all the details of the Tundish gold rush."

"I thought you heard most of that at the museum." Delta glanced at her grandmother.

"Oh, but he knew some anecdotes that are a little more obscure." Gran winked at her. "Very exciting about hidden treasure and all. Never mind making dinner, darling, I'll call for delivery."

"Are you sure?"

"Yes, I feel like splurging on something special tonight. How about stir-fried rice with beef and vegetables?"

"Sounds delicious."

Gran was already on her way to make the call with the vacation home's landline. Delta picked up her own phone to let the Posse know Gran had turned up. "She was out with a friend sightseeing," she put it. She didn't want to mention it had been a male friend, or the ladies would immediately feel romance in the air.

There might be some. A little...

After all, why would Gran be so cheerful? The news that she had to leave her beloved house had hit her hard, and, even as she enjoyed her time here and considering what her new life might be, Delta sensed those moments of quiet and sad introspection. Now, however, Gran was buzzing with energy.

"That's taken care of. They expect the delivery driver to be here in twenty minutes. Shall we grab some appetizers? I can mix apple juice and fizzy mineral water into our very own alcohol-free prosecco. You do have to drive home later, darling." Gran hummed as she was at it, looking for what she needed.

Delta looked at the flowers on the table and silently

thanked Major George Buckmore for having put a spring in her grandmother's step again.

—————————

When Delta came home to Hazel's cottage with a stomach full of delicious food and her cheeks stretched with laughter from her grandmother recounting all the anecdotes her new friend, the major, had shared with her, she found Hazel on the lookout.

"Oh, it's you," Hazel said as Delta stepped from her car. She sounded disappointed.

"Of course it's me," Delta replied, puzzled. "Who else would it be?"

"I was expecting uh…" Hazel looked pained to admit it.

Oh, I see. Delta grinned. "Ray? Did he let on earlier today that he might drop by? I can leave again and do a few laps around the lake while you meet up with him."

"No, it's not Ray. I wish people would stop pairing us off." Hazel waved her hands in a gesture of frustration. "Tilly Tay showed up here and asked for the key to Wanted. She was unhappy with a few details in the display, and, seeing as we're doing the grand reveal tomorrow…"

"You gave her the key to our business?" Delta asked in

disbelief. A sense of unease rippled through her. If she had been here when Tilly made that request she would have said no.

"Not just like that," Hazel defended her decision. "I told her she could come in early tomorrow and make the changes. I also offered to come with her. But she was very adamant that she couldn't work when someone was watching her and that she didn't want me there."

"But earlier we were there and watched her work."

"Exactly. That's why it didn't turn out the way she wanted, she said. I felt bad about the way we studied her every move as she was at it. It must be uncomfortable. Disturbs the creative process, Tilly explained. So I caved. I know it was stupid, but you know I can't say no to people. Especially if they push hard." Hazel hung her head.

"Cheer up." Delta stepped up and put an arm around her. "It's not that bad. I don't assume Tilly will fill up her van with washi tape and notebooks and drive off. She has a reputation to protect."

"That's what she told me too. That I needn't suspect her of rushing off with the contents of the till. I told her there isn't even anything in the till at night. For safety reasons. I felt rather silly being seen as suspecting a respected artist of not taking good care of a key to a building. So I let her have it. I made dinner and sat waiting for her. Then I decided I should maybe go and see how she was doing? And you appeared."

"It's okay." Delta patted Hazel's arm. "I'll go and see how she's doing. You pop back inside." She made a mental note to explain kindly but firmly to Tilly that she wasn't supposed to do things at the store on her own. As a matter of principle.

Shivering at the chill, Delta dived back into her car and drove from the cottage into the quiet town. A few residents were walking their dogs, and, every now and then, another car passed. In summertime, tourists hung out in town until late in the evening but, now with an insidious November wind breathing down Mattock Street, no one was out and about.

Delta parked her car in front of Wanted, grinning to herself that the deputy wouldn't be around now to come and try to fine her for it. Tilly's van wasn't there, so maybe the artist had become extra careful and left it at the church parking lot?

She stepped out and looked at the front. No lights on. How odd. Tilly wouldn't be working in the dark, right? She went to the door and peeked in through the glass pane. Nothing to see. She used the flashlight function on her phone to shine in. The beam crept across the interior, not revealing any person present.

Where's Tilly?

After a moment's hesitance she pulled out her own key, unlocked the door and stepped inside. "Tilly? Are you there?"

Was that light under the door leading into the pantry? Was the miniature maker in there having a cup of coffee?

Delta's heart rate sped up. Her muscles tensed as she walked through the dark store, waiting for something to pounce at her from the shadows. At this late hour, the familiar surroundings felt suddenly hostile. Her fingers trembled as she reached out to open the pantry door.

The light was on, but Tilly wasn't there. There was no scent of coffee in the air.

Having checked that the coffee maker wasn't on, Delta turned off the light and shut the door. She went over the entire premises, shining her phone's flashlight inside the old cells to see if anything was out of place. With everything as it should be, she left again.

Her breathing was still unsteady. She felt rather silly for having assumed something was wrong. Still, the silence ate at her nerves. Tilly hadn't come back to Hazel to return the key.

"Why not? Where is she?" Delta muttered as she ducked into her car and sat a moment. Then she pulled up her phone and called Tilly Tay's number. No one picked up. If she had been staying at a hotel, or B&B, Delta could have gone there to talk to her, but, right now, she had no idea where Tilly had intended to take her van for the night.

Could she message the Posse to ask them if they had spotted the van anywhere?

No, it would only alert them to something wrong, and, after the false alarm over Gran, she didn't want to ask them again. Besides, it was better they not know Tilly Tay wrangled their key from them. It might reflect negatively on the guest and honored creator of the display. The reveal in the morning was supposed to be a fun event, bringing joy to the entire town. As everything seemed fine at the store, she needn't worry about the missing key. Tilly would probably hand it over when they met at the store for the reveal.

With a sigh of resignation, she started the engine and headed home.

"I can't believe she didn't bring back the key," Hazel said as they were having breakfast. "I slept badly. I kept dreaming the store door was left open and raccoons got in and tore up all the notebooks."

"Raccoons?" Delta echoed, reaching for more jam for her toast. "Where did you get that idea?"

"From stress." Hazel rolled her eyes at her. "Things like this grand reveal this morning are fun, but they always make me feel jittery. What can go wrong? Maybe the whole display collapsed. We should really get there as soon as we can and check on everything." She seemed ready to run out of the door without having had a bite to eat.

Delta gestured at her. "Calm down. Sit and eat something. I checked the store last night, after Tilly left, and everything was all right." She didn't mention the light in the pantry that had been left on or the eerie quiet she felt.

"But what if Tilly went back later to change the display yet again? I read a newspaper article once about an artist who got up at all hours of the night to change details about his paintings. Or set fire to them when he had decided he hated them."

"Relax. Tilly won't have set fire to our shop. She has her ways, but she's perfectly nice and harmless." Delta washed down her toast with coffee. Despite her reassuring words to her friend, the evasive behavior of Tilly's workmen came back to mind, raising an unsettling question. Was Tilly *that* difficult?

Nerves fluttered in her stomach, and she decided against more toast. After the grand reveal had gone down well, they would all feel better and be in the mood for more food.

Hazel sat down, fidgeted with her hands, pulled the elastic band from her hair, and jumped to her feet again. "I have no peace. Can't we go into town and see? If everything is all right, I can eat."

Delta guessed nothing she could say would convince Hazel, so she rose and said, "Sure. Pack some food then."

While Hazel was at it, Delta slipped a banana in her pocket. No need to reveal to her worried friend that she wasn't perfectly calm either.

They drove into town in Hazel's Mini Cooper. Hazel was completely quiet, staring anxiously ahead as if scanning the air for smoke, signaling that Tilly had indeed set fire to the display and everything else inside. But the only clouds visible were sending fat drops pattering on the car's roof. It was a reassuring sound, and Delta yawned, wishing she could have stayed in her warm bed just a little longer. Maybe, instead of fighting the quiet season, they should embrace it and see it as a time for recuperation after the summer's crazy rush?

In town they parked at the church, and Hazel sprinted ahead to Wanted. Delta followed at a brisk pace, clutching her purse to her side. She knew nothing would be wrong, but still her palms were decidedly clammier than on a normal morning arriving for work.

Hazel had stopped at the shop and peeked in. She gestured to Delta. "Hurry up. I haven't got my key."

Delta closed in and unlocked the door. Hazel darted inside and made a tour of all the spaces, breathing hard like a hunting dog on a scent. "It looks okay," she said hesitantly, as if she could barely believe it.

"Told you so." Delta closed the door and locked it from the inside to keep early arrivals out for the moment. She went to the display and looked at the last-minute changes Tilly Tay had made. Two buildings had moved location, and several miniature people were doing a different activity than before. The added blacksmith looked very authentic lifting up a red-hot iron and a hammer to strike at it. At the boardinghouse...

What's that?

Delta leaned down to look better. A man was lying on his face, the tiny mattock that Tilly had showed to Ray stuck out of his back. *Grisly.*

But realistic, probably. There had been violence over the gold. Maybe Tilly had wanted to show some of that without it being too present in the scene. Delta had only spotted this detail because she had been looking hard. Most casual observers would probably miss this tiny murder scene. *Fortunately*.

Would it be one of the clues Tilly had mentioned earlier? Stuff she put in the displays on purpose, for her fans?

Well, Delta hoped people would sooner track Buddy than this murdered man.

"Everything seems to be in order," Hazel said behind her back, with more confidence this time.

Don't let her see it. Delta swung round to her. "What did I tell you? You worry too much. Raccoons. Really?" She wagged a finger at her. "Now you grab a cup of coffee in the back and have a proper breakfast."

"I'll have some after the reveal." Hazel stood and rubbed her hands together. She glanced at her watch. "Still an hour to go." She glanced down her clothes. "I don't like this sweater. I think I'm going back home to change."

Delta wanted to protest that she was running to and fro but realized her friend would be even more nervous if she was cooped up inside the shop for another hour. "Sure, you go back home and change. I'll mind the store. Why don't you pick that lavender sweater you bought last week? It looks great on you."

"I was thinking about the coral blouse. But I'll see." Hazel left, waving at her through the window.

Delta sighed. Her gaze wandered the floor, and she noticed some sand that had fallen from the display. She'd better vacuum it away before the guests would arrive for the reveal and hear their soles crunching across the boards.

They had managed to get the mayor's wife, rather last minute, to say a few words and cut the proverbial ribbon, so it would be a rather weighty occasion. Adding importance to it by inviting a guest of honor and the press had seemed logical, as the whole point of having the display here was promotion for Wanted, but, right now, Delta almost wished she had kept it low-key. It would have saved them a lot of stress.

Now that she was alone in the quiet store, the unease from last night resurfaced, and she glanced surreptitiously at the display with the murdered man. That gruesome detail seemed out of place, like those moments where friendly talkative Tilly had clammed up about her earlier visit to Tundish and the unknown man who had threatened her in the street.

What if that man turns up again, at the reveal?

Chapter Four

DELTA HAD JUST FINISHED CLEARING AWAY THE SAND WHEN someone tapped at the door. She rushed over and peeked out. It was Jonas Nord, a local wildlife guide and friend. *Well, friend...*

Delta flushed a little as she opened the door for him. There were moments when she wondered if he felt the same way about her as she did about him—that they were a little more than merely friends. After a quiet dinner, a while back, when he had taken her home, she had been almost certain he was going to kiss her, but he hadn't, and she didn't know whether he hadn't wanted to or had stopped himself in the last instant.

And, if he had, why.

"Good morning," Jonas said. He smiled at her. "I heard that you're having a little festive opening here later this morning. But I can't be there. Obligations at the Lodge. Providing stress relief to big businessmen and all that." He looked up at the sky, which was filling with more rain clouds. "I'm almost certain that traipsing around dripping forests won't relieve stress for most people, but okay."

Delta laughed. She leaned down to pat Spud, Jonas's loyal canine companion. The German shepherd had worked as a police officer for years before retiring and becoming Jonas's partner in helping other retired K9s adjust to civilian life. "How are you this morning, buddy? The rain isn't bothering you, huh?"

Spud shook his head, splashing a few cold drops in her face. She smiled and scratched him behind the ears. "You can outpace those businessmen any day."

Jonas said, "Anyway, I'm sorry I can't be there. Maybe we can uh…have dinner sometime or something, to catch up?"

"That would be great." Delta avoided having to look at him by focusing on the dog. "I feel like I'm spending too much time working. I set up this thing with a Tilly Tay display, and I'm not sure it was such a good idea."

"Why not?" Jonas asked, surprise in his voice. "People like something new in town. The tourists will certainly appreciate something related to the town's past. That is why they come here. If you can pull them into your shop, especially at this time of year, you've won half the battle. They'll buy stuff and tell their friends. If they take pics and share them on social media, even better. I think it's very savvy of you."

All the compliments made Delta blush, but her uneasy feeling lingered. "Yes, but... Tilly is different from what I had imagined. The woman I saw in the newspaper photograph was..." Delta caught herself wanting to say classy, and, suddenly, her attitude felt rather snobbish and wrong. She'd never judged people by their outer appearance, so why start now?

Because her business was involved?

She never wanted to become a judgmental person who didn't give others an honest chance.

"Never mind." She made a dismissive gesture. "You can't judge a person by their clothes or the car they drive. Maybe she's a bohemian, like artists are, right?"

"Has she caused any problems?" Jonas asked.

Alarmed again by the question, Delta faced him. "Why would you think that?"

"I don't know. Her name sounded familiar. I wondered if I had ever come across it in a case."

"I don't think so. She's a renowned artist. Because of her

miniature worlds. If you know her name, it must be from some news item about her displays."

"Could be, of course." Jonas nodded, but his eyes betrayed him; he wasn't convinced and was still scanning his inner database, wondering when he had come across her name and why.

The idea that Tilly Tay might have once been involved in a criminal case made Delta's stomach contract. Since Delta had come to town, there had already been several murders, and she wasn't eager to get caught up with someone who had been involved with the police, even if it had happened years ago.

"Listen, Delta…" Jonas touched her arm. "You better be careful around her. I mean, she can display at your shop, of course, but don't give her access to your lives."

Access? Why did he have to use that exact word? Delta thought about the key Tilly hadn't returned and swallowed. "Of course not. We're smarter than that." It sounded unconvincing in her own mind, but Jonas nodded. He checked his watch. "I'd better get going, or I will be late and Rosalyn will complain."

"Good luck leading the businessmen to calmer minds and wetter bodies."

Jonas huffed and walked away with a last wave of his arm. As Delta watched his broad shoulders, she wished he could have been present at the display reveal. But that was nonsense. It was a very simple town affair. Nothing she needed a former cop for.

"What a nice young man," a voice said.

Delta jumped at the sudden appearance of Tilly at the door. Today she wore a long woolen coat and red scarf wrapped around her head. She carried Buddy in her arms. The chihuahua still looked very sleepy, keeping his eyes closed. His human, though, stared at Delta intently, and, for a moment, Delta wondered, uncomfortably, if it was possible that Tilly had drawn near without them noticing, as they talked at the open door, and she had overheard something of Jonas's words about possibly recalling her name from a criminal case. But that didn't seem likely.

"Good morning," she said. "Do come in. That drizzle isn't strong, but it's still chilly."

Tilly followed her inside and put Buddy in the sheriff's chair. She unwrapped the scarf and unbuttoned her coat. Underneath, she wore a paisley dress in autumnal shades with a large gold-sprayed necklace ending in a pendant studded with fake gemstones.

"Let me hang your coat in the back," Delta offered, accepting the coat and picking up the scarf as well. "How are you this morning? Did you manage to find a good spot for the van?"

"Oh, yes, I always manage." Tilly smoothed her hair. As soon as she had pushed down a wiry curl, it popped back into the same position again.

"Did you have breakfast?" Delta asked. "I can make coffee."

"No, no, I'm jittery as it is." Tilly rubbed her hands together.

Delta noticed a scratch on the back of her left hand. It seemed very fresh, the blood hardly having clotted. "Do you need a bandage for that?"

Tilly looked down. "No, no, it is uh...I got caught behind a nail. Nothing special."

A nail? Inside a van?

As if Tilly read her mind, she said, "A nail sticking out of a wooden box I use for props. I would love some coffee, anyway. Can you get it for me?"

As Tilly had moments ago declined the coffee, Delta strongly felt like her guest only said it to avoid further conversation about her injury, but she could hardly be impolite and disappeared into the back.

Before she was done with the brew, Hazel breezed in,

dressed in her favorite red pantsuit. The color put a healthy glow on her cheeks and made her look less anxious than before. She greeted Tilly warmly and didn't pounce at once about the key.

Only after Delta had served the coffee and they were all sipping, Hazel said, "I totally understand you weren't able to return the key last night. It must have gotten late, changing things, and you didn't want to disturb me anymore."

"Key?" Tilly looked surprised. "I didn't want to disturb you, no, so I put it in your mailbox."

"Mailbox?" Hazel and Delta echoed.

"Yes. At the cottage."

Delta glanced at Hazel. Hazel shook her head almost imperceptibly to indicate she hadn't checked the box this morning. Neither had Delta. So, the key was in there. Might have been all night. And they had been so worried. *For nothing.*

Delta smiled at Tilly. "Great, thanks. I hope you could change the display to your satisfaction."

"Umm, well…" Tilly glanced at it over her shoulder. "It's never really done, in my mind. But it will have to do. I do appreciate that I could set it up here."

"Oh, we love having you," Hazel assured her.

There was a knock at the door. It was the mayor's wife, dressed in a navy-blue ensemble over a white blouse. She closed a huge umbrella and put it in the stand at the door. Having cooed over the cute chihuahua, she moved toward Tilly, enthusing about how she was a long-standing fan of her work. Soon, the two were in deep conversation about the best way to make miniature furniture for a doll's house. The mayor's wife complained about never getting her plants to look good, and Tilly launched into a long-winded explanation of how to make them true to life.

Delta cleared away the coffee mugs, and Hazel messaged the Paper Posse to remind them of the reveal. They all messaged back they hadn't forgotten and would be there soon.

Indeed, there was a crowd gathering in front of the store waiting for the grand moment. To Delta's relief, the rain had petered out completely, and their guests could wait without getting wet. She spotted Gran among the group, talking to Bessie Rider. She had put a flower from Major Buckmore's bouquet in her buttonhole, giving her outfit an almost summery look.

Close to the agreed-upon time, they went outside, the mayor's wife standing beside Tilly Tay while Hazel attached the ribbon to the store doors. The mayor's wife expressed her delight at Tilly Tay visiting Tundish and creating a custom-made display for their little town. "These creations may be tiny, but the thought and attention that goes into them is astounding. For many hours, our honored guest worked hard, hunched over her workbench, to create that lifelike appearance for both the buildings and the people who once populated them. I'm sure that, if there are longtime fans among you, you will know how to look for those little clues Tilly leaves in her displays for all of us to find and enjoy. Especially Buddy, her faithful canine companion, who is here in the flesh today, but also present in the Tundish display."

Tilly blushed and fidgeted under all the praise heaped upon her.

"But I will not keep you in suspense any longer," the mayor's wife said with a determined nod. "Let's officially open this wonderful exhibition of Tilly Tay's interpretation of our beloved gold rush Tundish."

The crowd hummed approvingly as the mayor's wife accepted the scissors Delta handed her and cut the ribbon. With applause, she entered the store, the guest of honor and the curious crowd pouring in after them, slowly pushing past the display and then dispersing into the cells to look at the other products. Delta saw Mrs. Cassidy leaning over the display at the exact spot where the murdered prospector with the mattock in his back was, and she expected the woman to come over her at once to ask about it. But the flow of the people steered Mrs. Cassidy in the opposite direction. It was all very tight, but people seemed willing to accept a little discomfort to be part of this moment celebrating their town's illustrious history.

Gran did manage to reach Delta and said, with a wide smile, "It turned out amazing. I can't see all the details now, because I don't want to block other people's path forever, but I must have a closer look some other time. I did recognize Tilly Tay's little dog. I think it's adorable she put him in there. Chihuahuas are a really old breed, so why wouldn't it have been possible for one of them to live in gold rush Tundish?"

"I'm glad you like it. Is your new friend the major not here?"

"No, but we are seeing each other later today." Gran's smile brightened even more. "I do hope you won't mind, Delta, but he's not into this kind of fidgety thing. He's more of an outdoorsy person, you know."

"Fine with me," Delta assured her. "I hope you have a great time together."

Mrs. Cassidy had managed to reach the artist and was

talking to her. She seemed to ask a question, because Tilly looked up at her with some surprise and then nodded and responded.

Delta wondered if Mrs. Cassidy also thought she knew Tilly Tay from a prior occasion. Tilly had said she'd been to Tundish before. And, even though Jonas couldn't have known her from a previous visit, only coming to live here recently, it was possible Mrs. Cassidy could have.

Delta mentally shook herself. It was none of her business. Everything had gone off without a hitch, and people seemed to like the display. They were taking pictures of it with their phones. Maybe they should even create a special hashtag for it. And then award a prize to the best photograph? A package with a notebook and pen? Something like that... She had to work out the prize bundle and then post a good shot of it later today.

Among the browsing locals, Delta spotted Sven LeDuc, editor of the *Tundish Trader*, the town's newspaper since 1887. He was an old-school newsman who always carried his notebook around and wrote in it with an extra-sharpened pencil. His son, Marc LeDuc, had been cast to take over, but a disagreement between them about how things should run at the paper had driven them apart. Now Marc had a website, called News as It Develops, where he tried to publish all the scoops before his father got to them.

But, apparently, Marc didn't consider this news, because he was nowhere in sight.

Good for us.

Delta disliked his tactics to get stories and could do very well without him poking his phone in her face to record a statement about something she didn't want to give a statement about. In the two murder cases earlier that year, Marc had been a real pain. Although, she had to admit begrudgingly, he had sometimes dug up some information that had helped them along the way.

Sven LeDuc maneuvered in her direction, waving his notebook. "This is fantastic," he called above the hum of crowd. "Reminds me of the model railway I used to work on in the attic. Gave up on it years ago, as I no longer had the time for it. But all the boxes are still there, somewhere. I should really look them up and dust it off again. Bring my track back to life. Fantastic."

Delta gave him a thumbs up. At least, the *Tundish Trader* would write a nice little piece about this. It could help business. Anything to get through this dry season.

Speaking of dry… Outside, the rain had started again, full force, pounding against the window. She imagined how Jonas would be walking through the forest now, the rain dripping down his face from his soaked hair. She knew he loved being outdoors, so he might not mind too much, but his followers? She had to ask him later how things went. Then he might also make a concrete date for that dinner he had suggested. She did want to spend time with him again. Soon.

People stayed a little longer waiting for the rain to ease, but then, gradually, they left, opening up umbrellas or crossing hurriedly to Mine Forever. Mrs. Cassidy came over to Delta. "I asked Tilly Tay to visit the gold-mining museum," she enthused. "I think it would be an honor to have her there. She can sign the guest book. She said she'd come right after the reveal here was over. I would love for you to be there as well. You are the one who invited her over to town."

Delta opened her mouth to say she had to help Hazel with the store when her friend popped up beside her and said that she was coming too and that they could close the store for an hour. Delta wanted to protest, but Hazel pointed at the weather outside. "There won't be that many people coming on a morning like this. We can afford to do it."

Delta sensed that Hazel wanted it, for a reason she couldn't quite fathom. Maybe to make a good impression with Tilly Tay? Did Hazel feel guilty for having distrusted the artist?

She agreed and, after they had said goodbye to their last visitors, they closed up and went to the museum together. Tilly praised the authentic look of the building, the mining cart placed outside, and the little gift corner near the reception desk. Delta was just brushing wet drops from her hair when she heard singing. Hazel caught her arm and led her into the nearest room where the entire Paper Posse was gathered with Gran and the mayor. Delta's eyes widened. "What is this?" she whispered to Hazel.

Her friend beamed at her. "Mrs. Cassidy arranged for it, so she has to tell you."

Mrs. Cassidy made a dismissive gesture. "It was really Jane's idea."

Jane said, "If we keep playing pass-the-parcel, we'll never get this done."

Bessie Rider stepped forward. "Okay, I'll tell you." She took a deep breath. "All the shopkeepers on Mattock Street agree that you are a real asset to the street. You and Hazel have made Wanted into a shop that attracts tourists. You have set up special events, like the display with Tilly Tay right now, to boost the town. For your tireless efforts and enthusiasm, you deserve a reward, so we have chosen you as shopkeeper of the season. The mayor will officially hand out your medal."

Delta flushed as the mayor stepped up and shook her hand, then passed her a box that held a medal resting against blue velvet. It had a silhouette of Tundish in the center with words written on the edges: *Tundish Shopkeeper of the Season*. The medal glittered in the light from above.

"It's not real gold," the mayor warned her, and everyone had to laugh.

"I'll put it on display in the shop," Delta said. "Thanks so much. I feel very honored. And I have to say that Hazel did so much as well. Together we are the best team ever."

She put an arm around her friend, who beamed with pride and whispered, "I'm so glad you came to Tundish."

Gran came over and kissed Delta on the cheeks. "You deserve this, darling."

Mrs. Cassidy passed around glasses, and they toasted to Wanted's prolonged success. Just as Delta touched her glass to Mrs. Cassidy's and thanked her again for nominating her, there was a bustling sound, and Sheriff West raced into the room. He stopped when he saw the festive gathering and cleared his throat. Everyone stood frozen with their glasses midair, staring at him. West said, "I'm looking for a Miss Tilly Tay. She has to answer some questions."

"About what?" Mrs. Cassidy asked.

Delta supplied, "If her van is wrongly parked, we'll have it moved right away."

Jane added, "We're celebrating Delta's election to shopkeeper of the season. As you can understand, Sheriff, we've not thought of parking violations. Or tickets." She gave him a pleading look.

West said, "I'm afraid it is a little more serious than that. This morning, outside the motel, a dead body was found. The man was stabbed in the back."

As he said it, an image popped up in Delta's mind. The dead prospector with the mattock in his back in Tilly's display. *Dead body, outside lodgings, stabbed in the back. So many similarities.*

She scanned the people present looking for Tilly to gauge her response to this news. The petite artist had been talking to Rita moments ago. Where was she now?

West continued, "As Ms. Tay was seen arguing with the victim, she must answer some questions."

Delta frowned. "Arguing with the victim? She only arrived in town yesterday."

"The argument took place yesterday, in the street. Several witnesses saw it."

"You're referring to that insurance salesman in the

oversized raincoat?" Delta asked. "I saw them together, and they were not arguing. That is, he tried to force her into taking his insurance for her van, and she refused. He was being obnoxious, but then lots of insurance people are and—"

"I don't need you to explain the situation to me," West cut her short. "I want to hear Ms. Tay's statement." He looked around. "Where is she?"

Rita pointed beside her and said, "She was here a moment ago." They all turned their heads, scanning the room, but Tilly was nowhere to be seen. She had certainly not walked past West, so...

Jane said, "She must have gone farther into the museum."

"She's trying to run!" West exclaimed. He raced into the next room.

"Wait!" Mrs. Cassidy followed him. "Let me try and find her. I'm sure it's all a misunderstanding. She will gladly answer your questions, so you can clear the matter up."

But why, then, Delta asked herself, had Tilly Tay slunk away instead of simply answering the policeman's questions on the spot? If she was innocent...

Of course she's innocent. She just got a scare.

Delta hurried after West and Mrs. Cassidy.

West had passed a display of hopeful prospectors buying

a map, and entered the history of law enforcement room. He seemed to have heard a sound, for he abruptly turned into a corner and collided, headlong, with the dummy on display there. It was a very good likeness of Earl Bolt, the Tundish sheriff who had caught a famous gang and had been awarded a regional medal of bravery. The dummy teetered on his legs as West tried to maintain his own balance.

"I don't know if you ever met," Mrs. Cassidy said drily.

West didn't appreciate the irony. "This place is crammed full of stuff," he growled. "She could be anywhere."

He raced on, into the next room.

Mrs. Cassidy called, "You only spooked the poor woman. Can't we talk about this?"

"Someone died." West sounded grim. "And she's running, so she must be the killer. Ah, there she is."

Delta was just in time to see West grab Tilly, who was two heads shorter than he was, and pull her arms behind her back. He clicked the cuffs on. The woman stood with her head down, panting.

"No need to be so rough," Mrs. Cassidy said. She tried to inch closer to West and Tilly, holding her arms up in a pleading gesture, but the sheriff wouldn't let her come near and growled, "Don't you try to help her escape."

Delta asked, "If you only want to ask questions about her argument with the victim, are you even allowed to cuff her?"

"I'm making sure she can't run again. If this is a misunderstanding, we'll sort it out."

"And you should apologize for the inconvenience," Mrs. Cassidy said. "You totally ruined our festive gathering to give Delta an award."

West didn't seem to listen, or care, as he continued, "I'm taking you in, to answer pertinent questions about your argument with the murder victim but also because you refused to cooperate when I first asked you and are obstructing the investigation."

Mrs. Cassidy glanced at Delta and whispered, "I don't know if all of this is legal."

West must have overheard her for he said emphatically, "You can call a lawyer once we're at the station. This is strictly by the book."

"I can't afford one." Tilly looked up now. Her eyes were panicked, but her voice sounded firm. "You have the wrong suspect, Sheriff. I was nowhere near that motel last night."

West narrowed his eyes. "How do you know the victim died last night?"

Good question, Delta thought.

"I don't know when he died," Tilly said in a rush, "but I was at the store working on my display until midnight, and then I went to my van and slept inside it. I've been nowhere else."

"Yes, you came back to the cottage to bring us the key," Delta pointed out.

Tilly ignored her. She said to West, "You're entirely mistaken, Sheriff. I have nothing to do with it."

"Then why did you run?"

"I didn't run. I was looking at the museum's displays. They can give me new ideas for my miniatures."

"You're panting, and there's sweat on your brow." West studied her with a suspicious look.

Tilly insisted, "I had already left the room before you came in."

Delta wasn't sure if Tilly had been there when West had stormed in. Focused on his arrival, she hadn't done a head count. Would Mrs. Cassidy know, or Jane or Gran? There had been plenty of witnesses.

"Don't worry," Delta told Tilly. "We'll arrange for a lawyer and have you out again in no time. This is obviously all a big mistake."

West shook his head. "I know things you don't, Miss

Douglas. I'd advise you to stay away from this case. You can only get burned."

Delta pushed her heels against the floorboards as West took Tilly away like some dangerous convict. That big sheriff with such a little bewildered middle-aged lady... Delta felt so sorry for Tilly. To get arrested in the town you had been invited to...

Tilly jerked up her head and cried, "Where's Buddy? He walked with me when I went to look around."

Delta peered around the room but didn't see the chihuahua anywhere.

"I have to look for my dog," Tilly insisted, trying to pull away from West. The metal cuffs clinked.

West shook his head. "It's full of people here. They can find your dog for you."

"Don't worry about it," Mrs. Cassidy said. "I have experience with dogs. I'll find Buddy." Tilly didn't seem convinced, but West ushered her along.

Mrs. Cassidy continued to Delta, "I also have a friend or two who know lawyers. I'll make a few calls to get some help for Tilly." She put a hand on Delta's arm. "I'm sorry your party turned out this way."

"I almost feel like I don't deserve that medal. Now the exhibition I brought to town is associated with murder!"

"We'll solve the matter. I'll have a look for little Buddy. You go to the others and tell them what happened. Go on." Briskly, Mrs. Cassidy turned away to start searching for the missing chihuahua.

Delta wished she could feel quite so in control of the situation. But her head was spinning, and a voice whispered in the back of her mind repeating West's words: *I know things you don't.*

What things?

Hadn't Jonas said he thought he remembered Tilly's name from a case?

Did I invite a criminal to town?

She dragged her feet back to where the others were. Gran asked worriedly, "Did Sheriff West really arrest Tilly Tay? How on earth can he think a frail woman like her could stab a man in the back? That's so unlikely."

"It might be possible if she was very angry," Bessie said. "I read in a book—"

Jane cut her short saying, "We need to prove Tilly didn't know that man. And where she was at the time of the murder. Can we do that?"

"If the time of death was before midnight," Hazel said in a hopeful tone, "and Tilly says she was in our store..."

Delta shook her head. "I went to check if she was still there, remember, and that was before midnight. She wasn't there anymore."

"So, she lied to the sheriff?" Jane sounded pensive. "I wonder why."

Delta took a deep breath. "I'm sorry to be the bearer of more bad news, but, if the murdered man is who I think he is, Tilly did argue with him. And maybe he wasn't trying to sell her insurance. That is what she told me to explain their altercation, but he did say she had to cooperate and she might be sorry if she didn't. He mentioned too much being at stake. I wondered at the time if he meant at stake for himself or for her."

"Or both of them," Jane supplied, "if they did know each other."

Rita said, "You mean he followed her to town to pressure her about something…"

"Yes." Delta looked at the other women. "If the sheriff knows about some connection between them that we don't, he might have a case in the making."

Jane clapped her hands. "All the more reason to get a good lawyer on this. And we can help. We've worked out murders before."

The other women nodded and started talking among themselves. Mrs. Cassidy came in to report she hadn't seen Buddy anywhere at first glance and would start a more thorough search. She said to Delta, "I know every nook and cranny of this museum. I'll find him." Lowering her voice, she continued, "I saw something in the display, back at Wanted. A man murdered with a mattock. Outside the local boardinghouse. Suspicious, right?"

Delta swallowed. "I know. I saw that detail this morning when we arrived at the shop. Tilly must have added it last night when she was working alone. But... If she is a killer, she wouldn't leave a clue in her own display, would she?"

"It would be rather risky." Mrs. Cassidy agreed. "But we hardly know her."

Delta bit her lip. "What have we gotten ourselves into now?"

Chapter Five

WHEN DELTA AND HAZEL CAME BACK TO WANTED, CURIOUS locals were in front, peeking inside. Hazel elbowed Delta. "They must have heard Tilly was arrested, and they want to know what's up. We can't tell them anything. The mere word 'murder' will cause commotion. We should pretend like we haven't got a clue."

Delta didn't know whether this was the best way to go about it, but, as they were already closing in on the crowd, she couldn't discuss it with her friend. Someone spotted them and called, "Nice, that is. You open an exhibition for us, and then you lock the door and go elsewhere. We want to see this tiny Tundish."

"Yes," another agreed. "I want to see if it's as good as they say Tilly Tay makes them."

Relief trickled through Delta's chest. "Of course. Sorry about that." She unlocked the door, and the people poured inside. They oohed and aahed as they walked around the display pointing out details to each other. "That tiny horse looks exactly like our Thunderbolt."

Grimacing, Hazel whispered to Delta, "That was a narrow escape. But the arrest is bound to become breaking news soon enough. And what do we say then?"

"That they should ask the police for more information. How can we know what West is doing? He sure isn't sharing anything important with us." Delta blew a lock of hair from her face. She was tempted to call Jonas and see if his tour with the stressed businessmen had already ended. She needed his advice on this matter. He knew more about police work than she ever would and could tell her what West was probably basing his charges on. At the thought, Jonas walked through the door with Spud by his side. He told the dog to stay at the door and wound himself past the people in his path to reach Delta. He grinned. "May I congratulate you? I heard that you were voted shopkeeper of the season. Sorry I couldn't be there when it all happened."

"Thanks," Delta said.

Jonas frowned slightly. "That doesn't sound very

enthusiastic. I assure you it's a big deal around here. And you're a newcomer at that."

"Oh, I do appreciate the honor. But there's a little problem." Her heart sank even further when she considered their predicament. How could the festive mood have turned sour so quickly? "Could you step into the back with me?"

With question marks written all over his face, Jonas followed her into the pantry. He looked her over. "What's up?"

"Tilly Tay was taken in by the police."

"Why? For a traffic violation or something? I heard she's driving around in a battered old van..."

"I wish it was something that simple. We could pay the fine for her, and that would be it. No, it's something rather more dramatic. Sheriff West thinks she killed someone."

Jonas's jaw sagged. "Sorry? He thinks she *killed* someone? How?"

"This morning, a traveling insurance salesman was found dead outside the motel. He was stabbed in the back. West found out somehow that the man had an argument with Tilly shortly before he died. I'm afraid that I have to admit that Tilly did argue with a man in the street yesterday, so, if that is the same guy as the murder victim, we can't deny the argument between them took place. However, Tilly seemed to be unintimidated by it, and I can't see her going after the guy later and doing something as drastic as stabbing him to death."

Jonas hemmed. "You don't know how bothersome he might have been. If he had her phone number, he might have kept calling her. Or he might have shown up at her van again? Stalking is a terrible thing. It puts an immense strain on those pursued. Maybe she felt like she couldn't take it anymore?"

"Then you're already assuming this guy had harassed her before?"

"It would be odd of West to assume Tilly killed him after one short altercation in the street. In public view and all."

"I see what you mean. They must have had more history than that." Delta nodded. West had warned her that he knew things she didn't. A prior connection between Tilly and the dead man could very well be among those things. "Anyway, West took her. Because she walked off when he came in, he thinks she tried to run and put her in cuffs."

"She walked off? Or she did run?" Jonas asked, tilting his head. His blue eyes had a searching expression as he tried to work out Tilly's personality.

Delta sighed. "I'm not sure, to be honest. Tilly has a mind of her own. The workmen who came to deliver the display seemed eager to avoid her." She wished with all her might she hadn't asked the eccentric miniature artist to exhibit at Wanted.

"Hey, listen." Jonas put a hand on her arm. "I can understand you're upset about someone connected with the store getting involved with the police. But it's really none of your business. They'll tell her to get a good lawyer and…"

"Tilly already said she can't afford one."

"Then they will get her a lawyer out of some program who works for free. Either way, she'll have a defense offered to her."

"I know. But the Paper Posse already jumped on the chance to start sleuthing again."

Jonas groaned. "Those women can't be stopped."

Delta felt bad he was judging her friends like that. "They did provide valuable information in the other two cases we worked on," she reminded him.

"Yes, they did, but this isn't the third case we are going to work on." His tone was firm as he repeated her words. "We're going to leave it to the police. A traveling insurance salesman stabbed at the motel has absolutely nothing to do with you and Hazel. The other times, it was different because you were on the scene when it happened, but this murder was miles from here. The prime suspect may have an exhibition at your store, but the exhibition itself isn't linked to the murder."

"I wouldn't be too sure about that."

"How do you mean?"

Delta took a deep breath. "It's not as simple as you think. Tilly was at our store working on her display the night of the murder. She was unhappy with some details and got Hazel to give her the key so she could work in Wanted on her own, have peace and quiet. Tilly says she was there until midnight, but she lied, because I came to see how she was doing, and Tilly wasn't there. Also..."

Delta looked for a way to put it that wouldn't sound rather insane. "I think there is a clue to the murder in the display."

"Excuse me? What do you mean?"

It does sound insane. But the genuine interest in Jonas's expression gave her courage to explain. "This morning I saw that there was a tiny prospector lying dead outside the miniature town's boardinghouse. He had a mattock stabbed into his back. It's so like the murder."

"And the main suspect added that detail to her display?" Jonas sounded incredulous.

"Yes, or someone else did."

"Who has access to the store? Except for you and Hazel, of course."

"Nobody."

There was a knock at the pantry door, and Gran put her head around it. "Can I step in and share some important information?"

"Of course," Delta said, waving her in.

Gran smiled at Jonas. "I'm so glad you want to help out. You know how these things work."

Jonas raised a hand as if to stop her. "I'm just explaining to Delta that she shouldn't get involved."

"She's already involved." Gran's face contorted with worry. "I went to the cottage to check inside your mailbox, find the key Tilly Tay allegedly left there. It wasn't in the box. It's missing."

Delta exhaled hard. "That can't be true."

"Yes, it is."

"So someone can get in here," Jonas said. "Someone other than Tilly Tay can have added the murdered prospector to the scene."

"But why?" Delta looked at him. "Do you honestly think a killer would drive across town to a stationery shop to leave a clue in a miniature display after murdering someone?" As she put it into words, it seemed to become more ridiculous by the second. "It makes no sense."

"Not to us, but, to the killer, it might be perfectly logical. If he or she knew Tilly would get suspected, it would be an extra pointer in her direction."

Gran said, "I wanted you to know. I'll leave again." She was at the door when Delta said, "But, Gran, you can stay in the store, if you like and…"

"I have an appointment. See you later, darling."

Jonas grinned at Delta. "Feisty old lady. Knows what she wants. Good thing she checked on the key. Now that it's not there, we have to figure that anyone could have come in here last night to change the display."

"How are we going to find out who it was?" Delta asked. "There are no cameras on Mattock Street."

"Well, not yet, at least." Jonas pointed a finger at her. "We can ignore the missing key for the moment. I mean, act like we don't know it's missing, and then we can put a camera inside the store and see if someone shows up."

"What for? They've left their clue. They're not coming back."

"You don't know that. Killers can be very jittery after the fact and start believing they left behind evidence on the scene or that they made another mistake that can give them away. They might return to assure themselves it's all okay. Let me arrange for a camera to be put up tonight after closing hours. I can watch the footage live from a nearby stakeout."

Delta suppressed a smile at his wording. "You were the one telling me this was definitely not a case we'd be working."

"That was before I knew about the missing key. It can really help. And, if nothing happens, at least I'll make sure your property is safe."

Delta sighed. "I'm not sure. Shouldn't we simply have a locksmith change the lock? That way, we keep any creeps outside and you don't have to keep watch all night."

"But I'd like to do it. For you." Jonas stared into her eyes. For a moment, she seemed to detect something tender there, a concern that ran deeper than friendship. Then he turned away abruptly. "I have to set up a lot to make it work tonight. I'll let you know later how it's all going to pan out."

"Okay." Delta watched him disappear. She leaned on the sink. It felt cold under her clammy hands. What a sudden, strange turn. From the happiness of unveiling their display and receiving the wonderful "shopkeeper of the season" medal, to another murder case. The killer walking around with the key to their shop in their pocket?

She shivered. If she were being honest, she wanted to call a locksmith right away. But she did trust Jonas's judgment. If he thought he could learn more, they had to try.

Also, for Tilly's sake.

Still, Delta didn't just feel sorry for the artist. She also knew that Tilly had been far from honest about what was happening here. If the key wasn't in the mailbox, what had Tilly done with it? Why had she lied about putting it there?

Or had she actually put it there and had it been taken by someone else who was keeping an eye on Tilly?

Delta raked back her hair and sighed.

Maybe Tilly would tell the truth to Sheriff West.

———————

Around three, Mrs. Cassidy rushed into Wanted and drew Delta aside. She was glad to see Mrs. Cassidy after messaging her several times to ask if Buddy was found and hadn't received a reply. The little dog's fate weighed on her mind. Where had he vanished to? Would he be okay?

There were still a good number of people admiring the display, and Mrs. Cassidy spoke softly so as not to be overheard. "I got a lawyer for Tilly via my contacts. She went to the police station to talk to her client. Seems Tilly is very upset, and it's affecting her memory. In fact, she was so incoherent that the lawyer asked a doctor to come and look at her, and he determined she was in shock and advised that they bring her to a safe place where she can be guarded during her recovery. The lawyer called me, I called Ray, and, to make a long story short, she is now at the Lodge Hotel, in one of their suites, with a deputy at the door to make sure she can't get away. The doctor gave her a sedative so she can have a good sleep, and they hope to get more from her in the morning."

Delta tilted her head. "Do you really think she's in shock?"

Mrs. Cassidy shrugged. "She was taken to a police station in cuffs. That's enough to upset anyone, and she's not twenty anymore, you know."

Delta nodded. "I'm just a little wary, Tilly seemed to have lied about a few things. In fact, when she was in the store unpacking and a deputy showed up to give her a parking ticket, she also lied to get away with it."

"A little white lie. Like all of us use from time to time."

"That's what I told myself. But I wonder now if she's prone to twisting the truth, just a little, to her advantage. She might not mean any harm, in general, but now that this is a murder case..." Delta took a deep breath. "I'm surprised Ray wanted to have her at the hotel."

"I told him he'd do you and Hazel a real favor, as your store was involved, and he's always keen on pleasing Hazel, so..." Mrs. Cassidy winked at her.

Delta didn't smile. "Rosalyn can't be happy with having a murder suspect at the hotel and a policeman guarding the door." Her gut clenched. The hotel's reputation meant everything to Rosalyn. If Tilly's presence caused trouble, Rosalyn would surely blame Hazel and her. "There will be talk."

"West assured me they would be discreet. He turned somewhat softer toward Tilly when he heard the doctor's verdict about shock and all. He doesn't want her to fall really ill and get blamed for police brutality as a result."

"Especially not with Tilly being well known," Delta supplied. "I can imagine."

"I can't really blame West for being frustrated with the way his investigation is going. He wanted to check Tilly's van for clues, but it's not parked anywhere in town."

"But how did Tilly get to Wanted for the opening of her exhibition?"

"I don't know. And we can't ask her now either." Mrs. Cassidy rubbed her temples. "Anyway, now you know the latest. I think we did the best we could so far. We're not sure she's guilty, so we must assume she's innocent and protect her interests."

Delta nodded. "That seems like a valid approach. Did you manage to find Buddy in the museum?"

"Unfortunately, no." Mrs. Cassidy sighed. "I heard him bark at one point, but he seems to be crawling from one hiding place into the next. Not even the dog treats Nugget adores can coax him out. I'm worried he understood his human was in danger, and he thinks he's now not safe himself. Actually, he'll probably only show himself if Tilly appears in person to look for him."

"But she's at the Lodge under a sedative."

"I know. But don't you worry about it. Buddy is secure inside the museum, not roaming the street where he could get hit by a car or catch a cold in the rain. He's safe and warm, and over time, he will get hungry and come out to get some food. If we can't catch him before closing hours, I'll sleep there myself to make sure he's not alone."

Delta smiled at her. She could have known that Mrs. Cassidy, as a real dog lover, would do her utmost to care for Tilly's dog. "Thanks so much."

Mrs. Cassidy waved it off. "I called the lady who works at the front desk at the motel—well, at least for a few shifts each week—and I asked her if she could tell me more about this murdered man. As it happens, he checked in when she was on duty. She could tell me his name and his occupation. Mr. Smith, a dealer in car parts."

"Smith?" Delta tasted the name as she spoke it. "Sounds suspiciously simple. Did she ask for an ID?"

"No. She told me, in the strictest confidence of course, that her boss isn't too particular about who rents the rooms as long as money comes in. The guy paid cash, for three nights in advance. That was enough for them to let him check in."

"And then he gets murdered, and they can't even tell the police who he is." Delta grimaced.

Mrs. Cassidy leaned down to pat Nugget who became impatient with the prolonged conversation. "I did ask the desk clerk if she had noticed anything particular about him. She said he had very little luggage, just a canvas overnight bag. Oh, and he had a tattoo on his left wrist. He had a big watch hiding half of it, but she saw it anyway."

Delta jerked upright. "Then it's definitely the same guy who fought with Tilly in the street. I also saw a little bit of the tattoo. I don't know if he likes showy watches or it was that big to hide the tattoo because it's easily identifiable?"

"Not necessarily," Mrs. Cassidy said. "A large watch may be a status symbol to him."

"Hmmm." Delta pursed her lips. She wasn't about to let

go of her theory that the man had been secretive on purpose. "He told the motel clerk he was selling car parts. But Tilly said he approached her about insurance. So which is it?"

"The lawyer will no doubt hear more details about the victim, so she can tell me what she learns."

"Will she do that?" Delta asked doubtfully. Wasn't there something like client confidentiality?

"I should hope so." Mrs. Cassidy straightened up. "I'm paying her."

Delta's eyes widened. "Why would you do that?"

"First of all, I was assured she knows what she's doing. Second, I want to help out. Wanted is involved in this case, and I don't want a stain on your reputation. Especially not after you got shopkeeper of the season."

Delta looked her over. Suddenly she understood. "You nominated me for that title."

"Along with other Paper Posse friends." Mrs. Cassidy smiled. "We thought you really deserved it, and so did all the other shopkeepers. The vote was strongly in your favor."

Normally it would be wonderful to hear this, but, under the circumstances, Delta's heart sank. "Now I feel super guilty. You all believed in me, and, on the very day I win that medal, the shop becomes the center of a murder investigation."

"Not the center," Mrs. Cassidy corrected cheerfully. "The dead body wasn't in the shop. You're only marginally connected to it. And, the sooner we can cut that tie, the better." She nodded briskly. "I'll keep you posted. Also, about my attempts to lure Buddy out into the open. Don't worry too much." With a squeeze of Delta's shoulder, she turned around and left.

Delta stood staring, with a burn behind her eyes. Her new friends here in Tundish truly believed in her and had wanted her to have this medal and the honorary title that went with it. But she was the one who had invited Tilly Tay to town. Who had, as it now turned out, invited only trouble herself. Whether Tilly had brought it along, or it had followed her, danger was now among them all. People were admiring the display only because they weren't aware yet that the artist was in jail.

Well, not exactly in jail yet. She was at the Lodge Hotel, sleeping so she'd feel better and could give a statement.

But did Tilly really intend to give a statement?

Or was another escape attempt in mind? She had to be worried about Buddy. Having seen her with the dog, Delta was convinced Buddy was Tilly's darling, her baby. She would be horribly anxious about what happened to him. At the very least, someone had to go and tell her that Buddy was cared for.

And what about her van? If Tilly hadn't brought it into town, it was left somewhere else, with all of her possessions inside. They had to find out where it was so they could look after it.

Acting quickly, Delta told Hazel she had an urgent errand to run and headed toward the Lodge. It was probably a bad idea. West would obviously not want them anywhere near Tilly. But maybe the deputy at the door would allow her to write a note for her?

Anything to make sure that Tilly wouldn't wake up and panic about Buddy and her van. People under emotional strain did the oddest things, and, if Tilly attempted escape, West would be furious and Ray and his family involved, which would have a ripple effect across town.

I have to make sure that Tilly Tay stays put.

Chapter Six

WHEN DELTA PARKED HER CAR AT THE LODGE HOTEL, SHE noticed a man in a jacket with elbow patches walking around in the parking lot, writing down all the license plates. She ducked to avoid being seen as he came closer to her vehicle.

Sven LeDuc, on the hunt. She had been pleased earlier that day to see him in their shop for the display reveal and had even appreciated his enthusiasm for the result, but now she would rather crawl into a hole and hide. He probably knew about the arrest at the museum and, perhaps, even about Tilly's transfer to the hotel. Why else would he be here?

A knock on her window made her straighten. LeDuc stood beside the car, peering in. Delta pasted a friendly smile on her face and opened the window. LeDuc studied her with a frown. "Did you drop something?"

"Yes, my car keys." Delta kept smiling so hard her jaw hurt. "I popped over to have a chat with Rosalyn about some crafting events Hazel and I are organizing here at the Lodge. But, in my hurry to get inside on time for the appointment, I dropped my keys and they got under the mat."

"I thought you'd have come over here to see your protégé Tilly Tay. She's staying here, right? I heard she had a nervous breakdown and needs to see a psychiatrist. It's the artist's way, I suppose. Genius coming close to madness. Beethoven was virtually certified. Or was it Chopin? Anyway, van Gogh did cut off his own ear." He nodded solemnly. "I want to write a background piece about mental strain and the arts, and I hoped for a short word with the person treating Tilly Tay."

That explained his skulking in the parking lot. Delta almost sighed with relief until she realized it wouldn't take long before he learned the true cause of Tilly's breakdown and would be on the case. She got out of the car. "I have to rush. Good luck with your article."

LeDuc looked suspicious as she passed him by, but he let her go without another word.

Inside the Lodge, at the reception desk, she found Rosalyn in deep conversation with the clerk. Rosalyn wore a burgundy pantsuit and had her hair swept back in a loose bun. The gemstones in her long earrings glittered in the light. She tapped at a paper on the desk with a meticulously man-icured finger. Everything about her was so perfect that Delta cringed at the idea of letting a murder suspect anywhere near Rosalyn's hotel. *This is bound to lead to disaster.*

As if Rosalyn sensed someone hovering, she turned round and spotted Delta. Her expression changed from animated to annoyed. "You're the very person I want to talk to. My office, right now."

She clicked ahead of Delta on her high heels and swung the door open.

Inside, sunshine poured in across her almost-empty desk, with a computer whirring and a sleek smartphone's screen lighting up as another message came in. Rosalyn threw a casual glance at it as she settled into her leather chair and said, "I don't appreciate you putting pressure on Ray to accommodate a police suspect at our hotel."

"I didn't put pressure on Ray. I heard about arrangements *after* the fact."

Rosalyn waved a hand. "I'm sure Ray offered of his own accord, but he did so because he's under the impression he has to step in and help out whenever one of you two falls into a puddle. However, I heard you made shopkeeper of the season. With so much support from other locals, you can no doubt take care of your own business. I'm entertaining some important families here this week, and I don't want police around or the guests to know we're housing a murder suspect."

"Tilly Tay has nothing to do with that stabbed salesman," Delta said, with more certainty than she herself felt. "She's accused because she had an altercation with him, but that's hardly enough to base any real accusation on. Sheriff West jumped to conclusions before. Remember Isabel?"

Rosalyn flushed at the reference to her sister's arrest during a previous murder investigation.

Delta said sweetly, "We should wait until the sheriff has a chance to look into the case more."

"Tilly Tay could have told him what she knows. Instead, she's pretending to be in shock."

"Pretending?" Delta echoed. That Rosalyn confirmed her own doubts about Tilly's integrity made her knees go weak.

"Yes. She was taken to her room, and, five minutes after the deputy and the doctor who came with her had left, I smelled cigarette smoke coming from under the door. Guests are not allowed to smoke in their rooms, and I wanted to barge in and tell her so, but there was a policeman standing guard."

Rosalyn crossed her arms over her chest. "I'm telling you that nice-looking little lady is playing games with all of you. She's *not* in shock. She knows more than she's letting on. I want her out of my hotel before the newspapers start writing about it."

"They won't," Delta protested, rather weakly, her mind flashing to Sven LeDuc already skulking in the parking lot. He claimed to be looking for Tilly's psychiatrist, but who knew what he was really up to? How much he already knew, or was about to find out...

Rosalyn said, "Since Ray agreed to this arrangement with the police, and I don't want to argue with West, I will tolerate it for one night. But one night only. In the morning, you figure out a way to get her unshocked and out of here, ready to make her statement or whatever. Or you take her into your own home. If you are so certain she's innocent."

Delta put up both hands, palms out. "I didn't know Ray would suggest it or that it would be inconvenient to you and your important guests. I'll make sure she leaves in the morning."

Rosalyn nodded and picked up her phone. Delta took this as her cue to leave. "Oh," she asked at the door. "What room is Tilly in?"

"319. But they won't let you see her either."

Delta went up to the third floor anyway and found the

deputy seated on a chair in front of the door marked 319. He was leafing through an old copy of the *Tundish Trader* with a bored expression on his face. Delta greeted him cheerfully. "Good afternoon. Can I talk to Tilly Tay for a moment? Her dog went missing this morning, when the sheriff came to take her to the station, and I'd like to update her on how he is."

"She's sleeping." The deputy turned the page and read on, obviously considering the discussion closed.

But she wasn't about to let him dismiss her like that. "Buddy is very important to her," she pleaded, "and knowing he's safe can really put her mind at ease and help prepare her for giving her statement to the sheriff."

The deputy considered this but still shook his head. "I was told not to let anyone in to see her. If those are my orders, I can't make any exceptions."

Understandable. But still... Delta's mind raced to come up with a counterargument.

In the silence that reigned in the corridor, Delta could hear a sharp click. As if a door was closing somewhere nearby.

"Can I write her a note?" she asked. "We don't want her worrying about her dog and getting upset again. That will only delay proceedings."

The deputy seemed to understand that she wasn't leaving

and said with a sigh, "You can write her a note if you want to, but I'll have to see what is in it before I pass it on."

"Fine, no problem." Delta opened her purse, pulled up her notebook and a pen, and wrote a short message to Tilly explaining that Mrs. Cassidy was caring for Buddy and that they had also arranged for a lawyer, free of charge, for Tilly.

Again, she heard that click, but now it was farther away. What could it be? The central heating maybe? Guests entering and leaving their rooms?

The deputy accepted the note, glanced over it and put it in his pocket. "I'll give it to her later." He stretched his shoulders and stared in the direction of the elevators as if he wished he could get away from this dull chore.

Suddenly, a rough scraping sound like wood across stone interrupted the quiet. The deputy listened a moment, but then sank back into his lethargy. The sound hadn't come from Tilly's room but from somewhere down the corridor.

Delta waved goodbye and ran to the staircase to get down quickly. She walked through the lobby and the dining room onto the terrace. There she looked up and tried to determine what room was 319. Her grandmother had stayed at the Lodge for a few days when she had just arrived in town, and Delta tried to work out the layout from memory.

As she scanned balconies, she spotted wiry gray curls peeping out over a balcony railing. Instinctively, Delta scooted backwards and hid herself behind a large pot with a ball-shaped box sprouting out. She crouched and took a deep breath before trying to peek at the balcony where she had seen the curls.

Now a head was visible, peering to see inside the adjoining hotel room. Delta blinked to clear her view. Tilly Tay. Not sedated in bed, but secretively spying outside of her own hotel room doors. But no, Delta started counting, calculating quickly. That couldn't be the balcony of 319. It was more likely 323. What was Tilly doing on someone else's balcony? And how did she get there?

The artist quickly tiptoed past the doors and opened the gate to get onto the next balcony. A click resounded, like the ones Delta had heard when talking to the deputy. Of course. The Lodge's balconies were constructed so that, in case of a fire, the hotel guests could easily go from one balcony to the next to reach the fire escape on the side of the building. Tilly was opening the connecting gates one by one and hurrying across the balconies to reach the staircase leading down onto the terrace.

She's trying to get away. I can't let her do this.

Delta's mouth went dry. She ran from pot to pot, keeping

her eyes on the figure above, but Tilly was focused on reaching the fire escape without being seen from one of the rooms. She stopped at one point and peered in, waited, and then quickly ducked past, rushing across the next balcony in a mad dash.

A voice rang out from behind a half-opened door. It opened further, and a man looked out. He spotted Tilly and called out to her. "Hey, lady, what are you doing?"

Tilly was at the fire escape and started to climb down. The metal creaked under her steps. Delta crouched behind the last pot close to it, waiting for her to reach ground level. Then, as Tilly stopped to look round the corner of the hotel, Delta jumped at her and grabbed her shoulder.

Tilly yelped and swung round. As she spied Delta, she said, "Oh, it's you. Let me go. I have to take care of Buddy and my van."

The anxiety in her eyes seemed genuine enough.

"Buddy is still at the museum," Delta rushed to say. "Mrs. Cassidy is taking care of him." She thought it better not to mention the dog was hiding.

"He doesn't understand what happened," Tilly said with a catch in her voice. "Why I was taken away by this loud, angry man. I have to go calm him. And my van... Someone might come and steal all my models. My life's work."

"Where is the van? I'm sure the police will want a look at it, and, once they've taken it over to the station, it will be perfectly safe there."

"Taken it to the station?" Tilly echoed with disbelief lining her voice. "What for?"

"They'll want to search it, I suppose, for evidence or something. Unfortunately, you're a suspect."

"For no reason." Tilly's cheeks turned red. "I have nothing to do with some guy who died."

Delta's emotions bounced between sympathy for the woman and annoyance that she wasn't being forthcoming about what she knew. Couldn't Tilly see she was harming her own interests by being so reticent? If she really didn't know anything, she could be upfront about it.

"He talked to you on Mattock Street. I myself saw that. He wasn't trying to sell you insurance either. He mentioned too much being at stake." She decided to bluff a little and see if that got any answers. "You knew him."

Tilly's eyes flickered a moment with panic and uncertainty, deliberating how best to respond. But, suddenly, she turned away from Delta. "I'm going to see to my dog and my van, and you can't stop me."

"Yes, I can." Delta tightened her grip on her shoulder.

"Friends of mine vouched for you." Frustration with Tilly's stubbornness clogged her throat. "Ray arranged for you to stay here to recover, against his sister's wishes. He is just rebuilding his bond with Rosalyn, and I'm not letting you ruin it for him. Mrs. Cassidy also got you a lawyer, at her expense, and..."

"So I should be grateful? Because you all want to help Tilly Tay, the famous artist? I know what it's like. People are only kind when they want something. They're all selfish and intrusive. Maybe you also want a look inside my van to tell the newspapers how I live. But that is my business. Not yours, or anyone else's."

Delta blinked at Tilly's tone, which was sharp and emotional. She had no idea what it was like to live in the public eye and feel scrutinized and judged all the time. Maybe Tilly felt she had to defend herself because she couldn't believe people genuinely wanted to help her?

She must be incredibly lonely.

Delta said slowly and emphatically, "I don't want to intrude into your life at all. I just want to clear up this mistaken suspicion that you had anything to do with the murder. We believe in your innocence. That's why we're helping you. But you're making it hard, if not impossible, for us. You can't walk away now. West will surely think you're guilty."

"I've never met such an incompetent man." Tilly huffed.

"It wasn't very smart to walk away when he wanted to talk to you."

"I have nothing to say about it."

She isn't denying she walked away. "Tilly, please." Delta released pressure a fraction to show she meant well, but not give the woman a chance to suddenly dash off. "We're all on the same side. You may have had unpleasant experiences with people coming after you for a scoop or whatever, but we are a nice small-town community here. People genuinely care."

"Really?" Tilly gave her a sad look. "Maybe they care for you and Hazel. They are worried your shop will be involved in this, and they want to ensure you aren't hurt by the publicity that is surely to follow. But no one cares about me. I can be accused, maligned, dragged through the dirt in all the media, and everything I worked for will be ruined." She burst into tears.

Delta put an arm around her narrow shoulders. "Tilly, please, believe me, we don't want to harm you in any way. We want to help clear your name. Mrs. Cassidy got that lawyer for you so she can sort out what happened and get you released. We don't believe for one moment you had anything to do with this murder. All you have to do is tell the police what you know and then..."

Tilly pulled herself away. She hung her head. "I'll go back into my room. I'm sorry I was so silly." She started to climb up the fire escape.

"Wait!" Delta called. "Where is your van parked? I'll go find it for you and make sure that nothing happened to your models."

Tilly hesitated, her hand around the fire escape railing so tightly the knuckles turned white. Then she said, "There's an abandoned campground north of town. I parked the van there, behind the old groundskeeper's cottage. But be careful; it's a dilapidated lot."

Delta watched as the artist walked back across the balconies and entered her own room. She took a deep breath. If it was so easy for Tilly to get away, she might try again as soon as Delta left. If she had lied about the location of the van, Delta would be going on a wild-goose chase while Tilly took off to where the van really was. She could leave town and cause a lot of embarrassment for everyone involved.

But she'd never leave without Buddy. So, if she ran from here, she'd have to go to the museum to find her dog.

Delta bit her lip. Whether Tilly would be capable of

making a run for it or not, there was really nothing else to do but inform the police and ask them to guard the fire escape as well.

Delta reached for her phone. She could tell West that she knew where the van was and ask him to send a deputy to meet her near it. She wouldn't reveal the exact location so the officer didn't get there ahead of her, and she could ensure he didn't damage any of Tilly's property. The models did have commercial value, not to mention how attached Tilly was to them. They were her life's work. And, with her reputation under threat, her legacy needed protection more than ever.

To prevent the eager policeman from rushing ahead of her, Delta had told him to meet her at the junction where the sand road led to the abandoned campground. From there, she drove ahead with the police car following her. She parked outside the old groundskeeper's house, which looked ready to collapse. Windows had broken and the roof sagged. The deputy who came over to her as she locked her car shook his head. "Place should be ripped down completely. Look how dangerous it is. You're not saying we have to get inside?"

"No, definitely not. I think the van is parked around here."

Delta walked briskly ahead of him, rounding the building at a safe distance. The wind breathed through the tall trees above their heads, and an ominous creaking sounded every few seconds. She wasn't sure if it was branches rubbing together or the crumbling construction of the building singing its swan song.

Relief swept through her as she spotted the van. But the happiness faded just as quickly when she saw the side door was wide open. Had someone been here ahead of them?

"Let me handle this," the deputy said. His voice was tight and his hand went to his gun. "There could be someone inside."

"I'll wait here," Delta offered at once. "But be careful." The idea of a confrontation happening before her eyes made her skin crawl, and sweat trickled between her shoulder blades.

"I'll take my time," the deputy assured her, approaching the vehicle slowly. Delta kept scanning the length of the van, looking for suspicious movement so she could cry out and warn the officer if need be.

But nothing stirred. Only the eerie creaking from above and behind could be heard, driving goose flesh up her arms.

The deputy was at the door of the van and looked in. He

muttered something, then turned to her. "Someone ransacked it. Everything is overturned."

Oh, no! Delta bit her lip. Tilly had been worried about her models being broken. She walked up to the deputy and asked, "Is there a lot of damage?"

The deputy gestured to her to stand back. He went inside, still moving cautiously and with his weapon at hand. After a while, he came out. "I need a team in there to look for fingerprints. DNA, maybe, if we're lucky." He pulled up his phone. "You'd better leave. We have a lot of work to do here."

Delta desperately wanted a peek inside to see how bad it was but realized the policeman wouldn't let her near it to preserve possible traces. "I appreciate that. Could I ask you for just one favor? Tilly Tay's dog got spooked when she was arrested, and he's hiding in the museum. We haven't managed to draw him out yet. If there is a dog toy inside or his bed, could I maybe take that along to try and lure him?"

The deputy shrugged. "I saw an old bed and a chewed-on bone. I'll get it for you."

While he went back inside, Delta peered through the open door. Boxes were overturned, and scattered models lay on the floor. Clothes had been thrown over them, and a saucepan rested in a corner. Even with the little she could see, it was evident that the van's contents had been overturned by some-one who was determined to find something. What had they been looking for?

And could the ransacking help Tilly's case? Could it prove she was a victim herself?

Having talked to Tilly at the Lodge and sensed her raw emotions, Delta wanted nothing more than help her to sort out what had happened. Get her off the hook with West, for the moment, and reunited with her beloved dog.

Delta's thoughts were racing, but at least she now had the bed, which might be a way to track down Buddy. If the idea she had would work...

Pacing up and down, she called Jonas. As soon as he picked up, she explained the situation briefly and asked him whether he could bring Spud to the museum to help look for the missing dog. "He's so small he can crawl into spaces and behind objects, and Mrs. Cassidy had no luck locating him so far. She even offered to sleep at the museum tonight so the poor creature isn't left alone, but it would be better to find him before closing hours. I have a dog bed here, with Buddy's scent on it. Can you use it for tracking him? I know Spud used to track cash, and he might not be used to finding a fellow dog..."

"I've got a friend with just the dog you need. Let me ring her, and I'm coming out as quickly as I can."

Her? Delta thought. That little stab of jealousy was silly, she knew. Jonas probably had lots of female friends. She wondered if maybe she was simply one of them. Maybe he didn't consider her special. The way he looked at Delta, or what connected them, it could all be in her head.

Chapter Seven

HALF AN HOUR LATER, JONAS ARRIVED AT THE MUSEUM. HE studied Delta's expression a moment. "What did you think when you found the van ransacked?"

"I wasn't worried about me; I had the deputy with me. Luckily, I hadn't decided to go it alone." She shivered a moment. "But Tilly will be so upset when she hears about this. That van is her home. Now some bad guy went through all her possessions, and the police are turning everything over again."

Jonas patted her on the shoulder. "Don't you worry about it. The fact that someone ransacked her belongings makes it more likely she's innocent in the murder. After all, why would someone come and look through her things, unless they wanted something?"

Relief trickled through her. Jonas drew the exact same conclusion she had. Surely, this would give West a different view of the case?

"Ah, there's Paula." Jonas gestured to a statuesque brunette sportily dressed who came up to them with a black Labrador on the leash. "Paula's dog used to track people and pets who got buried under rubble after earthquakes. He's retired but still got a great nose."

"Hello." Paula reached out a hand to Delta. "So nice to meet you. Jonas told me you got shopkeeper of the season. That's a huge thing in town." She shook back her brown curls. "I live on the outskirts, so I'm not really that involved with all the Tundish activities but..." She smiled widely. "I'm glad I might help out. It's a dog missing, right? Inside this building?" She scanned the gold-mining museum's front.

"Yes. It might seem a bit odd to bring in a tracking dog for something like this, but Buddy is rather small—he's a chihuahua—and very smart. He's crawling behind things and going from one room into the next, and, so far, they haven't been able to lure him out. I got his bed, and I thought we could use it somehow."

Paula led her dog over to the bed. His tail began to wag as soon as he realized what they were going to do. Jonas grinned. "Spud's just like that, can never resist an opportunity to work."

"Didn't you bring him?"

"Might have distracted Prince." Jonas nodded at the Labrador who had sniffed the dog bed from all sides and now looked at his handler for an order to begin the search.

Paula took him inside the museum where Mrs. Cassidy welcomed them and led them into the room where West had arrested Tilly. "I'll leave you to it," she whispered to Delta. "Too many people around can't be good for the search dog. And he'll need every ounce of attention. Buddy's like Houdini. One moment he's there, then he's vanished."

As soon as Paula gave the signal, the Labrador started to sniff the floorboards. He seemed to have some trouble picking up the scent, and Delta was worried there were simply too many smells from all the visitors. But then he went to the door leading into the next room and disappeared into a far corner sniffing behind a model of a miner with lamp.

"Mind the objects," an elderly male volunteer said, who was following their actions with concern.

"I wouldn't dare break anything," Paula said with a winning smile.

The volunteer turned red under his collar and offered

to get Paula a cup of tea and a snack. Paula declined with another dazzling smile.

Delta wondered if Jonas thought Paula was attractive. She was, in any case, energetic, for, as the Lab sniffed at a display, she dropped herself flat on her stomach to see underneath. "I think our little runaway hid here," she called. "I can see scratch marks."

She let go of the lead, and the Lab rounded the display and ran into another room. He sniffed here and there, going in a circle, then tracking back to the previous room.

They called Buddy repeatedly. But there was no bark in response. Prince was working precisely, every now and then taking his time to determine where the trail went.

Paula checked her watch. "We can't go on forever," she whispered to Jonas and Delta. "There is a limit to search dogs' attention span. Also, with people having walked around here all day, the trail gets vaguer as time goes by. Prince isn't the youngest anymore." She smiled down on her canine companion. "His left back leg can get painful after we've walked for a bit. I don't want to push him too far."

"You have to tell us when to stop," Jonas said. "You know him best."

Paula nodded with a serious expression. "Thing is, I don't

like to give up before we've found whoever we're looking for. Nothing worse than an unsuccessful mission."

Jonas put his hand on her arm a moment. "You're doing all you can."

Paula sighed. "Sometimes that's not enough." Her eyes were dark as she turned away from them and focused fully on the dog again.

Jonas watched her through narrowed eyes. Delta wondered if he knew how Paula felt. He himself had to have experienced cases that didn't go the way you wanted them to. Failure was always unpleasant, but especially when lives were at stake.

Suddenly there was a sound in the distance. Vague and indistinct, but...

"Was that a bark?" Paula asked with suppressed excitement in her voice.

"I think so." Jonas stood listening, but the sound didn't repeat itself.

"Could have been outside," Delta said, pointing at the nearby window to prevent them from getting overenthusiastic about nothing.

They kept listening intently as they walked on. There it was again.

Prince seemed to zero in on it, walking faster and lifting his head every few paces, trying to focus on any sounds he might catch. Delta watched in fascination.

Suddenly Prince stopped at the reception desk, where a box stood on the floor. The label of the postal delivery service was still on it. Prince stood at it, looking in.

Delta came to stand beside him. Inside the box, rolled into a ball, was Buddy. "How did he get here?" she exclaimed. "We were certain he was inside one of the rooms, hiding."

"He must have made a dash for it earlier," Paula said, "and hidden here."

"I bet he wanted to get out of the door, if he could." Jonas pointed at the entry doors. "He wants to find Tilly."

"Good boy," Paula praised her dog. Prince lowered himself to the ground and peered inside the box. He made a low whirring sound.

A head popped up from the box. With perked-up ears, Buddy peered with interest at the big dog and then reached up to stand nose to nose with him.

Paula whispered, "Look at that little diva."

Prince rolled over, and the chihuahua jumped at him, touching his paw. Soon they were running around, chasing each other and playing as if they had been best friends for years.

Jonas said, "Well, so much for having to coax a frightened dog from his hiding place. He doesn't seem traumatized to me."

"Still, he ran away," Paula reminded him. "He must have known something was off. He's just releasing tension now, but he'll still be on edge."

"You found him!" Mrs. Cassidy appeared and clapped her hands. "I'll take him home and keep an eye on him. Once he makes friends with Nugget, he won't feel alone anymore."

"I doubt Nugget wants to share her human's attention with someone else." Jonas grinned. "But we can see how they do together. If it doesn't work out, you can let me know, and I'll come and take him off your hands."

"Do you hear that?" Mrs. Cassidy smiled at Buddy. "Everyone loves you, little fellow, and wants to have you near."

Jonas patted Prince, who rubbed his head against him and then leaned down farther, reaching toward the chihuahua. Buddy was reluctant at first, carefully sniffing Jonas's hand before allowing him to scratch him behind the ears. Then he threw himself on his back for a belly rub and, soon, let himself be lifted into Jonas's arms.

"Isn't he a little treasure?" Paula enthused. She came to stand close to Jonas and cooed to the dog snuggled against Jonas's chest like a baby.

Delta felt another stab of jealousy suddenly seeing the two dog handlers and their rescue cuddled close.

She almost shook her head to dispel the idea. Paula had helped them immensely, and she should be grateful for that. "I'm so glad Buddy is all right. I'll let Tilly know. And Hazel. She'll be wondering where I'm at."

Mrs. Cassidy said, "As Buddy seems to have taken to you, Jonas, why don't you keep him tucked against you for the moment and let Delta drive you to my place? I'd rather not risk him making another dash for it."

"Fine with me."

They all set out to leave for Mrs. Cassidy's home.

"So have you known Paula long?" Delta asked as she put her car in gear.

"We met years ago at a weekend for handlers. I had no idea we'd one day live in the same town."

"She knows her stuff." Delta glanced at Jonas and his proud smile gave her that weird feeling inside again. That he had helped find Buddy said very little about their relationship status. It was the act of a friend, or maybe even a dog lover who was worried about the chihuahua's safety. It might have nothing to do with her.

And that was fine, because she didn't intend to start a relationship with him anyway. Romance just made everything so complicated. And she had her shop to think of, finding the perfect place for Gran and her...

"Have you contacted Zach yet?" Jonas asked. "You wanted to use the upcoming holidays to casually get in touch, right?"

Delta flushed. He even remembered something she had told him a while ago. Her brother Zach had caused trouble by scheduling his wedding on the very day when her other brother, Greg, a renowned athlete, competed for an important prize. That way Zach had wanted to force their parents to choose which event they attended, to find out who they thought most important. Delta did appreciate that Greg's career had taken up a lot of time and energy, and their parents might not always have been there for Zach in the way he wanted, but to play it like that had made her raving mad. Confronting him about it had caused a fight, and, since then, they hadn't been in touch.

"I might send a Christmas card. I still need to let him know about my address change." As always, her throat clogged when she thought of Zach, the argument, and the deep silence after that. "I don't really know how to handle it."

"You just put it into words. Send a card, tell him you moved. That way he knows you want him to have your current address so he can be in touch. That's an open door."

"I doubt it's enough for Zach."

"You should try. The breach hit you harder than you want to admit."

Delta glanced at him. Jonas returned her look and smiled. "I do know you that well."

A warm feeling filled her chest. Having these moments with Jonas, feeling his genuine interest in her life, reaffirmed to her they were indeed friends and nothing—or, rather, no one—could come between them.

At Mrs. Cassidy's home, they discovered their hostess had managed to get there ahead of them and welcomed them from her porch. "Bring him in. I'll point out where you can settle him."

Mrs. Cassidy let them inside into a cozy living room with large sofas around a fireplace, Old West photos on the walls, and a desk with a computer in a corner. Mrs. Cassidy opened a cupboard and got a metal fence out, which she used to fence off a little area for Buddy. Nugget circled Jonas and jumped up against his legs trying to see her new friend closer. "Put him behind the fence," Mrs. Cassidy advised. "Then they can get used to each other without any kind of uh...fight."

"Fight?" Delta echoed.

Mrs. Cassidy sighed. "Nugget is quite possessive of her toys. Last time I had a friend's dog over, he went straight for Nugget's ball, and she bit him to get it back. She isn't very strong, so it wasn't a serious wound, but still... I felt terrible. I wouldn't want Tilly to worry about the safety of her dog as long as he's with me."

Buddy looked at Nugget through the wire. She tilted her head and barked. Buddy sat down and eyed her melancholically. Nugget nuzzled the wire. Then she ran to her basket and picked up a teddy bear toy and dragged it over. She put it at the fence and pushed it with her nose so it touched the fence.

Mrs. Cassidy clapped her hands together. "Unbelievable. She's actually offering her favorite toy to him. She must sense he's sad and stressed out, and she wants him to feel better."

She snapped a photo with her phone. "I'll send this to Tilly's lawyer to share with Tilly when she next sees her."

"Thanks. Tilly will feel much better when she can see for herself that Buddy is in good hands," Delta said. "Hopefully, it will soften the blow of her ransacked van. Seeing those scattered models made me wince, let alone the person who created them with such loving detail."

"But it's good news," Mrs. Cassidy enthused. "It proves she has nothing to do with the murder. The killer came to look for something in her van. I have this perfect theory that fits the case."

Jonas threw Delta a warning look as if to say, *We were leaving, remember?* But Mrs. Cassidy was already launching into her hypothesis. "That man who came to town and talked to Tilly Tay in the street was involved in a scam to get money out of Tilly. Because she's well known, people think she has money or valuables. When Tilly didn't want to cooperate, the guy reported back to a companion, and they got into an argument. The companion killed the guy who argued with Tilly and then went to search her van for whatever they wanted off her. Whether he got it or not remains to be seen. But whoever searched her van has to be the killer. Sheriff West must find that person. Surely there will be fingerprints?"

"Not if the intruder wore gloves," Jonas said. "And the woman at the motel said Mr. Smith checked in alone."

"Yes, but his companion could have checked in alone as

well, a few hours before or after. Did you look into other guests, traveling alone?"

"No," Jonas said in a hesitant tone as if he had half-decided to reject this theory outright but also was half-intrigued by the possibility.

"You do that, and you'll see it helps." Mrs. Cassidy nodded and then turned her head as, inside the house, a phone rang. "I have to go answer that."

"That's our cue," Jonas whispered, taking Delta's arm and pulling her along. "Bye, Mrs. Cassidy." He waved a hand as he kept walking. He said to Delta, "I do appreciate the Paper Posse's input, but they tend to have these wild ideas. Tilly Tay may be famous, but she doesn't strike me as a woman who has money to spend or who had something incredibly valuable in that van. Why would two criminals come after her? And have a deadly argument about her?"

"True," Delta said as they got into her car and buckled up. "But it's a fact that the guy threatened Tilly to cooperate about something. Her van was ransacked, and someone may also have been inside the shop. Since there were no traces of a break-in, they must have used the key that Tilly put in our mailbox. If they took the trouble to retrieve that key and come to the shop, there must have been something for them to do there. Just leave the clue of the dead prospector in the display? Nah, it doesn't make sense. It would be more logical to assume they were also there to look for something. Maybe they thought Tilly had left a bag of stuff at the store."

"Did she?" Jonas asked with tension in his voice.

"Not that I know of. Just empty boxes that held the models from the display."

"The display." Jonas glanced at her. "I haven't seen it up close. Does it have hollow spaces? Inside, underneath? Can something be hidden in it?"

"Hidden?"

"Yes. Inside the models even?"

"Maybe, but we can hardly go and destroy models to search for some mysterious hidden item. Unless you know of ways to see inside without having to open them up?"

Jonas grinned. "I can think of something if need be. But let's first see if someone turns up tonight for another search of the place. Maybe that will answer some questions."

Chapter Eight

AFTER THE SHOP CLOSED, JONAS INSTALLED HIS CAMERA AND explained to Delta where he would keep watch. There was an empty shop space on the other side of the street, and he had contacted the owner about using it for the night. Delta thanked him again for all he was doing for her, but Jonas waved it off. His phone beeped, and he pulled it out, looking at a message that had come in and grinning as he typed a reply.

Delta wondered who it could be from but didn't ask.

She went home with Hazel to eat dinner and tell her all the details of her visit to the Lodge, the discovery of the ransacked van, and the hunt for the missing dog inside the museum. Hazel laughed at Mrs. Cassidy calling Buddy Houdini but then grew serious, pointing her fork at Delta, as she said, "I don't know what worries me more: Tilly's attempt to get away from the police custody or her van being searched. I mean, she's obviously not in as much shock as she pretended to be. What if she knows very well what the culprits are after?"

"I don't follow," Delta said, cutting up her pizza slice.

"Suppose Tilly owes someone money. That wouldn't be odd, considering the old van she drives, her clothes. The creditors followed her here to let her know she has to pay them back. When she refused, they broke into the van to take whatever valuables were there to sell them for money."

"But how likely is it that anything in there was worth any substantial money?" Delta mused. "And if Tilly did have something of value, perhaps an heirloom or something, she wouldn't have it lying around a van that she parks at an abandoned campsite."

"I don't understand how she got into town if it wasn't with the van," Hazel waved her fork in the air. "Tilly was arrested at the museum after being at Wanted all morning. If she had come to town in her van, it would have been parked in town. But, apparently, she left it at the campsite when she came over for the grand display reveal at Wanted. How, then, did she travel? On foot?"

Delta shook her head. "It's six miles, at least. I can't

imagine she'd walk that stretch. Maybe she biked? She could have had a bike in the van."

"Or she took the bus." Hazel jumped to her feet and got her phone, looking for something online. "The bus stops close to the abandoned campsite. There might no longer be any camping done there, but the bus stop is still there. That would have been a quick and affordable way into town. Still the question remains: why not take the van? Why leave it where someone could get into it unseen?"

"She had been admonished about parking it in the wrong place." Delta shrugged. "If she's low on cash, the idea of a ticket would naturally worry her. She'd rather not risk it."

"I'm not convinced." Hazel put the phone away and picked up another slice of pizza. "Tilly knew she could park at the church. She had moved the van there yesterday. If she wanted to keep an eye on it, she would have brought it. It almost seems like she wanted to keep it out of sight."

"That is peculiar." Delta nodded thoughtfully. "She seems to be pretty protective of her models. Worried something would get displaced or broken. An abandoned campsite isn't exactly a secure site to leave something you consider precious."

"Tilly is a mystery." Hazel leaned back with a sigh. "I

can't believe we have another murder case in town. That's really not normal."

"Mr. *Smith*," Delta put an ironic emphasis on the name, "came from out of town, so he really doesn't have anything to do with us. Mrs. Cassidy seems to think he was here for some shady business and a criminal associate did him in. Might be. Then it's just a case of one crook bumping off another, and it happens to be outside a motel near Tundish."

Visibly relieved, Hazel nodded. "Sounds logical enough to me. Now we just have to convince West of it."

Delta checked her watch. "You know what? I'm going to pack a few snacks and visit Jonas at his stakeout. I do feel a bit guilty about the plan that makes him sit up all night."

"It was his idea, right?"

"Yes, but I doubt anything will happen. Why would the perp return to Wanted? But Jonas did mention to me earlier that he believed he remembered Tilly's name from an earlier case. I want to ask him if he can find out what that case was. I don't suppose he still has access to police files, but he does have contacts among PIs. Maybe the case she was involved in earlier offers a clue."

"Good thinking. You do whatever you have to do." Hazel winked at her, suggesting she believed that the case information was merely a thinly veiled excuse for going to see Jonas.

Feeling a little caught red-handed, Delta flushed and went to collect some cheese, potato chips, and marshmallows from the kitchen. When she peeked into the living room area to say goodbye, Hazel had settled on the sofa with a book. She waved at her. "Take your time."

Delta's cheeks turned warm again. Of course Hazel thought she wanted to spend time with Jonas, but, honestly, it was just an act of friendship. He was being so kind to help them out, not just with this camera surveillance of Wanted, but also in recovering Buddy. The thought that the chihuahua was curled up on his own bed at Mrs. Cassidy's, perfectly safe and sound, warmed her heart.

She drove into town, noticing how quiet it was on this November night. There was no one stirring. The few tourists were safely tucked away at their hotels dining, drinking, or turning in early to have a good night's sleep before another day trip tomorrow while the locals were probably sitting in their houses, watching the news. She wondered if it would feature Tilly Tay's arrest.

She turned on the car radio and flipped past a few channels before she found a regional newscast. It mentioned a landslide, an election update, and a story about a traffic stop that had led to the accidental discovery of fifty thousand dollars in cash in someone's spare tire. Whether he had a good explanation for having that amount of money or was part of a money-laundering scheme was still under investigation. The weather followed, and Delta turned the radio off. Nothing about Tilly. The mention of hidden money made her wonder again what Tilly might have hidden in her van. Or in her display and models, as Jonas mentioned.

Maybe, instead of watching Wanted from across the street, we should go inside and check out Tilly's things?

After Delta parked the car, she pulled out her phone and went to Marc's site, News As It Develops, to scroll through the headlines. She held her breath waiting for the name she dreaded to see there. Not just Tilly Tay but also Wanted.

But there was nothing. Not a beep about the arrest or Tilly being at the Lodge for the moment, recovering from a nervous breakdown. Not even a single sentence about the murder at the local motel. That was decidedly odd. Marc could hardly be in the dark about it. His moles were everywhere.

Has he actually decided to be prudent for once?

Delta lowered her phone with a feeling of bewilderment. And a niggling sense something wasn't right here. Marc couldn't have suddenly seen the light. He was a reporter to the core, and he always wanted to beat his father to every juicy story. Why would he ignore a murder in town, which also seemed to involve a Montana celebrity?

Puzzling at these questions, she walked through the empty street, turning up her collar against the light drizzle descending from the dark sky overhead. The eerie silence got on her nerves. Two times, she stopped because she was certain there were footfalls behind her, but, the moment she listened intently, she didn't hear anything anymore.

She walked on faster, clutching her phone in her pocket. At last, she reached the empty building and knocked on the windowpane. It took a few moments before anything stirred inside. Had she come to the wrong building?

No, she detected movement, a low creak rang out, and the door opened. Jonas said, "What are you doing here? Come in quickly. I don't want to draw attention to myself."

"Whose attention?" Delta asked cynically. "There's no one around. It's so quiet it gave me the creeps." She slipped out of her damp coat. "I wanted to bring you some snacks and keep you company for an hour or so. Just for fun. But if you don't want me here…"

"Of course you're welcome. I'm just…" Jonas shrugged.

"I've been looking out and seeing absolutely no one in the street. I began to think it was a bad idea to install that camera and seriously believe we'll catch anything on the footage. And then you turn up and miss sleep as well, because of my wild idea."

"Nonsense. I kind of enjoy this. Reminds me of that time when I had just moved into town and we watched over Wanted together. After someone broke our window, remember?"

His eyes turned warm and he leaned over, saying, "With that brick marked LEAVE in painted letters. Sure, I remember."

He reached out and touched her cheek a moment, running his warm fingertips from her cheekbone to her jaw. "You look cold. I've got a thermos with hot coffee."

He turned away from her. Her cheek burned where he had touched it. Why did he always manage to confuse her? He was kind, concerned, then just friendly and… It made her head spin.

This is friendly too. Hey, you're cold, let me get you coffee. Nothing to it. Leave it be.

She paced the room. "It's chilly in here because the heating hasn't been on for ages, I bet. How long has this been sitting empty, anyway?"

"Since spring. The owner is quite desperate looking for someone to take it off his hands and do something with it. Anything."

"But he's not finding any ready takers? I mean, this isn't the best season to start a business here. And Tundish has been in the news with two murders recently. People might feel like the crime rate is too high."

"Are you having doubts about moving here?" Jonas handed her a paper cup. "Careful, it's hot."

"Thanks." As the warmth seared into her fingers, she realized how chilly she had been walking that empty street. "Doubts? Why would I?" Did he worry she might move away again?

"I don't know." Jonas stared at the monitor with the footage from Wanted. "If we had some early snow, it would help with the tourists. But the forecasts aren't showing any change. Can you two survive when sales don't pick up?"

"Hazel did it before, so I'm counting on her business savvy." Delta tried to sound cheerful, but the fact that Jonas was bringing this up said a lot.

"Still, you have to live off the store now, and you're planning to get a place with your gran. It all costs money." Jonas half-turned to her. "It does mean you consider Tundish your home now, right?"

The look in his eyes confused her. It seemed he was eager to know her answer. But why? Did he feel the same thing she did, want to take their friendship to a new level?

Jonas glanced back at the monitor. "Hey!" He froze and stared at the monitor intently. "I see something."

"Inside the shop?" With quick steps, Delta came to stand beside him.

"Yes, there's someone there. That's an arm."

Her breathing grew shallow. Someone was in her shop. A stranger, an intruder.

The killer? Having come back to look for...

For what?

The cold sense of shock faded under a rush of anger, and she felt like running across the street to confront whomever had invaded her privacy. You didn't do that, break into a place under the cover of darkness and touch things that weren't yours.

"I can't see his face," Jonas said, watching with focus. "It's a man, though. Don't you think?"

"He's rather tall and slim for a man. But maybe a younger man?" Delta leaned closer to the monitor. "I wish there was a zoom function."

"But there isn't. We'd have to go over to see who it is." Jonas sounded determined.

"Are you crazy?" Her heart skipped a beat at the idea. "That wasn't the deal. He could be armed."

"But this footage isn't conclusive," Jonas retorted. "West can't use it to find the culprit. If we let him get away, we got nothing."

"We got proof of a break-in. That can help Tilly's case." Delta said it knowing it wouldn't be enough. West would want a clear suspect, and this was all but clear. "I'll call West." She reached for her phone.

"That'll take too long. He can be done any moment and vanish." Jonas was at the door already. "I'll go and catch him. You stay here. Don't interfere."

Wait. What? Delta's heart sank. How could he do this? What if she stayed here and then a shot rang out and Jonas was killed? While she was close by, doing absolutely nothing to support him?

She raced after him and grabbed his arm so he couldn't walk away from her. "I'll call West, and then we're going out there together. I'll peek in to see if I can identify the intruder. You make sure he can't come out and run."

Jonas didn't seem eager to try it her way, but Delta was already calling the station while she nudged him on. "Let's go now. If we do nothing, he could be gone." Then, into the phone: "Hello? This is Delta Douglas. Someone has broken into my store, Wanted. Yes, he's still on the premises. Please come out at once." She disconnected the call, and they crossed the street in a half-bent position, slinking through the shadows of the buildings. Jonas signaled her to stay behind him.

They were now close to Wanted's entrance. Delta could hear the blood drone in her ears. Part of her didn't want to be here and wished fervently she was in her bed, sleeping soundly. But she also did want to be here, right behind Jonas to help him. Make sure he wasn't hurt.

Jonas took an audible breath. He peeked in. "He's kneeling down, looking and feeling under the display."

"So it could be a hiding place for something like you suggested. It must be the same person who ransacked Tilly's van." A wave of excitement washed through her. A breakthrough in the case. *The* proof Tilly was innocent. "This is huge," she whispered. "He shouldn't get the slightest chance to get away. While he's still distracted, you can run in and knock him to the ground. He's trespassing."

"That doesn't give me permission to hurt him. You've called the police, and we should leave it to them. If I jump the intruder, I can hardly claim it was self-defense."

Delta sighed. She didn't want a fight and injuries, Sheriff

West blaming Jonas. "Maybe but..." She stared over Jonas's shoulder. "He does look familiar. Those white sneakers..."

"You can't identify a guy by his sneakers," Jonas protested. But Delta tilted her head, her thoughts racing. Could that be the reason why he hadn't written about the murder?

Yes, it had to be. It was so unlike him to keep quiet. Unless he was after an even bigger story. Something he, and he alone, could take credit for.

The stupid idiot! "I know who it is," she said, the adrenaline squeezing her voice now from anger sooner than fear. "Let's go in and say boo."

"Are you sure that is such a good idea?" Jonas protested, but Delta already opened the door. The figure stirred, shooting upright and banging his head on the display's edge.

Delta closed the distance quickly. "Hello, Marc. Find what you're looking for?"

Chapter Nine

Marc LeDuc stared at her with wide eyes. "Delta. I uh...hadn't expected you here." He rubbed the spot where he had hit his head. He hadn't even bothered to wear gloves. But, with everyone in town touching the display and with the Wanted key in hand, he probably thought he didn't have to worry about the police dusting for fingerprints and finding his.

Delta glanced at Jonas, who had followed her in and was studying Marc with a challenging look. "We didn't trust the situation and kept watch," he said without specifying how, exactly. "You're caught red-handed. Now give me a good explanation for your presence here and fast before I call West and have you arrested." Jonas pulled out his phone and held it up, his finger posed to punch in the number.

Delta knew West was already coming, but, if they said

that, Marc would surely try to dash. They had to get some information out of him, fast.

"Arrested for what?" Marc asked challengingly. He held up something that shimmered in the light from the streetlight outside.

It was the key.

"I didn't break in. I had legal access."

"Excuse me?" Jonas huffed. "Letting yourself into someone else's property isn't called legal access. Even if you have a key, you didn't have permission. Or do you have the nerve to claim Hazel told you it was okay?"

"No," Marc said slowly, clearly racing for a clever reply. "But I did receive this key with a message to come and have a look, so..."

"A message?" Delta echoed, and Jonas said, "Come on..."

"I'm not making this up." Marc put his hand in his pocket and pulled out a piece of paper. "I brought it. See for yourself."

He held it out to Delta, who peered at the paper closely. The lines on it were typed. "This is the key to Wanted. The display there holds a key as well. See if you can work it out. Good luck."

Jonas read over Delta's shoulder. He raised an eyebrow

at Marc. "You can't be serious. You actually received this message? Or did you type it up yourself to use as an excuse in case you got caught?"

"I didn't plan on getting caught," Marc said with a sour expression. He was still massaging his sore head. "I received it. With this key."

"It must be Hazel's missing key," Delta mused. "But who sent it to Marc?"

Jonas shook his head. "That doesn't matter. You knew when you got it that it had to do with the murder. That makes it evidence relating to a serious crime. You should have turned it over to West at once."

"West and I aren't exactly best friends." Marc grimaced. "Why help him? He can figure it out for himself. Or not."

His disparaging tone seemed to irritate Jonas. He gestured at the self-assured reporter. "Look what you did now. You ruined possible fingerprints on both the note and the key. You came here and broke in the shop to look for evidence. You also put your prints all over this display. That's wrong in so many ways."

"Spare me the lecture," Marc spat. "I used a key to get in. I wasn't burgling the place. I'm a concerned citizen, a journalist, having a look at something suspicious."

"That won't fly with West." Jonas held up the phone again as if he was about to place the call.

Marc scoffed. "Do you really want them to come racing in with blaring sirens and everyone watching and talking about Wanted like this? Not good for your girlfriend's business."

"Delta is not my girlfriend," Jonas growled.

"Oh? Then why are you together in the middle of the night?" Marc tilted his head. "Seems like you're awfully close."

"It's not even midnight, and we were on stakeout, to catch someone like you."

Delta's face was on fire. She didn't dare look at Jonas to see how he took this. She quickly asked Marc, "Did you find something special inside?"

Jonas hitched a brow. "Do you think he's going to tell us?"

"Actually, I'm going to tell everyone about it. The whole of Tundish and beyond." Marc laughed softly. "You can read everything on my website, first thing tomorrow morning. Cross my heart."

"That sensationalist website of yours, full of wild guesses, not facts." Jonas's eyes flickered with anger. "If you write anything incriminating about Wanted..."

"Sue me." Marc pulled back his shoulders and walked out of the store.

Jonas followed him, calling, "Hey, you can't leave like this."

In the distance sirens blared. As soon as Marc heard them, he broke into a run and vanished into the night. Jonas and Delta were left on the sidewalk, eyeing each other uncertainly.

"What do we tell West?" Jonas asked. "He will be livid that we intervened and the intruder got away."

"We'll say we saw who it was. Then he can go after Marc. But it won't do the sheriff much good, I reckon. Marc already ruined any possible prints on the key." Delta frowned and continued thoughtfully, "I'm trying to work out what it all means. The killer probably had the key if they were the ones who changed the display to show the murder outside the boardinghouse and incriminate Tilly. But why, then, pass the key to Marc? Only locals know that he runs a sensationalist website. Does that mean a local is involved in the murder? But why would a local person kill Mr. Smith, a stranger to town?"

"Maybe he wasn't a stranger. Maybe he came here more often and we just don't know that yet."

Delta swallowed. Tilly had also mentioned, in passing, she had been to Tundish before. She seemed to have been guarded speaking about it. How did that connect to the murder?

A police car raced up to them, and West jumped out. He glanced at Wanted, then focused on Delta and Jonas standing outside it. "Is the intruder still in there?"

"Unfortunately not," Delta said. "But we saw who it was. Marc LeDuc. He entered with the missing key."

"You talked to him?" West growled.

"We tried to reason with him and persuade him to share what he knows with you, but he's convinced he has some major scoop," Jonas said. "Maybe you can find out what it is before the rest of the world does? And ask him to return the key?"

Delta could've kicked herself for not demanding that Marc turn it over, but the clue in the note was the only thing on her mind in the moment.

West snarled, "I would love to arrest that nosy journalist and lock him up for the night. If I do, your key goes into evidence and you won't get it back right away." His phone beeped, and he took the call. The speaker sounded very animated and spoke so loud Delta could catch the words "break-in attempt" and the name Cassidy.

Cassidy? Oh, no. "Is that Mrs. Cassidy?" she asked.

"Looks like it," West said. "Sorry, got to go. Talk to you later." He dove into his car and raced away.

Her heart pounding, Delta stared at Jonas. "A break-in attempt at Mrs. Cassidy's? How odd."

"Maybe Marc had more addresses on his list for a nightly visit?"

Delta frowned. "What could Marc want at Mrs. Cassidy's?"

"We don't know what clues he discovered here in Wanted. Come on." Jonas waved her along. "We're going over to see if she's all right."

While they drove to Mrs. Cassidy's place, Delta played nervously with her bracelet. "I do hope she's fine. And Nugget and Buddy. Tilly was so concerned about her dog earlier." She sucked in air. "Can that be the connection? Tilly's things at Wanted and Tilly's dog at Mrs. Cassidy's."

Jonas glanced at her with a doubtful expression. "What would anyone want with Buddy?"

"I don't know. But the link between the store and Mrs. Cassidy seems to be Tilly." Delta rubbed her face. "I'm wishing more and more I never invited her to town."

They reached the house and parked at the side of the road to avoid blocking in a police car in the driveway. Delta spotted

Mrs. Cassidy standing in the hallway talking to a deputy with Nugget in one arm and Buddy in the other. The two dogs were vying for her attention, both licking her face and neck. Delta waved at her, and Mrs. Cassidy called, "Hello there. What made you turn up? Not the news of my house being under attack, I hope? It wasn't a big thing, really. A dark figure was rattling at the back door. Both dogs went frantic, and, since I was still up, I went over to see what the commotion was about. Then the figure fled through the garden. With the wet weather, there might be a footprint or two left there in the mud."

"It's unusual," the deputy said, "for burglars to strike this early in the night. Usually they wait until people are fast asleep and there's no risk of being overrun by the owners."

"Well," Mrs. Cassidy said, "I wonder if he thought I was out. You see, I was supposed to be at bridge tonight. I always am this day of the week, and I never get home before midnight. But I decided not to go because of Buddy's arrival; I wanted him to settle in and feel safe."

"If the burglar came assuming you were out, they must have known your routine," Delta said. She glanced at Jonas.

"Know my routine?" Mrs. Cassidy shrugged. "I guess that wouldn't be hard. It's no big secret. In fact, I mentioned my bridge game today at the museum with dozens of tourists around." She looked ruefully. "I never thought I owned anything worth coming after."

"I'll just finish taking your statement," the deputy said. "Then you can have a cup of tea with your friends here to calm down."

"I'm perfectly calm," Mrs. Cassidy assured him, but Delta said it was a good idea. She and Jonas stepped aside for a moment to let the policeman finish up.

Jonas said, "Burglars sometimes keep tabs on people for a while, and, once they've worked out their routine, they try to strike. It was bad luck for this guy that Mrs. Cassidy changed her ways tonight."

Delta shook her head. "It's too coincidental that someone comes to try and break into her house on the very day she took in Tilly Tay's dog. Remember the ransacked van?"

Jonas didn't seem convinced. "If the van didn't yield the wanted item, why come for Buddy?"

"He could be the wanted item. Maybe he's valuable somehow?"

"How, then?" Jonas laughed softly. "He's not a very special breed. And he's not wearing a diamond-studded collar either."

"I know." Delta shrugged and shivered in the cold evening air. "Maybe I'm getting paranoid. It could be an impromptu, clumsy attempt at a burglary by someone who thought there was nobody home."

"Could be." Jonas nodded. "You do have these opportunistic crooks who pass a house and think: why not? They hope to find a wallet left out or snatch a smartphone quickly. No big score necessary, just some money to get through another few days on the road. Let's keep it at that for the moment." He came to stand closer to Delta. "Are you cold? Or worried?" He studied her with a searching look. "First the shock of finding Marc snooping around in the store, with this far-fetched story about the key being sent to him, and now this."

Delta hugged her shoulders. "I'm fine, really."

Jonas put his arm around her a moment and pulled her close. His warmth swept around her, assuring her that, whatever was happening, she wasn't facing this alone.

Then the deputy said he was done, and Mrs. Cassidy invited them inside to have tea with her. "No coffee," she said, "or we won't sleep a wink. Not that I feel like sleeping at all myself. Odd how something so silly can still give you a spook."

Delta patted her shoulder. "The dogs saved you, barking as they did."

"Yes, they were great." Mrs. Cassidy walked into the kitchen and put the dogs on the floor. She went to fill the kettle with water. Jonas sat on his haunches fondling Buddy's ears.

Delta sat down on a chair at the table with the checkered tablecloth. "We had our own odd little experience in town." She told Mrs. Cassidy about finding Marc inside Wanted after receiving Hazel's missing key.

As she had hoped, Mrs. Cassidy grew lively at the revelation, asking questions, and throwing out theories. "If the killer had the key," she said, getting out the cookie jar, "and he sent it to Marc inviting him to come and see the display in Wanted, it must hold more clues than just the murdered prospector. Maybe we are dealing with a killer who likes to leave difficult puzzles for the police or other interested parties."

"Spare me," Jonas said. "That sort of thing only happens in books and movies. In my experience, killers come in two varieties: the mad ones who kill without rhyme or reason and certainly don't take the time to use a miniature display to advertise a hidden message and the occasional ones—I mean those who are not mentally disturbed but who resort to killing for a very real reason, like getting rid of a rival or a threat. They kill for practical or passionate purposes and try hard not to leave clues. In Mr. Smith's case, I'd go for the latter. I assume, judging by his behavior—you know, checking into a hotel without showing ID and paying cash and all—that he was trying to go unnoticed. He could have had some shady business here in town. Maybe a victim of his dealings, whatever those could be, killed him. Or a business associate at that."

Delta nodded in his direction. "Did you manage to discover whether any other lone people checked into the motel around the same time?"

"I asked questions and am waiting for answers." Jonas gave Buddy a final rub across his back and took a seat at the table. Mrs. Cassidy poured the boiling water into the teapot and asked what flavor they'd like. They agreed on Earl Grey, which she fetched from the cupboard. "Take whatever you like from the cookie jar."

The inviting scent of butter rose as Delta looked into the jar. She fished out a pretzel-shaped cookie with sugar and shoved the jar over to Jonas. He seemed to want to decline but then glanced at Mrs. Cassidy, busy making them feel welcome, and chose a cookie with an almond in the center.

Mrs. Cassidy sat down and cradled her own tea mug in her hands. "I'm glad I didn't go to bridge. What if the house had been broken into and the dogs had attacked the intruder and gotten hurt? I'd never have forgiven myself."

"But it's not your fault when an intruder comes to your home," Jonas pointed out gently.

Mrs. Cassidy waved a hand. "I know, but maybe I should take the dogs with me wherever I go? If they're not safe here."

"You could also think about having an alarm installed." Delta bit into her cookie and chewed quickly.

Mrs. Cassidy sighed as she sipped her tea. "Winter is of course the perfect season for such criminals. It's dark early, there are few people around. Yes, I think I will look into getting some sort of alarm. It'll make me feel better."

Delta touched her hand. "I do hope you'll forget about this soon. I always had the impression you felt so safe and at home in Tundish."

"Oh, I do." Mrs. Cassidy squeezed her fingers. "This small incident won't ruin that for me. It's just a bit much on one day. The murder, Tilly Tay being arrested, her van ransacked, her dog missing for hours and entrusted to me..." She fell silent and sat up, looking from Delta to Jonas. "Could that be the connection? Is someone after the dog?"

Jonas raised a hand. "We asked ourselves the same thing, but Buddy doesn't seem to have any immediate value."

"Maybe Tilly Tay was married, and they didn't agree on who should have the dog when they got divorced. I read a story about that in a magazine. People go very far for their pets."

"A case of dognapping?" Jonas asked, obviously incredulous.

Mrs. Cassidy sipped her tea again. "I do want Tilly's dog to be safe with me. I will call an alarm company in the morning. I've got a card in the drawer."

As she spoke, a beep rang out. Buddy started to bark, and Nugget jumped up against the legs of the chair Jonas sat on. "Yes, yes, I'm getting it," he said as he pulled out his phone. He checked a message on it. "A friend of mine looked into Tilly Tay's financial situation. Seems she doesn't have much to her name. The van, and that's about it."

"But she must have made money off her exhibitions. Doesn't she have some savings account?" Delta asked.

"Not as far as my friend can tell right now."

"Does that mean," Mrs. Cassidy asked, "that the victim wasn't after her for money?"

"Not necessarily," Jonas retorted. "He might have assumed she had money."

"He asked me if I was a relative," Delta said. "Why would he want to get in touch with her relatives?"

"Interesting." Jonas typed a message on his phone. "I'll ask my contact to keep looking for a possible savings accounts but also check out Tilly Tay's personal relations."

"You know what?" Delta pointed a finger at him. "Tilly mentioned having been here, in Tundish, before. Maybe she does have family here? Or there's some other connection to town that can prove useful in the case."

"On it," Jonas said, typing furiously.

Mrs. Cassidy yawned behind a politely raised hand.

"Maybe you will be able to sleep, anyway," Delta said with a wink.

Chapter Ten

Delta herself had no trouble sleeping after she got home from her adventures. She did have muddled dreams about Buddy running through a forest leaving a trail of miniature prospectors with Jonas and her following. In a clearing was a wooden hut where the trail ended and a dark figure slipped away around it, but, before Delta could draw Jonas's attention to it, the door of the hut opened, and Paula stepped out in a wedding gown with a veil folded back over her dark hair and a gorgeous smile on her pretty face. She walked over to Jonas reaching out her hand to him, and, as Delta saw Jonas wanted to take it, she cried out to stop them and woke with a start.

She lay very still, willing her thundering heartbeat to calm. She hoped she hadn't really cried out and would find Hazel knocking on her door to ask what the matter was. She would never admit to having this silly dream. Even if Paula and Jonas were close, it was none of her business.

But the tight feeling in her chest told her that, aside from her strong words about her not caring at all, she did care. Why hadn't she acted sooner, letting Jonas know how she felt about him? Maybe the attractive Paula had managed to snare him because he had felt uncertain about his relationship with Delta?

Nonsense, she told herself, *if Jonas had been in love with me, he wouldn't suddenly have fallen for Paula. So, if he did fall for her, he never felt anything for me—a truth I'd have to accept.*

Deep inside she knew it wasn't that easy and that she really should do something about her feelings for Jonas. Unless she wanted to be forever sorry she had let this chance pass her by?

She checked her alarm clock, saw that it was close to seven, and slipped out of bed to take a shower and dress. When she came downstairs, hoping Hazel already had some breakfast going, she found the kitchen empty and the sink clean. She took a deep breath and set to work, making toast and coffee and cutting up a few oranges and a grapefruit for juice. She heard the sounds of Hazel upstairs, indicating she was out of bed.

While waiting for her, Delta pulled out her sketchbook and created a case file in the back, as she had done before with the other murder cases. She drew the silhouette of a man and wrote in it, "Mr. Smith, car part dealer, staying at local motel, had altercation with Tilly Tay in town." She drew Tilly and connected her to Smith with some washi tape, writing on it: "connection?"

As she stared at the two figures, she realized that the rest of the sheet looked dauntingly empty. There wasn't anyone she could readily put in and connect to the victim. Which was exactly why Sheriff West was focusing all of his attention on Tilly Tay. But there had to be someone, or even several people considering all the odd happenings after Tilly had been taken in by West: break-ins, cryptic notes...

She drew the van with the cute crocheted curtains and wrote beside it, "who ransacked it?" She drew Buddy on his dog bed with a note: "burglary attempt at Mrs. Cassidy's, was it about Buddy? Is he valuable in some way?"

And, of course, she added the key to Wanted, with questions: Did Tilly put it in the letterbox? Who stole it from there? Why give it to Marc? What was he supposed to find in Wanted?

When they had talked to Marc last night, he seemed ready

to reveal something major. Would it be on his website right now?

Delta reached for her phone just as it beeped, and she decided to check her messages first. Wild Bunch Bessie wrote, "Last night I was at a birthday party, and the conversation happened to touch on history. I mentioned that I had heard, via a friend, of this history buff Major George Buckmore, and someone said to be careful with him. Apparently he tells tall tales. I laughed at first, because I had the impression that it was innocent, but then I was told he's been able to convince people to invest in less-than-profitable schemes. He wins their trust first and then gets them to let him handle part of their savings. As your gran knows him, I wanted to let you know first thing. It need not be true, but just to be on the safe side…"

Delta read and reread the message. Her stomach sank. Gran didn't just know this man; she seemed to like him. This new acquaintance had brought a breath of fresh air into her life, helping her get over the loss of her beloved home.

Telling her this news about Buckmore would…

Well, perhaps it wasn't even factual. It was someone simply gossiping at a party.

Right?

Calamity Jane responded, "I know this is none of my business, but I heard a lot recently about these charming elderly men who worm their way into the confidence of gullible ladies and take their money. It has been in papers and magazines. All the victims say that they never thought they'd fall for something like that and that, even when they were in the relationship, they sometimes had doubts but dismissed them because the person concerned was so charming and they were so lonely and in need of this attention. So your gran better be careful because none of us knows this Buckmore type really well."

Now he was suddenly "this Buckmore type" as if Jane was already distancing herself from him.

Rattlesnake Rita wrote, "Maybe you can ask Jonas to look into him? He has contacts, right? You only want to protect your grandmother."

Delta lowered the phone. The idea that she would ask Jonas to check up on a friend of her gran's didn't sit well with her, but just letting Gran strike up a friendship with someone who might be unreliable was worrying. What should she do?

"Good morning," Hazel called as she dashed in. "I'm sorry for being so late. Oh, you already prepped all the stuff. Thanks so much. I wouldn't know what I'd do without you."

If she and Gran bought a house together, Delta would be leaving Hazel alone. A sense of guilt washed through her. What if Hazel thought she had used her by moving in and staying with her after coming to town, because it was convenient, and then leaving her alone when it suited her better? Of course it wasn't like that at all, but what if Hazel felt that way?

She sipped the juice, the taste suddenly more bitter than before.

Hazel put jam on her hot toast. "You're looking pensive."

"Oh, I'm just thinking about last night. Marc at the store and all."

"Yes, he must have breaking news this morning. What did his site say?" Hazel eyed her expectantly.

"I haven't checked yet."

"Really? I thought it would be the first thing you'd do."

Delta's face grew warm. "I was writing down everything we know so far..." She gestured to the sketchbook. "And then I'll add what Marc has to say. If it's even relevant." She couldn't admit how the dream about Paula as Jonas's bride had distracted her, and then the messages about Major George Buckmore.

She quickly scrolled to Marc's website. "Did famous Montana resident and artist Tilly Tay kill her husband?"

Husband?!

Delta almost choked on the mouthful of juice she was about to swallow. Her eyes widened as she raced across the next lines. Marc wrote that the deceased Mr. Smith was really Bob Weatherspoon, the man who had married Tilly Tay when she had been just nineteen.

Had West known this right away? Was that what he had meant referring to things she didn't know, emphasizing she shouldn't get involved?

Hazel eyed her expectantly, her hand with her cup of coffee stalling midair. "What did he write?"

"The victim was…" Delta's throat burned from the juice that had gone the wrong way, and she coughed, tears rising to her eyes. "Tilly's husband."

"What? Did you say Tilly's husband?" Hazel looked as bewildered as Delta felt herself.

None of this made any sense. Tilly had been face-to-face with her husband on Mattock Street, pretending she didn't know him, that he was trying to sell her insurance! Why?

And why keep her mouth shut once the police had become involved? She would have known that they would establish the victim's true identity, and the tie to her, soon enough.

"That's terrible," Hazel exclaimed, half-rising from her

seat as the news sank in. "If Tilly knew him a lot better than she let on, she might actually have a motive to kill him."

She lowered herself again, looking deflated as she added, "What will the townspeople say about us now, springing to the defense of someone who could very well be guilty?"

"We don't know that," Delta protested. "Tilly may have been married to the victim, but that doesn't mean she killed him."

"She should have told the truth right away. After the altercation in the street you witnessed, she might have felt embarrassed to admit who he was, but when the murdered occurred, she made herself all the more suspicious by keeping quiet." Hazel waved her knife in the air. A bit of jam flew off and stuck to the wall.

Delta pointed it out, but Hazel was too deep in her argument to notice. "Why not tell of her own accord if there was nothing special to their connection?"

"They could have been estranged." Delta tried to find some reason to explain Tilly's behavior. Anything other than her being actually guilty. "She didn't want him here and ignored his presence. Or something." But Jonas's words about stalking came back to her. About people growing desperate and striking back. A fight gone wrong? A murder Tilly had never meant to commit?

"Anyway..." Delta focused on the article on Marc's website. "I'll read this first to see where he gets this fantastic twist. Maybe he's basing it on absolutely nothing." But, inside, she knew Marc was smarter than that. And, at the store last night, he had told them so smugly that he knew something big.

Marc wrote that Tilly Tay and Bob Weatherspoon had gotten along well at first, but, over time, the bond had deteriorated and Tilly had moved away. The marriage had never been annulled or ended in divorce, even though the spouses hadn't lived at the same address for the past twenty years.

"Listen to this." Delta read the closing section out loud to Hazel: "Where Tilly Tay went on to make a name for herself as miniature artist, gaining reputation and wealth, Mr. Weatherspoon was less fortunate, rolling from one job to another and eventually ending up in the criminal world. He has been in and out of prison for offenses ranging from the sale of fake luxury goods to insurance fraud."

Hazel said cynically, "An insurance salesman after all."

"Wait for it," Delta said. "It gets even better. He had been recently released after serving five years for conducting an elaborate pyramid scheme. The money put up by his many victims was never recovered. This missing loot is rumored to amount to millions of dollars."

"Millions?" Hazel pushed her plate away. "I'm done eating. This is too much. The guy was a serious criminal. Not a small-time crook but someone who was smart enough to set up a pyramid scheme and hide the proceeds so cleverly that the police never recovered them. And Tilly knew that." She thought a moment and added, more reluctantly, "At least I assume that she knew that he was in prison from time to time. Why didn't she warn us that he was in town? It could mean nothing but trouble."

"Look," Delta said, trying to find some defense for Tilly's choices, "it says here that they haven't lived together for two decades. She probably considered the relationship ended and the man out of her life. He might have turned up every now and then to ask her for money or something, but... It must have been embarrassing. She wanted to avoid any and all association with him. I can understand that."

"Hmmm." Looking skeptical, Hazel leaned back against her chair. "I suppose so."

"Tilly couldn't know he would be killed right here in Tundish and she'd be suspected." Delta studied the item on Marc's site again. "I don't understand how Marc's visit to Wanted last night led him to this information. The display will hardly have held a marriage certificate, right?"

Hazel pursed her lips. "Maybe Marc also ransacked the van and found information there?"

"If Marc went through the van's contents, the fact that it was searched doesn't prove that Tilly had nothing to do with the murder." Delta sighed. "There goes our way out of this mess."

She updated the case file putting behind "Mr. Smith," "real name Bob Weatherspoon, married to Tilly Tay, con man, used to do small stuff, but did a major pyramid scheme five years ago, millions still missing."

Writing it down, the incongruity hit her between the eyes. Why would a man who had access to hidden millions need to bother his ex for money?

That doesn't make sense at all.

Her phone rang, and she picked it up. It was Ray. "I thought you'd want to know," he said in a solemn voice, "that the police took Tilly Tay to the station for questioning. They already planned on doing that after she had a rest and all, you know, but I wonder if it has to do with the news Marc LeDuc spread on his website. That the victim was Tilly's husband. The sheriff mentioned something about confronting her with irrefutable evidence." He sounded as if he'd like her to tell him more about this so Delta rushed to say, "I read that, yes, but I can't confirm whether it's true. Tilly certainly didn't mention anything like that to me. In fact, she said the man who spoke with her in the street was a salesman."

"She must be embarrassed by his criminal lifestyle." Ray sighed. "Well, anyway, Tilly has left the hotel, and Rosalyn is glad for it. She seems to think that, after the revelation about the victim being related to her, the case is about closed and Tilly will soon be charged. I'm not too sure, though. Marc is usually very free with his facts. Let me know if there's anything else I can help you with. I have to run now. It's rather hectic here." Ray disconnected.

Delta told Hazel that Tilly was at the station again. "Maybe we should pop by on our way to Wanted to ask if she needs anything. Just to show that we're not abandoning her."

Hazel looked doubtful. "Mrs. Cassidy got her a lawyer, right? That should be enough. I'd rather stay out of it." She smoothed the tablecloth. "I don't want to abandon her, as you phrase it, but, if she has really been married to the victim, the media will eat it up. I already had a taste of that when Finn was accused of murder at the Lodge."

Finn was Hazel's brother who had worked at the Lodge Hotel and been suspected of involvement in the death of a guest just after Delta had come to town. Delta nodded. "I understand. It was my idea to invite Tilly to the store. You know what? You go and open up, and I'll drive by the station."

"Are you sure?" Hazel tilted her head. "I don't want you to feel like I'm bailing on you."

"Oh, no, it's fine." Delta stood up and picked an apple out of the fruit bowl. "I'll go right away." She didn't want Hazel to know she had an extra reason for visiting the police station in person. She wanted to ask a few innocent questions about other possible swindling schemes being reported in the region. Any signs that maybe Major Buckmore wasn't the history-loving gentleman friend he seemed to be. What Bessie heard might just have been gossip. But Delta owed it to her grandmother to check and see if there was a kernel of truth to it.

Chapter Eleven

At the station, Delta found a tall, dark-haired woman at the desk explaining with flourishing hand gestures that she wanted to be admitted to Tilly Tay. The deputy retorted that Tilly was being questioned, but he barely got a chance to explain anything before the woman emphasized that she was allowed to see her sister.

Sister?

So Tilly did have a connection to Tundish. Her sister lived here. Or had she come in especially to see Tilly? Delta couldn't remember having seen her before.

"Good morning." Delta stepped up to her. "I'm Delta Douglas. I run the stationery shop in town. Tilly is exhibiting her miniature version of Old West Tundish there. Do I understand correctly you are her sister?"

"Yes." The woman turned to her and reached out a hand. She was dressed in a riding outfit with spotless white pants and gleaming black boots and had her hair pulled back in a simple ponytail. Her makeup was immaculate, and she wore both a sleek golden watch and a ring on her finger full of shimmering precious stones. There could hardly be a greater contrast with Tilly's bohemian appearance.

As she shook Delta's hand, the woman introduced herself. "Tabitha Tay VanderHurst. They used to call us Tilly and Tabby. People often mistook us for twins, although I'm in fact a year older."

"How nice. Did you come to town to support Tilly now that's she suspected? Or were you already here for the exhibition?" Mr. "Smith" had asked about relatives. If he had been married to Tilly, he had also known her family at the time. Maybe he had thought Delta was a cousin?

Something adamant flickered in the woman's eyes, but then she said, "Yes, yes, indeed, we were already in town. It's so nice to see my sister's work. She's so talented. I wouldn't have the patience to sit down and spend hours on creating such tiny fiddly things."

The deputy seemed relieved that the demanding woman was distracted by an innocent conversation and wanted to step away, but, as soon as Tabitha noticed his movement from the corner of her eye, she shot at him again, "I want to see my sister. You have to let me talk to her. I can actually help you with the investigation. I'm the only one who can get through to her and convince her to face the situation. I'm sure she's not doing well. She must be so upset about that louse turning up again."

"You mean her husband?" Delta asked. If Tabitha could tell them more about the elusive Mr. Smith, or rather Bob Weatherspoon, it might indeed help the case.

"Ex-husband," Tabitha corrected sharply. "They were never formally divorced, but it was over between them. She despised him for his swindling. He also took her money when they were first together. It was appalling. I'm glad he's dead."

Delta blinked at this rather firm statement. Unperturbed, the woman continued, "Tilly should have stood up to him more, I suppose. But she was sentimental about him. He was her first love and all. Even with his behavior, she was always kindhearted about him. Not about his actions, of course; she didn't condone those. He popped up occasionally to ask her for money. Which was ridiculous, really, as Tilly didn't have any."

"She seemed to be living a simple life," Delta said.

Tabitha huffed. "Simple? She was about reduced to poverty. She never had a real job, so she hadn't built up any pension either. I guess that, in time, when it would have become too hard for her to live in that van, she would have turned to us to ask for money. My husband is rather well-to-do." The latter statement came out with a quiet satisfaction.

Delta wasn't quite sure how Tabitha felt about Tilly, whether she wanted to help her because she cared or because she felt a little smug about her sister's situation. This called for a closer examination. "I'm sorry that your sister is in such trouble now. That must be upsetting to you."

"I can't say I'm not used to it. We're trying to persuade her to get off the road for good."

Delta wondered what that meant exactly. It sounded a bit ominous.

But Tabitha was already continuing, "It's just too taxing. We've had to step in before and bail out Tilly. I just hope I can save her this time when it's something as serious as murder."

The deputy said, "I'd like to get a statement from you about Ms. Tay's financial situation and your knowledge of her relationship with the deceased. Also, anything you might know about recent activities of your brother-in-law."

"Brother-in-law?" Twisting her diamond ring, Tabitha grimaced. "I'll never call him that, and we hadn't been in touch with him for years, but if you insist…"

Delta said to the deputy, "If Tilly is being questioned right now, did the sheriff bring in her lawyer?"

"Of course. He's eager to do it by the book." The deputy focused on Tabitha again. "Could you come into the sheriff's office? I can take your statement there. Would you like some coffee? We have very good mocha."

Delta almost had to laugh at how accommodating he had suddenly become while he had first been eager to dismiss Tabitha.

So Tilly has a well-to-do sister. Delta couldn't remember having seen her in any photos of past exhibitions. There were lots on Tilly's website, and, in them, Tilly was usually surrounded by people, but a sister had not been mentioned in any byline. Perhaps the bond was less close than Tabitha had suggested?

It was too bad the deputy had now left, because she had intended to ask him her innocent questions about Major George Buckmore to sleuth out if he may be unreliable. She did want to know before Gran fell in with him any further than she already had.

Delta chewed her lip. It was a very delicate matter. She

didn't want to upset Gran, so she wasn't going to tell her anything. And she didn't want to go behind her back checking up on her new friend either.

But, on the other hand, it would be terrible if Gran got taken advantage of. Especially now, on top of the sale of her beloved home.

Delta felt obliged to do something. *Anything.*

"Can I help you?" The woman who took incoming calls came over to her, with a friendly smile. "I see no one else is there at the desk."

"The deputy just stepped into the sheriff's office to take a statement." Delta gestured in the direction of the door that had closed behind the deputy and Tabitha Tay. "I'm waiting for Tilly Tay if she's free after questioning. I want to tell her her dog is fine after all the commotion the other day."

"Oh, I hope he's not too shaken. I have dogs myself. I love them. What's his name?"

"Buddy. He's a chihuahua."

"How cute."

Delta gave some more details, and, as the woman started to beam, Delta felt assured she might get something here. "It's so sad Tilly got arrested," she said. "After all, she was only here to show off her miniatures."

"Yes, but the sheriff takes it very seriously that she has been here before. A couple of years ago, in the same summer where a rash of charges were filed, actually. Locals had been conned into buying luxury vacations, paying down payments via a website that went off air from one day to the next. The con men vanished with the money. Sheriff West believes that one of them was that man who died and that maybe the wife helped him at the time."

"Oh, I see. And now there was a falling-out among thieves, so to speak?" Delta asked. It made her uncomfortable to realize that Tilly might have had times where she wasn't making much money and still had to provide for herself, and her husband had come back into her life with a good plan to score a quick buck. It was speculation, of course, but it was possible. Had Tilly said she had never believed she'd come back here because she had been part of a fraudulent scheme last time she had been here?

"I understand the sheriff's reasoning."

The woman nodded solemnly. "He also wants to avoid the impression that he's not looking at her as possible suspect because she's well known. He doesn't want people saying the law has favorites."

Delta hemmed approvingly. "Say, speaking of tricksters

in the area years ago, how are things right now? I overheard talk at a birthday party that there was a charming elderly gentleman asking ladies for money?"

"Really? I wouldn't know." She frowned as if trying to recall any word about it. "If anyone has reported it, I haven't heard. But many people avoid reporting when they get tricked like that. Feel too mortified, you know. Oh, phone call…" The woman rushed off to attend to the ringing phone.

Delta exhaled. That hadn't delivered much. The woman was right that victims of fraud often felt bad about having been so gullible and might not turn to the police. That meant that George Buckmore might have had his hands free until now.

She'd have to ask Jonas to help her, even if it felt weird to put a friend of Gran's under investigation. Jonas would have to be extra careful to ensure Gran didn't find out. If the suspicions were totally unfounded, Gran might blame her for having assumed Buckmore capable of something criminal.

The mere thought of getting Gran angry with her made her wince. They had always been super close, and she couldn't imagine them arguing and not seeing eye to eye.

But hurting her bond with Gran wasn't her only concern.

What if Buckmore got wind of her looking into him?

If he was innocent, it would be super awkward.

But if he was guilty… What would a con man do when he ran the risk of being caught?

No. Delta didn't want to think that far. Jonas knew how to handle this sort of thing. She had to rely on him to get it right.

When Tilly Tay's lawyer appeared in the station waiting area, Delta asked her if they could talk. The woman—late twenties, blond, and brisk—seemed hesitant until Delta explained she was both a friend of Mrs. Cassidy and the shopkeeper who had invited Tilly to town to exhibit her miniatures at her shop. The lawyer said, "Oh, you sell all the paper goods. I really should take a look around in your shop sometime. My mother-in-law is a huge scrapbooking fan." She reached out her hand and introduced herself as Marjorie Brenning.

Delta asked the lawyer if she'd care for pancakes at Mine Forever, where they could discuss how Tilly's case looked. Luckily, Marjorie had skipped breakfast to race out to the station that morning, so she readily agreed.

In town, they snagged a window table and sat down to enjoy their lattes after ordering their food. Delta had pulled out her sketchbook and updated her case file with the figure of Tabitha Tay VanderHurst in her riding outfit, saying in a text bubble that she wanted Tilly to stop living out of boxes in an old van. A second figure without clear features yet denoted her husband.

Delta also created a box with information about Tilly's past in Tundish, noting that she had been in town when the luxury vacations had been sold. But her gaze kept returning to the words "missing millions" she had written down before. Something about those didn't sit well with her.

Putting down her pencil, she said to Marjorie, "I'm hoping, with you here, we can make progress to clear Tilly and Wanted's reputation."

The lawyer replied thoughtfully, "Tilly had a good night's rest and could tell a bit more about what happened. The sheriff confronted her quite bluntly with the deceased being her husband and all. I wished he had done it more subtly, or just given her a chance to get to the point herself. But, of course, he told me after the session was over he thought she would never have told him of her own accord." Marjorie grimaced in a way that made Delta suspect she had experience with types like Sheriff West always thinking the worst of a suspect.

"Anyway," Marjorie continued, "she admitted it was her

husband, or, rather, her ex. She said they hadn't lived together in decades. The marriage had been a big mistake she wanted to forget."

"Still, it is odd," Delta noted, "that, when you are married to someone who is a criminal or who starts to act like one, at least, you don't divorce them to put a clear end to the connection and avoid being involved in any of it."

"Involved how?" the lawyer asked, raising a perfect blond eyebrow. "They didn't have joint bank accounts or assets. There was no divorce, so no alimony, and Tilly says Weatherspoon never gave her any money. But, on the contrary, it was her slipping him some whenever he was out of jail again and trying to make a fresh start of it. That he did contact her from time to time doesn't prove anything. He could have done the same even if they hadn't been married. He didn't exactly have a lot of people who still wanted anything to do with him. Besides, Tilly is someone who abhors paperwork and bureaucracy. She wants to live in freedom. She considered properly filing for a divorce a hassle she could do without."

"Off the grid, yes." Delta nodded. "I already had that impression with her van and simple lifestyle. She likes to be able to move from town to town and not be tied to any set place."

"Exactly, and that's not forbidden." The lawyer crossed her arms. "Tilly couldn't help the sheriff at all with the investigation. She worked at the shop and left, took the key back to your friend Hazel's mailbox, and then she slept in her van and came to the store for the opening of the exhibit."

"How did she come to the store?" Delta asked.

"Sorry?"

"She left the van at the abandoned lot where it was later recovered. How did she come to the store? And why didn't she just drive?"

"She left the van on purpose. Weatherspoon knew what it looked like, and she didn't want him skulking about town and snatching something off it."

"So, if she assumed he might lurk during the opening of the exhibit, she didn't know he was already dead," Delta mused.

Marjorie sighed. "I think so, but the sheriff said she might have made it all up. Tilly says she came into town by bus. And she never saw her husband again after the short moments in the street, the day when she arrived in town. You were there, I understand, so you also saw that no violence took place. She never came near him, let alone stabbed him to death."

Delta admitted that Tilly hadn't seemed violent when she

had met the man in the raincoat on Mattock Street, but she had obviously been annoyed with his presence. "He said to her there was too much at stake. Did she tell you why?"

Marjorie looked puzzled. "No. But I guess the victim meant that his new life was at stake if she didn't give him some money."

Delta wasn't sure Weatherspoon had meant it that way but didn't argue. Tilly had apparently not shared fully with her lawyer. *On to more pressing issues.* "She confirmed she didn't meet him later in the day?"

"She did, and I believe her."

Delta nodded. "So, her case is looking good."

"I wouldn't say good. The sheriff really doesn't have any other suspects. Seems the victim traveled alone and had no dealings with anyone in town. I mean, Weatherspoon might have been here to do another con, but we can't ascertain that he actually took anyone's money. At least there were no charges filed. Staff at the motel saw or heard nothing relevant. The only connection the sheriff has is the one to Tilly. So he's holding her at the station for the time being, looking to get even more. There are continued searches for fingerprints and DNA at several sites." The lawyer pursed her lips as if she considered Sheriff West rather reticent with his information.

"I told him in return that I expect my client to be released before nightfall. Unless he can come up with something substantial to charge her with, of course."

"Did Tilly say anything to you in private that can help?"

"She wasn't very forthcoming. She wanted to know how her dog was, and that was about it. I showed her the photo Mrs. Cassidy sent me, and she brightened a bit, even saying she'd be hugging him soon. I didn't have the idea that the reality of her situation had sunken in yet."

"Denial?" Delta suggested.

The lawyer nodded and explained, "She simply doesn't want to face what might be ahead of her. She still thinks it is all a misunderstanding, and the sheriff will come to her cell to tell her she can go without further consequences. But I'm telling you that, even if he has to release her because he has nothing to hold her on for the moment, he will still consider her a suspect and prevent her from leaving town. Only finding another viable suspect can really give us a break."

Their pancakes appeared, and they ate in silence for a few minutes. Then the lawyer said, "Oh, there was a card left for me from a lady claiming to be Tilly Tay's sister. She wanted to talk to me. I'm not sure I should call her. I mean, Mrs. Cassidy is paying me, and I don't need to tell the relatives anything just yet. Besides, Tilly mentioned to me that she didn't want any interference from her family."

Delta frowned. "Tilly said that to you? But you only saw the card left for you *after* you saw Tilly. Did you go back to tell her her sister was in town?"

"No. She knew. I guess they had already been in touch before the exhibit?" Marjorie shrugged. "How do you know Tilly's sister?"

"I talked to her at the station. Seems she rushed out to help Tilly when she heard about her being in trouble."

"But she was staying in town already, right? With her horse."

"*With* her horse?" Delta echoed.

"Yes, the deputy who gave me the card said that the lady mentioned staying at the Lodge Hotel because it has a facility where guests can bring and stable their own horses. She's a keen rider."

"How coincidental." Delta frowned. "Her sister staying here for her horseback riding, and then Tilly coming to town to exhibit here. Tilly's husband also showing up and getting murdered. Tabitha claimed she hasn't seen him in years, but she could be lying. What if Weatherspoon knew she was in town and approached her? It would certainly make more sense to try and get money off someone who vacations with her horse than off Tilly who barely owns anything."

"Hmmm. I just mentioned being low on other suspects," Marjorie said, dipping her fork into the chocolate sauce on her pancake. "But I doubt my client would want to shift suspicion to her own sister, even if they're not that close." Delta wrote beside Tabitha in the case file: "When did she let Tilly know she was in town? And did she know Weatherspoon was here as well, before he died?"

Was this seemingly concerned sister truly worried about Tilly? Or did she have another reason for being here?

Her phone beeped, and she pulled it up and checked the screen. Mrs. Cassidy messaged, "I had a good night except for the moment where I was suddenly certain I had seen the light. I ran downstairs and fell down to my knees to check the dog bed Buddy came with. I was certain there were valuables hidden inside that the perp who came to my home had been looking for. Remember he ransacked the van and didn't find what he was looking for? What if he didn't check the dog bed and then later thought he should have and came to my house? All the volunteers at the museum knew we looked for Buddy there, and he was later brought to my house with his things. If that got around, the person who ransacked the van might also have heard about it."

Delta's mind raced to process Mrs. Cassidy's reasoning. Would a person from out of town have been in the loop with local gossip about a missing dog at the gold-mining museum?

Mrs. Cassidy's message continued to say, "To my chagrin, I felt nothing solid hidden in the bed. I checked from all sides, but no luck. Buddy seemed okay with my inspection, even licking my hands as I was at it. I can report that the bed holds nothing I can feel from the outside. There could be a piece of paper in the bed maybe, a check or other document, but I don't want to take the whole thing apart to prove a rather tenuous point. So I guess I have to accept that I was wrong. I took myself to bed again, quite remorseful that I have become so sensationalist."

Delta laughed out loud and typed a reply. "You were only careful and have excluded a possibility. Thanks for checking. Now we know neither Buddy or his things have a special value someone might be after. That's a relief. You should be safe now."

Mrs. Cassidy replied that she would call the alarm company anyway.

The lawyer checked her watch. "Thanks for the breakfast, but I have to run. Other clients to attend to. Keep me posted if new developments reach you before they reach the sheriff.

I have the impression you are well informed." She nodded at the phone that beeped again.

Delta flushed and waved goodbye to the lawyer. The pancake breakfast had been super helpful. The idea that Bob Weatherspoon might have approached Tabitha Tay VanderHurst to get funds was certainly worth a closer look.

Chapter Twelve

As the Paper Posse seemed intent on studying the Tilly Tay case from all angles—going as far as getting up in the middle of the night to search a dog bed for valuables—Delta felt she should involve them as much as she could. So she shared that Tilly's sister Tabitha had come to town and asked whether anyone knew anything about her.

As she typed it, she realized that it would be hard for her friends to know the woman, since she hadn't even described how she looked, but, immediately, Bessie Rider of Bessie's Boutique reported, "She was in my shop the other day. Bought two rather expensive scarves with a horse and horse-shoe print. She also asked about out-of-stock dresses that she wanted delivered in the next few days while she stayed at the Lodge Hotel with her husband. She had stayed there before, she said, and really loved how authentic it was. I hope I can really make a few sales while she's in town."

"How wonderful for you," Delta responded, knowing that all shops ached for customers this time of year and especially the kind of customer that had money to spend. "Did she mention anything about Tilly?"

Bessie replied, "When she gave me her name, I asked whether she happened to be related to the Montana artist. She said, a little reluctantly, that it was her sister. I can imagine that a woman of her position isn't too keen on admitting she has a sister who drives around and lives in an old van. I'm not in favor of any kind of snobbery, but, well, people tend to be a bit judgmental. I mean, her friends and relations may be."

"But she was at the police station wanting to talk to Tilly," Delta wrote. "That is odd if she doesn't want to be associated with her. I mean, she doesn't want people to know she's the sister of a woman who lives out of a van, but she does want people to know that she's the sister of a suspected murderer?"

"She told the police she is; she didn't advertise it in the *Tundish Trader*," Jane commented reasonably.

"Well, if Sven LeDuc gets wind of it, it will be in the

Trader. On the front page." Rattlesnake Rita added plenty of exclamation points and wide-eyed emojis.

Delta sighed. That was true enough, of course.

Jane wrote, "I heard a rumor among customers that Sheriff West is asking around at local banks whether Weatherspoon had a safety deposit box there that might hold clues to the missing millions from the pyramid scheme."

Interesting. Delta stared at her case file, her gaze flitting from the ransacked van to Buddy on his dog bed to the words "missing millions" connected to the pyramid scheme.

A new suggestion came to mind: what if whoever had killed Bob was after the money and thought Tilly had it?

"Do you want more coffee?" the waitress asked. Delta had almost forgotten she was still at Mine Forever poring over the Paper Posse's messages after the lawyer had left. "Umm, no, I'd better be going." She quickly shut her case file.

"I'm sorry the exhibition is now a bit tainted," the woman confided. It wasn't the waitress Delta had talked to on several occasions but an older woman with gray curls held back with a black studded headband. Her name tag read GRACE. She said, "I love how it all turned out. I even posted on social media to invite people to come on over to Tundish to see it. There are special groups for fans of miniatures, you know."

"Thanks for promoting it," Delta said, pocketing her case file and pulling out her wallet to pay for the meal. "I do hope the confusion surrounding Tilly Tay will be cleared up soon. I'm sure the sheriff arrested the wrong person."

"That could be." Grace nodded. "I heard that the victim was seen arguing with a younger man that same night."

"Oh, really?" Delta perked up. "What young man? Another motel guest?"

"Hard to tell. The son of a friend of mine has an odd job there doing dishes, and he ran across the pair of them when he took out the trash. They were ready to come to blows, he said."

"Did he tell the police?" Delta asked, her breath catching. Perhaps another viable suspect for Marjorie Brenning was just within reach.

"I don't know. I bet West has been to the motel to question the regular staff, not some teen who only works a few hours at night."

"Then the boy should go to the police himself," Delta urged. "His testimony can really help."

"He doesn't particularly like West after the good sheriff caught him drinking while underage. Besides, what does he actually know?" Grace spread her hands in a helpless gesture.

"He can't identify the other guy. He only glanced at them and then went about his own business."

"Still, I think it would be good if West knew about this. Can't you persuade your friend's son to tell the police?"

Grace pursed her lips. "I can try, but I can't guarantee he will listen to me."

"Could you ask your friend then? He'll listen to his mother."

The woman held back her head and laughed, her curls shaking. "At that age, he doesn't listen to his mother about anything, so why would he about this? But I can see this is important to you with Tilly Tay being accused and all, so I'll do my very best. Deal?"

"Thanks so much." Delta tipped her and went out, standing in the street a moment, breathing the November air. The chill of winter coming was detectable, but the sun was trying its hardest to warm the pavement and give a glow to the authentic wooden storefronts. Delta let her gaze wander and realized how at home she felt in this little town.

A year ago, living in the big city, she would never have believed she could fit into a small-town community. She might have even thought she'd feel bored and alone if removed from all the bustle and the ready opportunities to pop into art galleries and attend concerts.

But, here, life was full of new adventures as well. She loved outdoor activities, if only a walk or a ride on her mountain bike. And the great sights all around fueled her creativity. She was currently designing a notebook idea with mountains and wild animals on it. She might not have trusted herself earlier to draw a deer well, but, having had the chance now to see animals up close and how they behaved in their environment, she felt more confident. Still, she needed Jonas's input. He could tell her where to erase a bit or add some bulk. It would be a sort of joint venture, even if he didn't know it.

Delta caught herself smiling at the idea, but the corners of her mouth sagged again when she remembered Paula. Even if Jonas regarded the pretty brunette merely as a friend, it proved that he was friendly with more women than just her, and his attitude could be the same to all. How would she know? She wasn't there when he went to dinner with others.

It stung, and she hurriedly crossed to Wanted to get her mind off Jonas. Hazel greeted her briefly as she served a mother and two daughters buying watercolor supplies. A family with young children were admiring Tundish in the display. "Daddy," the little boy asked, "why is that man lying on his face?"

Delta feared he meant the dead prospector and quickly

said, "Well, they were all looking for gold and, if they found some, others wanted it and sometimes got into a fight over it. Do you want to see the scales they used to weigh the gold? And maybe a real nugget?"

The little boy nodded eagerly, and she directed the group into one of the old cells where they had a bit more information on the gold rush. The mother bought a set of gel pens and some washi tape for a scrapbooking friend by way of "payment for the fun tour," as she put it with a wink. The family left smiling, the kids asking for ice cream, which was denied because of the cold.

Hazel had served her customers and said to Delta, "I remember always asking for ice cream. Didn't matter to me what time of year it was. You?"

Delta grinned. "I'd love some right now. Too bad we haven't got a freezer in our pantry."

Hazel stretched her arms up to the ceiling. "You've been busy. Did it pay off?"

"I thought of a plausible reason why Tilly's van has been searched. But I don't know if that scenario is good news for her case or bad." While Delta updated her friend, they unpacked two boxes with new pencils and collectible erasers that had come in. The pencils were put in see-through jars so the customers could see the different patterns on them, whereas the erasers—shaped like jungle animals—got a little display with paper fences like a tiny zoo. Delta took some pictures to upload to their social media channels.

"Let's hope this entices someone to buy a whole lot," Hazel said. She gnawed her lip a moment. "I had this nightmare last night where we hadn't paid our bills and the company came to cut our electricity."

"At the cottage?" Delta asked, rearranging the eraser elephants. Hazel's anxiety tore at her heart strings, as she wanted her friend to feel secure in their venture together. During this slow season, the store could easily be handled by one person so maybe Hazel thought sometimes that she'd rather still do it by herself?

"No, here at the store. Everything went dark. The only lights on where those in Tilly Tay's small houses. I remember getting quite irrationally angry that it was her fault we got into such trouble and now her lights were burning and ours had gone out."

Delta swallowed hard. She wondered a moment if, maybe, Hazel wasn't blaming just Tilly but her also for inviting the woman to the shop. She wanted to ask something to gauge Hazel's feelings, but Hazel was already saying, "We should give some of the Christmas items a more prominent place. People are really getting ready to write their cards, and we should be there to offer them all the pens, paper, and stickers they need to make theirs extra memorable."

"Yes, Gran will also want to send some," Delta said. "I should ask her to come have a look here before all the good stuff is sold out."

Hazel cast her a glance as if saying, *sold out, really?* but she only said, "The oddest thing happened while you were away." She removed herself a few paces and studied the pencil display. "This woman came in, I don't think I've ever served her before, but then she didn't stand out: forty-ish, short brown hair, sportily dressed. She could have been here before, and I just don't recall. But she asked for you, and, when I said you weren't here, she looked about her and whispered she might as well tell *me*. I felt like I should know her, I mean, you don't talk like that to a stranger, do you?"

"I don't think so." Delta's heart skipped a beat. The woman's behavior sounded rather mysterious. What could this be about?

Hazel said, "She said your gran was in danger."

"In danger?" Delta echoed. She knocked over the two eraser pandas she had just put up. "How did she mean that?"

"I asked the same thing. I was, of course, very surprised that she would put it that way."

Hazel brushed a lock of hair from her face and continued, "She said she did cleaning for elderly people around the area and that she had noticed several of her clients being very cheerful suddenly. They had met a charming man who took them out and..."

Oh no. Major George Buckmore. Delta's knees filled with jelly. A stab of guilt shot through her that she hadn't acted as soon as she knew of his existence, asking Jonas to look into him. You couldn't be careful enough these days.

Hazel was explaining what the woman had said, "He gives them flowers and bonbons and woos them the old-fashioned way, and they eat it up. She thinks he's after their money."

"Then she should tell the police." Delta felt anger rush through her veins at her own lack of action but also at this woman's choice to come gossip about it at Wanted instead of taking it to the proper authorities.

"Oh, but she did," Hazel said with wide eyes, "but the deputy told her they can't do anything as long as there is no criminal activity. I mean, he has to do something first, like ask them for money or steal from their homes before they can act against him. Until then, their hands are tied."

"I see." Delta was in no mood to appreciate that the police wanted proof. Right now, it felt like they were letting down her grandmother and other vulnerable elderly people by allowing this man do whatever he wanted. "And these women she mentioned, the ladies on the receiving end of his attentions, have they already experienced anything suspicious?" *If there's a clear instance of deception, I can use it to warn Gran.*

"Not to my knowledge, but she was eager to get away from the shop. She said she wanted to warn you, but, in case people asked, we didn't hear it from her. Because she doesn't want to lose her job cleaning at their homes."

"Well, we can't tell anyone we heard it from her, as we have no idea who she actually is. Or did she give you a name?"

Hazel shook her head with a rueful expression. "I was too surprised to ask for one. Sorry." She hung her head. "I already felt stupid about lending the key to Tilly Tay and now this. You must be mad at me."

"Of course I'm not mad at you." Delta went over and pretended to want to shake her friend by the shoulders in mock rebuke. But, instead, she grabbed them and looked her in the eye. "Are you mad at me?"

"At you?" Hazel seemed puzzled. "You weren't here when

the woman came in. You would have asked smart questions. I always think of those too late. After the fact." Hazel grimaced. "I could only think that if you had been here, it would have worked out much better."

"But I'm feeling lousy about asking Tilly over. I thought you were mad at me because of that. Inviting someone who's a murder suspect now."

"Just because West hasn't looked beyond her. There must be other suspects. I do admit Tilly has been reticent about a lot of things, but..."

"She is married to a convicted con man. Weatherspoon didn't commit crimes just once, but regularly, and served several sentences. That does make West wonder if Tilly was ever involved in his fraud and if they fell out when he came after her to Tundish. It makes sense that he asks those questions."

"Of course. But what about other people who might have been interested once Weatherspoon was out of jail? A former partner in crime? Someone he duped? He must have dozens of victims. What if your life savings went down the drain? Wouldn't you want revenge?"

Delta nodded. "Good thinking. We should have the lawyer look into that. The police can get access to Weatherspoon's criminal record and find out who his known associates or his

victims might be. I wonder if they're any living in the area."
She squeezed Hazel's shoulders. "So you're not mad at me? I
felt so bad getting shopkeeper of the season right before the
artist I invited for an exhibition was arrested for obstructing
justice. In a murder charge, no less."

"Not at all. I'm glad you're here. You're fantastic with
all that social media stuff. I never got it set up properly,
but, since you're taking care of it, we've got hundreds more
followers. From all over the country. Even internationally.
And I love your gran. Which is why that woman's visit and
her accusations against Buckmore rattled me. What if some
mean-spirited man who takes advantage of little old ladies is
now after her?"

"Gran can take care of herself," Delta said more posi-
tively than she felt inside. "If she knew other victims, they'd
get together for sure and find a way to draw him into a trap."

"Hey, that's an idea." Hazel pointed a finger at her. "What
if *we* try to lure Major George Buckmore into a trap? We can
make it super easy for him to steal something. We invite him
over and have money lying around. Or a valuable necklace or
some other thing. We can see what he does."

"Invite him over?" Delta repeated. "You mean to our
place?"

"Yes. We cook a special dinner and invite both your gran and him."

Delta hesitated. "If he preys on old ladies, he won't steal from us."

"You don't know that. He might take any opportunity. We can also invite some others so it's extra busy and there are distractions. Ray and Jonas. We'll be with six people. How about that? And, if he does take the bait, Jonas can arrest him. He knows how that works."

Delta was still doubtful. "Shouldn't we first find out if there is truth to this woman's story?"

"She warned us for a good reason. She's concerned about the vulnerable old people she cares for. I can understand that."

"Yes, but she doesn't clean for Gran. Why involve her at all? That doesn't make sense."

Hazel shrugged. "Maybe she saw them around town together. She knows him, and then she was worried who this new victim might be and found out who your gran is. She came to us because she knows that the victims themselves won't listen; they're probably so blinded by the man's charms."

Delta had to admit that Gran was very fond of her new

acquaintance and did spend a lot of time with him. A little digging into who he might really be wasn't a bad thing, right? She had already wanted to do that, and now she had a good reason for it. If Gran found out and wasn't pleased, she could tell her that a local woman had expressed concerns and they had felt obliged to look into it.

"Okay." She nodded at Hazel. "When do you want to do this special dinner?"

"Tomorrow night? I have to check whether they are free to join us of course. And look up some recipes."

"And arrange for some cash to put in conspicuous places," Delta provided. "Plus a valuable necklace." She pursed her lips as she considered this part of Hazel's plan. "I don't have any. If Buckmore is a thief, he won't be tempted by my beaded jewelry. Yours isn't much better, right?" She couldn't recall having seen Hazel with anything that would tempt a professional thief who knew the value of stuff at a glance.

Hazel thought hard. Then her expression cleared. "I know just the thing. You wait and see."

Later that day, as they were closing down the store, Jonas dropped by. He wore his heavy-duty raincoat, dark green to blend into the forest and not disturb the animals, and Delta asked him with a grin whether he was working with stressed-out CEOs again. Jonas rolled his eyes. "Spare me. I had enough of that to last me a lifetime. They weren't dressed for the occasion, despite the emailed instructions explicitly stating that they should bring comfy shoes and rain clothes. So the first guy was already complaining about blisters after we had walked half a mile. And, when it started to pour, no one had any rain gear on hand. They came back soaked. Rosalyn snarled at *me* for treating guests that way."

"Next time ask them, before you set out, whether they have a raincoat or something, and, if they don't, hand out those plastic poncho-style things."

"I'm not their mother, am I?" Jonas sighed. "These are grown men who run companies that make billions worldwide. If they can organize their agenda, they can also organize this walk in the forest."

Delta wanted to say that actually they didn't organize their agendas—their assistants did. But, before she could suggest this, Jonas asked with a worried frown, "Do you know if Mrs. Cassidy intended to really do something about that alarm she wanted to get?"

"Huh?" Delta had to refocus a moment.

Jonas gestured as he explained quickly, "She had a prowler around her house, remember, and then she said that she wanted to get an alarm and she already had a card from some guy who offered her an alarm. I thought about it, and it struck me as rather suspicious he offered to install an alarm and then she suddenly had a prowler."

Delta widened her eyes. "You think the two are connected?"

"That's possible."

"She did mention wanting to do something about it today."

Jonas nodded. "Then I'm going over to see her and tell her my suspicions. I'd rather do it face-to-face."

"I'm coming with you, to see Buddy. Tilly's lawyer told me that the only thing cheering up Tilly was good news about her dog. I'll snap some more photos for her."

Saying it, she cringed. It was a very bad excuse as Mrs. Cassidy could easily do this. But Delta felt like she urgently needed to spend some time with Jonas, both to gauge his feelings for Paula and to invite him to the dinner with Gran and Major Buckmore.

The mere idea made her stomach tighten. Gran really liked her new friend. It would be such a blow to her if he were found to be a con man. She'd rather forget about the whole trap idea and let Jonas do some quiet inquiries instead.

Delta told Hazel she was going with Jonas to see Buddy and would do their grocery shopping on the way home. "I'll also cook dinner to make up for running out on you all day long."

"Great. I'll have a soak in the tub while you're out. Gives me a chance to finish the book I started ages ago. Just give me your key so I can lock up. Despite Sheriff West's promises, I still haven't heard anything about getting mine back."

Delta handed over the key and waved goodbye. Jonas let her into the Jeep's passenger seat and got in himself, buckling up. Delta said, "Do you really think Mrs. Cassidy wouldn't see through this man's intentions? She's usually very sharp."

"I want to warn her, and then it's off my back. Whether she believes me or not is her business." It sounded curt.

Delta said, "You really didn't like the CEO thing. You sound seriously out of sorts."

Jonas waved a hand. "Just personal stuff."

Delta bit her lip. A real friend would probably ask more questions and find out what was wrong then, but she asked herself whether she even wanted to know. What if Jonas started to explain to her that he was in love with Paula or that Paula was in love with him and...

No, she could never talk about that without giving

something away of her own feelings. Sitting beside him in the comfort of the Jeep, with the rain pattering on the roof, she felt so at ease, so at home with him that the thought of losing that confidentiality hurt like crazy. Even if they'd still meet, it would never be the same once she knew he was in love with someone else.

Jonas said, "How is the Tilly Tay thing unfolding? Any new leads?"

"Maybe. Have you heard about the sheriff looking into safety deposit boxes at banks? To find the missing money from the pyramid scheme?"

Jonas seemed uncomfortable a moment. "Yes, I heard it in passing. How come?"

Delta kept her gaze on his profile as she asked, "Is he looking into boxes that belonged to Weatherspoon or also to Tilly?"

Jonas's expression showed the smallest slip, but Delta still noticed. "He is," she concluded. "So he wonders whether Tilly was involved in Weatherspoon's cons."

"West put two and two together. Why ransack the van of an elderly lady who owns nothing worth stealing? Yes, her models are valuable because of the time and effort she put into them, but they can't be readily sold for cash like jewelry or a laptop. It was no ordinary theft. That person was looking for something specific."

"Like the key to a deposit box?" Delta asked.

"For instance," he nodded.

"I have an idea who the intruder might have been." Delta told Jonas about the information the friendly waitress at Mine Forever had given her that morning, concerning the man Weatherspoon had argued with at the motel before he had died.

Jonas huffed. "That is a very vague statement. The police can't find the man in question based on that little information."

"Still, it's a lead. I also wanted to share something else. Tilly's sister showed up. Tabitha Tay. She is married to some wealthy man called VanderHurst and has horses. Keen rider too. She claims to be staying at the Lodge, with her horse. I guess she exercises him in the woods. Have you seen her there? She's a rather tall commanding type..." She described the woman better but still felt it was rather vague.

No wonder Jonas shrugged. "I don't have a lot of business with the guests who come for horseback riding. There is an instructor who accompanies the less-experienced riders. Why? Do you think the sister is somehow important?"

"I don't know. I was wondering why she showed up at the police station wanting to talk to Tilly."

"Maybe she is the protective sister who wants to get Tilly out of trouble. Or maybe she sees it as a chance to tell her to change her lifestyle. Often relatives use the brush another has with the police to point out what could be done better. Sad but true."

"Sad?" Delta queried. "Isn't it good if someone cares?"

"Obviously, but let's be honest. If you were in the cell, and suddenly your brother turned up telling you that he had always known running a stationery shop in a small town was a bad idea and hopefully you'd see that too, now, and change your ways, would you think he cared?"

"Not really. I would be annoyed and feel attacked."

"Exactly." Jonas turned the wheel to let the Jeep run smoothly through a bend in the road. "But, if you want me to look into the sister further, I might find out a thing or two."

Delta stared ahead. "Can you look into anyone you want? Suppose I met someone and I want to know if he's reliable? I mean, you're not a policeman, so you need not have a concrete suspicion to do some quiet research, right?"

"Wow, wait a minute." Jonas raised a hand. "If you met a guy and want to know if you can safely date him, I'm not going to check him out."

"No? I thought we were friends." Delta pretended to pout. In truth, her heart was racing at the idea that Jonas thought about her possibly dating and even sounded a little... jealous? "Don't you care at all for my safety?"

Jonas glanced at her. "Is there some guy you want to date?"

Delta held his gaze in that brief moment before he focused on the road again. What did those eyes tell her? Was he worried? Surprised?

Envious?

She couldn't quite tell. She fidgeted with her hands. "There's more to life than work, you know."

"Maybe." It sounded dismissive. Jonas took his time to look in the rearview mirror at some car coming up behind them at high speed. He let him overtake them, muttering, "Idiot." before saying to Delta, "I don't want to tap into my contacts too often. For a good cause, of course, I mean, Tilly Tay's case now and all, but..." He held the wheel tighter, judging by the tension in his knuckles. "Still, if you feel unsafe and it would help... This raises the question of why you'd even date a guy you don't trust. Just because he's good-looking?"

"It's not about me," Delta admitted with a sigh. "It's Gran. She met this charming gentleman who sweeps her off her feet with dates, flowers, and exciting stories about local history. They seem to share so many interests it's almost too perfect. I like him, I honestly do. But some woman showed up at the shop today claiming she cleans for old ladies and has heard stories about this man wooing several women with bad intentions. She came explicitly to warn me about the danger to Gran."

"Do you know that woman?"

"No."

"Odd, then, don't you think? Why her concern?"

"She's mainly concerned for her own clients, I gathered. And the police aren't doing a thing, as they claim nothing criminal has happened yet."

"Which is true. If there had been any charges, they'd look into it, I'm sure."

"Of course." Delta nodded. "But Hazel, who talked to the woman while I was away to look into Tilly's case, is now certain we have to do something to find out more about the intentions of Major George Buckmore, and she is setting up a trap."

"Trap?" Jonas echoed with a worried look at Delta.

"It's a dinner. For Gran and the major, Hazel and Ray... and you and me." She didn't dare look at him as she said it.

"Hazel thinks that if there's a hundred bucks around, he will steal it, and you can catch him red-handed."

"That's not how it works. Con men like that don't typically act when there are others around."

"I told her that, but she says it will work. I think she feels somehow guilty about lending the key to Tilly Tay that gave her and the killer access to the shop, and now she wants to make up by exposing this supposed threat to Gran. She means well, and I do want to know what he's about. But I'm not too sure about this particular plan."

"I'd say don't do it," Jonas said. He drove into Mrs. Cassidy's driveway and parked the Jeep behind an unobtrusive beige car. "Know whose that is?" he asked Delta.

She shook her head. "Not a clue."

"Let's have a look." Jonas got out, and Delta followed him around the house. At the back door, which stood ajar, they heard voices inside.

Mrs. Cassidy said, "I do appreciate you can do it on such short notice."

"I hope it will make you sleep better," a male voice said.

Jonas looked at Delta, then knocked, pushed the door open, and stepped in. In the kitchen they found Mrs. Cassidy and a man attaching a small black device to her kitchen window. "Hello," Mrs. Cassidy said, startled by the sudden intrusion. "I didn't hear you until you were already inside."

"We wanted to tell you some good news," Delta enthused to explain for their rather rude behavior. "But you have company, so it can wait." She kept smiling widely.

Mrs. Cassidy gave her a curious once-over and said to the man, "You can take care of this, Mr. Criggs? I will take my visitors into the living room then." She led the way, Buddy coming to jump at them and bark. Nugget sat in her basket looking too dignified to join in this overexcited greeting ritual. Mrs. Cassidy clapped her hands together and said, "What is it?"

Jonas lowered his voice and asked, "Is this the man who left you a card in case you wanted an alarm?"

"Yes. I feel quite silly now. I told him explicitly when he was here first that I don't need it or want it." Mrs. Cassidy flushed. "But now I asked him to come, and he made space in his schedule especially for me. I do feel that I should pay him extra for his service."

"Not necessarily." Jonas informed her, still speaking low, of his suspicions. Mrs. Cassidy's eyes went wide. "You mean that he urges people to get an alarm, and then, after they decline he breaks in... No, that can't be right. The intruder here was after Buddy."

"We thought so," Delta said, "because of Tilly's van and all, and you happening to be the one who accepted the dog into your home. But the two things might not be related. He" she gestured in the direction of the kitchen, "could be the very person who…"

Mrs. Cassidy shook her head. "I would never have thought of it. Especially because I'm so distracted by Buddy's presence, Nugget feeling ignored and all the talk in town about the shop…"

"The shop?" Delta pounced. "You mean, our shop, Wanted?"

"I'm so sorry." Mrs. Cassidy looked dejected. "I hadn't meant to tell you."

"What is it?" Delta urged her with a hand on her arm. "Come on, you can tell me."

"You might as well; she'll hear it anyway through the grapevine," Jonas supported her.

Mrs. Cassidy took a deep breath. "The shopkeepers aren't happy I advised them strongly to give shopkeeper of the season to you and Hazel. They feel like it's now a stain on their group and the town. With the murder having happened and being connected to Wanted. I tried to explain to them how silly that is, but they aren't easily swayed."

"I can give it back," Delta offered, but Jonas held up a hand. "Not so quickly. If Tilly turns out to be innocent, it was just false suspicions. You shouldn't have to hand back an honor you fully earned."

Delta blushed under his praise.

Mrs. Cassidy nodded firmly. "My ideas exactly. But this unpleasantness does gnaw at my nerves."

"You're right." Delta rubbed her palms together. "To be honest, I'm worried that we are so focused on finding criminals we might be seeing them where there aren't any." She glanced at Jonas. Were they making a mistake setting up a trap for Major Buckmore? Would it only hurt her bond with Gran if it got out?

Jonas wrapped his arm around her shoulder a moment and whispered in her ear, "Don't worry, Delta. We'll protect your gran together. I promise."

She looked up into his eyes, seeing the warmth there and the determination to stick to that promise. For a brief moment she felt totally protected, safe, in place.

"Excuse me…" The man popped his head around the entry. "I can't back up. There's a Jeep behind my vehicle."

"I'll move it," Jonas said. He left the room. Mrs. Cassidy leaned over to Delta and said, "When you told me you had some exciting news to share, I thought for a moment you were going to tell me you were in love. I know it's fast, as you've only lived her for two months, but still... There's been a strong connection between the two of you from the beginning."

Delta flushed. "We're just very good friends."

Mrs. Cassidy said, "Feelings are nothing to be ashamed of."

"I'm not ashamed of what I..." Delta bit back the rest. She didn't feel like explaining how complicated all of this was. "Like you just said, I've only lived here for two months. You can't really know someone in so short a while."

"And you can't fall in love?" Mrs. Cassidy asked with a tilted head. "I've heard people say it can happen at first sight."

"Not for me. I need to know that I can trust someone."

"I don't think that's an issue with Jonas."

"Car moved." Jonas appeared in the entry. "I took the liberty of mentioning to him that I hadn't seen him around before, and he assured me he's been working this area for years. Now I will check up on that statement as soon as I can and let you know. Just an extra precaution, free of charge." He said to Delta, "Ready to leave?"

"Yes, we must be going. I have my shopping to do."

"I can drop you off at the supermarket, if you want." Jonas leaned back on his heels. "I mean, I can wait while you do the shopping and then take you home."

Delta smiled at him. "Thanks, that would be great."

Once in the Jeep, she wondered why he was being so nice to her. Did he feel guilty because he knew he was in love with Paula and didn't want to tell her?

She looked for a way to start chatting about the pretty brunette, but nothing came to mind. In fact, her thoughts didn't want to focus on anything but an intense sense of loss at the idea Jonas was marrying someone else. They could still be friends, of course, but it wouldn't be the same.

Which said enough about her so-called friendship with him. It was more. Much more that she wanted to keep.

At the supermarket Jonas said he might as well do some shopping for himself, and they went inside together. Picking lettuce and tomatoes and even arguing about what the best orange juice was, Delta felt they were just like a couple. What would it be like to be some place with Jonas and look at him and know he was hers?

She had never before felt so possessive of a man. It was

exciting and intimidating at the same time. His opinion mattered to her, a lot, like when he had said she should really take action about Zach. But she didn't really dare to allow herself to feel it. People you cared for could hurt you. By their actions, like Zach had done, or when they got into trouble, like Gran was in now with the loss of her home and the possible threat coming from the charming Major George Buckmore. No, Delta didn't want to add more people to the list she had to worry about.

Chapter Thirteen

OVER THE QUICK BUT DELICIOUS PASTA MEAL DELTA PREPPED for Hazel and herself, they talked about Tilly Tay's case. Delta told Hazel about the teen working at the motel who had allegedly seen the victim argue with a younger man. "We should really find out who that was," she said. "Maybe he killed the victim?"

"If he did, he will be long gone. Why stick around?" Hazel dug her fork into the grilled cheese on top of her spaghetti. "This is great, thanks for cooking."

"I owed you, for being away all day. I do feel like I'm doing too little for the shop."

"You got shopkeeper of the season. That's a real honor."

Delta grimaced. "Yes, but the tide is turning." She told Hazel about what Mrs. Cassidy had reluctantly revealed to her and Jonas.

Hazel sighed. "I hope no one throws another rock through our store window."

To cheer her up, Delta said, "Let's make some plans for workshops we can do in January and February."

The December ones were fully booked, offering ways to make exclusive glass markers and place cards for the Christmas dinner table, creating your own Christmas crackers and a special one with an out-of-town guest crafter teaching paper poinsettias.

"January is a sort of 'meh' month," Hazel observed. "The festivities are over, the weather is usually kind of gray, you don't have a lot of money to spend."

"Hmm, maybe we should build on that. Teach people how to make a budgeting planner for the new year. We can use scrapbooking techniques and offer an outside budgeting expert as our guest. I've been thinking about this for a while, you know, how we can pull in more people. By combining the crafty aspect with something practical. I mean, something people are interested in, like tips to save money or to be more active."

"Great idea." Hazel sat up. "We can do a workshop where we make a household planner to hang on your kitchen wall and ask an expert to do a short item on quality time."

"I'm getting a notepad to take down some ideas," Delta said.

Soon they were writing down lots of ideas, some more wacky than others, laughing a lot as they were at it. Making all these plans gave the pair energy, and, as Delta maneuvered through the kitchen to make some coffee, she felt decidedly better. She had come to Tundish for the store, to be in business with her best friend and craft her way through life. She shouldn't let herself be sidetracked by murder cases or complicated feelings for a man who might not see her as girlfriend material. Her phone beeped. A message popped up from Calamity Jane: "My husband put all the photographs and videos he took at the opening of the exhibition in an online album. You can see them by clicking this secure link. If you want any to share on your social media channels or website, let me know. Hope you like them."

Delta clicked on the link and looked at the photos and videos of enthusiastic villagers looking at her display. It was a bit souring to realize that the people who had loved it then were now angry at her because of the murder.

Suddenly, in the last video she looked at, her gaze detected a familiar face. Tabitha Tay VanderHurst. She stood at the entrance of the shop, looking about her as if she searched

for someone in the crowd inside. Then she talked to someone Delta couldn't see on the footage, presumably outside in
the street. Her expression changed from animated to annoyed
and she suddenly stepped back and exited the shop in a hurry.

Why had she not come in to look at the display? Who had
been with her?

Frowning hard, Delta replayed the video. From Tabitha's
behavior, she got the distinct impression that she had appeared
at Wanted's door merely to check if a specific person was
present inside. Tilly? Busy with the exhibition? What had
Tabitha been up to?

Earlier they had assumed Tilly had left the van at the
campsite to protect it from Bob Weatherspoon's intrusion,
but what if she had tried to hide it from her own sister?

After all, Tilly had known Tabitha was in town; she had
mentioned it to her lawyer emphasizing she didn't want her
family to intrude. And, at the sheriff's station, Tabitha had
said they had been trying for years to persuade Tilly to quit
with the off-the-grid lifestyle. How?

And why?

Too bad Delta couldn't see in that video who had been
with Tabitha.

The next morning, while they were having a hurried break-fast, there was a knock at the back door. Delta went to open up and saw Gran standing there, all smiles. She was dressed in a smart three-quarter-length coat with a new hat on. "Come inside," Delta invited. "There's fresh coffee."

"I can't stay long. I wanted to say I'm going away for a few days."

"Away?" Delta echoed.

"Yes. George asked me to accompany him." Gran blushed like a schoolgirl. "He's giving a lecture about gold rush history, and he wants to explore the surroundings. With me." She smiled even wider. "I haven't been so excited about something for a long time. I hope you don't mind me leaving."

"If it's just for a few days..." Delta tried to look happy, but, inside, unrest, hesitation, and outright suspicion scrambled for the upper hand. Why would Buckmore want to take Gran away from Tundish? Did he have some sneaky plan for her?

What is he up to?

"Take care, darling," Gran stood on tiptoe to kiss Delta on the cheek. "I do feel like I'm abandoning you with the trouble you're in..."

"Nonsense. I'm not in trouble at all," she lied. "Sheriff

West is looking into the whereabouts of the pyramid scheme proceeds. No doubt he also knows which associates Weatherspoon may have worked with at the time who might have come after him at his release. Tilly Tay will soon be cleared of all suspicion, and everything will be fine, trust me. You have a good time."

Delta hugged her grandmother. Her throat was tight with fear that the man she was leaving with had some evil plan and she might be hurt. But she couldn't say that now.

It's too late.

Gran stepped back. "I'll call you."

"You do that." Delta watched her walk away, thinking this must be how a mother felt taking her toddler to kindergarten. Wanting to hold on tight and never let go.

"What's up?" Hazel asked stepping up from behind.

"Gran is going out of town for a few days, with Major Buckmore."

"What? How about my plan for the dinner where..." Hazel touched Delta's arm. "The guy could have something sinister up his sleeve."

"I know, but I could hardly ask her if he's a con man. She adores him." She might be in love with him. Hadn't Mrs. Cassidy said the other day that people fell in love at first sight? And this man was so charming, with his flowers and his fun ideas.

Delta felt lightheaded and went back into the kitchen to sit down. She clenched her hands together. "I'll call Jonas and discuss it with him. Where is my phone?"

Hazel looked about her. "It must still be upstairs. I'll get it." She ran from the room.

Delta sat breathing deeply. She didn't want to jump to conclusions, but she couldn't control the panic swirling inside. Gran was the dearest relative she had in the world. She was closer with her than with her own parents. If something happened to her...

Buckmore isn't taking her to the south pole, she admonished herself. *It's just a small trip, and they will be back soon. You can call her. You can check whether they arrived safely at the location.*

Wait a minute.

Gran hadn't said where they were going. And Delta hadn't asked.

The cold feeling inside intensified. Why hadn't she asked for the address of the hotel or wherever they'd be staying?

Hazel burst back in. "Here's your phone. Call Jonas. He'll know what to do."

Delta pressed the buttons with trembling fingers. She felt as if her gran had been kidnapped and she might never see her again.

When Jonas answered the call, Delta said in a shivery voice, "Hello, it's me. Gran was here a minute ago…"

"Is something wrong?" he cut in. "You sound upset."

"She's fine, but she told me she's going away for a few days with a new friend she made. The guy I told you about, the one whom the woman in the stationery shop warned us about."

Jonas was silent for a moment. "You think he has some plan for this trip?"

"I don't know. Maybe."

"Did you tell your grandmother about… No, of course you didn't. You wouldn't have wanted to hurt her feelings if you weren't sure the allegations were true."

"I wanted to check him out better," Delta said, her voice strangled with tears. "I didn't know I wouldn't have the time to do so."

"Calm down," Jonas sounded softer, as if he was moving closer to her. She could feel his arm around her shoulders again. "We can still make sure he doesn't mean her harm. Where are they going?"

"I don't know. That's the stupid…" Delta swallowed hard. A tear ran down her cheek. "I didn't ask. I was so taken off guard by her appearance and news that…"

"No problem. We can find them."

Delta rubbed away the tear with an impatient gesture. "I do know something. He is giving a lecture about the gold rush. Maybe you can find out online where that is?"

"Perfect. I'll call you back as soon as I know more and made a plan to ensure she's safe. Take care." Jonas disconnected.

Delta took a deep breath. "I feel so silly."

"Because you cried?" Hazel asked. "Maybe Jonas won't mind seeing a softer side to you."

"How do you mean?"

"Well, you're always so self-assured and independent. Maybe he thinks you don't need him at all."

What? Delta's jaw sagged. She always viewed Jonas as the independent one who didn't need her. Did he feel the same way? Was that why he had been keeping his distance? While he did want to…kiss her?

This really isn't the time to think about that, she admonished herself. *I must focus on Gran.*

As she thought it, her phone rang. She almost dropped it and accepted the call with a pounding heart. A male voice said, "Is this Delta Douglas? Are you arranging for the defense of Tilly Tay?"

"Yes, umm, well, more or less." Delta hesitated. Mrs. Cassidy had hired the lawyer, and she really didn't know whether... But the man gave her no time to explain anything. He spoke urgently, "We must meet. I have important information for you that can clear her. But I don't want to come to your house or your store. We must meet at some neutral place."

"Why?" Delta asked, determined not to be overwhelmed again. Two shocks in one morning were too much. "Besides, if you know something relevant about the murder, you should go to the police and tell them."

"I don't want anything to do with the police. I will tell you, only you." He sounded ready to hang up on her.

"Okay," Delta said quickly. Her curiosity was stronger than her reluctance, since it may help Tilly's case.

And, consequently, also restore Wanted's damaged reputation with the shopkeepers who were upset about the scandal. "Where do you want to meet?"

"I'll message you instructions. I don't want to take any risk of the police showing up. Get into your car, and I'll send the first directions." He disconnected.

Lowering the phone, Delta felt goose bumps on her arms.

This was kind of creepy. And dangerous. She had no idea who this guy was. He claimed to want to clear Tilly, but he could have something far different in mind. She could be meeting...the killer?

She turned to Hazel and explained quickly what was up. Hazel said, "How does he know you're involved in Tilly's defense? And where did he get your number?"

Delta shrugged. "There's plenty of talk in town. My number is on our business cards."

"Maybe he took a business card from the shop when he planted the clue in the display to incriminate Tilly," Hazel suggested. She crossed her arms over her chest. "You're not going alone. I'm coming with you. Or, better still, Jonas should come with you."

Delta pursed her lips. "Is there time to arrange that? The caller said he'd text me the first direction right away."

Her phone beeped. She almost dropped it. "That must be him now."

"Call in Jonas fast." Hazel squeezed her shoulder. "Good luck."

Delta sighed and called while she walked to her car. Jonas said, "I can't find information that quickly, Delta," The half smile in his voice warmed her insides.

"It's not about Gran. I had a call from an unknown man, he wants to meet me with information that can clear Tilly. He's texting me directions to a meeting point."

"And you're going there? Not even knowing who he is or what he wants? Are you crazy? How can you agree with something like that?"

"We can discuss that later. Are you coming?"

"You bet I am. Where to?"

———————————

Delta followed the caller's instructions. She switched her phone so incoming messages were read aloud, and, with Jonas listening on speaker, they were both headed out of Tundish. "Did you hear that?" she asked after another curt direction.

"Yes, and I'm close to you. You should see me after ten, five... Now."

Delta saw the Jeep appear from a side road to her left and turn onto the road she was driving on. It came to follow right behind her vehicle. A sense of intense relief rushed through her, leaving her knees jittery. Jonas was there; it would be all right now. Whatever the unknown man wanted, they'd face it together.

"I'm still not a fan of this," Jonas said.

"I know. But I can't let this chance pass. Tilly needs the break. West is focusing solely on her."

"I doubt he is. He did ask questions at the motel and is trying to find people who were in contact with the victim. He's also checking whether any victims of the pyramid scheme lived in this area, to find out if the murder was a revenge killing for damages done through that con. Weatherspoon was released, and he came *here* right away. To ask his ex for some petty cash? Not likely."

Delta sucked in air. "If we can prove he was in touch with someone local before he died...maybe via his phone records?"

"No doubt West is on that. But it takes time. He doesn't get calls offering him information on a silver platter."

"Don't be so cynical."

"Think about it. Why would this guy offer it to *you*? Who is he? What can he know?"

"Maybe it's the son of the woman Grace, the waitress at Mine Forever, knew. Remember? The one who worked at the motel the night of the murder? He saw the victim arguing with another man. Grace said that a young man like him might not want to turn to the police. If he can tell us what he knows, at least we can determine if it's important or not."

"But we'd still need an official statement to get anywhere in the investigation."

"We can see about that later." Another direction came in, making them turn left and follow the dirt road.

"This guy knows these surroundings pretty well," Jonas observed. He didn't sound happy with that.

"Logically," Delta tried to reason, "if he's a local kid." The idea that they were meeting a teenager who didn't want to go to the police with what he knew was a lot more reassuring than the possibility it was the murderer. They had wondered before if Bob Weatherspoon had met anyone at the hotel. Another lone traveler. Another criminal?

Finally the caller demanded her to turn into a half-gravel parking lot in the forest where several walking routes began. A large sign gave a map of the area and the routes while a picnic bench offered a place to eat a bite. A mountain bike stood leaning against it. There was no one in sight.

Delta got out and stretched her tight shoulder muscles, taking in the surroundings quickly. It was a beautiful place if you came here for some downtime, but, when meeting with someone about a murder case, the remote location and the sound of the last leaves rustling on the trees carried a sinister edge.

Jonas came over and stood beside her. "I don't think he's here. He's probably observing from another spot."

Delta's phone rang. It was still in the car, and she rushed to get it. The caller said, "You are not alone." It sounded on edge, but not vicious.

She swallowed before answering, "I was worried about the remote location."

"You didn't know it would be a remote location."

"I could guess. Else you'd come to the store to talk to me."

"Who is the guy?"

Her mind racing, Delta took a deep breath. She could tell him Jonas was a wildlife guide, but the association with official rangers might spook him. She said, "He's my boyfriend." She didn't dare look in Jonas's direction to see if he was close enough to overhear and, if he was, what his reaction was.

"I see. Did you tell him secrecy is key?"

"Of course, and he agrees. He just wants to make sure I'm safe."

"All right. Walk down the path marked with the red picket fence poles. I'll text the rest."

Chapter Fourteen

DELTA LOWERED THE PHONE AND TRIED TO LOOK INNOCENT as she turned to Jonas. "The path with the red poles."

Jonas said, "He must be able to see us." He turned his head slowly, scanning the area. "It's higher there."

"Don't point or nod." Delta tried to maintain a neutral expression as she started to walk. "He wasn't happy I'm not alone." She refused to look at him as she added, "I had to call you my boyfriend to explain. It was the first logical thing to come to mind. I don't want to spook him."

"All in the interest of the case?" There was tension in his voice she couldn't quite place. Was it about the situation they were in or her impromptu lie?

"It's more than the case. I mean, you are a very good friend, and I totally rely on you in this situation so..." *This isn't exactly making it better.* But what could she say? That she wanted him to be her boyfriend? If he didn't share her feelings, she'd ruin their friendship and she couldn't bear to think of that.

Jonas's voice broke through her contemplation. "There's a wildlife observation point up ahead," he said. "Maybe he's there?"

Delta's legs felt rubbery, and her hands were trembling. She held them beside her, turned to fists to hide the shaking. She had been to an observation point before with Jonas, but that had been a real hut. This one was just a simple woven screen to hide the human presence. In the dense natural material were holes to see through. Scanning the construction, Delta suddenly saw a pair of eyes watching them through the hole. She sucked in air.

"He's on the other side," Jonas said softly. "That is forbidden."

"I don't think he'll care." Delta couldn't stop her voice from shivering. "He could be a killer."

They came closer. Delta focused on those brown eyes peering at them. They were friendly enough. Not the eyes of a madman. But, then, the other killers she had been confronted with had seemed like normal people at some point too.

Jonas said, "That's close enough." He put his hand lightly on her arm to stop her. Delta felt his touch like a wave of warmth traveling through her arm straight into her chest where it was icy cold. She drew a shaky breath. "Who are you?"

The man behind the screen seemed to step back. "That's not relevant."

"We're not here to cause trouble for you," Jonas said in a level voice. "We only want to know what you know to help a friend."

"Is Tilly Tay your friend?" It sounded incredulous.

Delta rushed to say, "I invited her to my shop to show off her miniature display. So she's my responsibility, at least. Besides, she's merely an artist with a van and a cute dog. She doesn't hurt a fly. I'm sorry she got into such trouble because of her problematic ex-husband."

"Ex? Since when did they get divorced?" the man asked sharply.

"You know something about them?" Jonas shot back.

"I should know everything about them." It sounded wry.

"So you weren't just another guest staying at the motel?" Delta tried.

The man was silent for a moment.

"Please don't walk away," Delta said. "We really need your help. Tilly didn't kill that man, I'm sure. Why would she?"

"He was harassing her." The man sounded both certain and sad.

Delta's breath caught. "You know about that?" If West found other witnesses to testify that Tilly had been pursued by the victim, it would strengthen her motive for murder.

"Yes." There was a brief silence, and then he added, "He told me."

"I see." Delta glanced at Jonas, at a loss with how to proceed. She wanted to know much more but asking the wrong questions, asserting too much pressure, could ruin everything. The guy could run off, and they'd be left with nothing.

"What do you want to tell us?" Jonas asked.

Delta felt a surge of relief that he took this approach. It gave the man space to share what he wanted and nothing more, removing the pressure.

The man said, "I'm sorry for what happened. I mean, not only the murder, but him harassing her. It was a bad idea. I told him so, but he wouldn't listen. He never listened to anything I said."

Jonas stiffened, and Delta bet he was thinking the same

thing she was. This man could have been an accomplice. Someone working with the victim against Tilly. Was he the one who left the clue in the miniature display?

"I told him on the day he died that he would only get into trouble if he pushed on with it. That he might end up behind bars again. But he didn't care. He was determined to do it. He said she owed him. That she had been free all those years to travel and make money while he had been locked up."

"He blamed her for his imprisonment?" Jonas asked softly.

"He blamed her for not standing up for him." The man sighed. "Tilly was happy when it all ended. The lies, the cheating, the hurting other people. When he went to jail, she was free of him."

"Until he got out again," Delta said.

"I told him not to go after her. But he insisted."

"And you went with him?"

"We met here. But I never participated in his games. I didn't see her." It sounded tense. "I can't see her now. It would be too painful for both of us."

"So she knows you?" Jonas asked.

"No!" It sounded shocked. "And that has to stay that way."

Delta could hear the man's rapid breathing. "If you push me," he warned. "I will walk away and not say anymore."

"We're not pushing you," Jonas assured him. "We just don't understand the situation. Please have a little patience with us."

Delta didn't know if it was hard for him to take this accommodating approach, but, whatever Jonas did feel, his soothing tone was very convincing.

The man said, "I don't blame you for not understanding. It's all very weird and complicated. But I don't want her to suffer for what he did. It was all his fault. He had done his time, and he should have started over, but he couldn't. He blamed people and wanted to get even."

"He wanted to hurt Tilly?" Jonas asked.

"No, not physically. He wanted her help to get money."

"But she didn't have any and told him so," Delta suggested.

"It wasn't her money he was after." The man sighed. "He went to her van that night."

"The night he died?" Jonas asked with tension in his voice.

"Yes."

Jonas shot Delta a look. Tilly had assured her lawyer she had not met the victim again after the altercation on Mattock Street when she had been moving her van. Had she lied? Why? If she was innocent...

Delta's thoughts raced. Was she really innocent? Or were they mistaken about her? Was it possible they were coming to the defense of the murderer?

Jonas said, "Are you sure they met that night?"

"I said he wanted to go to the van. He might have. While Tilly was at the store working on her models. If she returned early, they might have met."

Delta clenched her fists. Tilly had lied about being at the store until midnight, that much Delta knew. "You know she was at my store?"

There was just silence. Jonas said, "Did he come back alive and well after seeing her?"

Delta held her breath waiting for the reply. If this man could testify that Bob Weatherspoon had returned from a nighttime meeting with Tilly unharmed, it could help her in a major way.

"I don't *know* if he saw her again. He had been to the van. I do know that. He was looking for money or checks or anything he could get." The voice sounded almost hurt.

Delta said, "So he ransacked the van... No, that doesn't make sense. After Tilly left the store, she went back to her van to sleep. If she had found it ransacked, she would have called the police or something."

"I wouldn't be too sure of that. She wanted to keep his presence in town a secret. Because of their past."

"You mean, her having been married to him," Jonas amplified.

"Yes," the man said, "and his scheming and all. It has always been whispered she had a part in it."

Jonas said, "Is it possible that she had? That she kept loot? That he's after something he thinks she has? A precious stone, maybe? Gold jewelry?"

"The money from the pyramid scheme..." Delta whispered, remembering, with a chill, Jonas's words on the way over here. If Weatherspoon had hidden millions before he went to prison, he need not have come to his ex to ask her for a pittance. Unless *she* knew exactly where the missing money was. Had she helped him hide it?

"I don't know," the man said. "I don't know what he did with the money he conned people out of. The trial said there had to be millions. I don't know where it is."

"But you wanted to know. That is why you contacted him when he came out of jail," Jonas said in a calm, conversational tone. "He agreed to meet you here in Tundish to talk it over. He told you Tilly had it all. That he would get it back and then share with you."

Delta held her breath again, desperately wishing the man would deny that Weatherspoon had claimed Tilly had the money or knew the way to access it.

"He wasn't the sharing kind." The man sounded bitter. "Especially after he found out what I intended to do with it."

"Which is?" Delta asked.

A branch broke farther down the path. The man startled. "What is that?"

"Probably just a deer," Jonas said quickly. "This area is full of them."

"No. No." His voice took on an angry note. "You called the police anyway. They're here, closing in. I have to run." And, in an instant, he was gone. They heard his footfalls race away.

Jonas rushed around the screen, but it took him too long to get around it, and the man was already out of sight. Jonas came back to Delta with a sigh. "There's no point in pursuing him. I can't arrest him without causing trouble for myself and for West. He'd be livid if his investigation was ruined because I interfered. We have to let him go."

Delta exhaled. "What bad timing with that branch. I had a feeling he was just about to tell us something really important. What did he plan to do with the money from the pyramid scheme?"

"We'll never know." Jonas spread his hands in a gesture of surrender. "But what he did tell us is very interesting. Was Tilly Tay a part of her husband's scheme? Did she keep money or goods for him while he was in prison? Did he come here to get them back? That would make a good reason to argue."

"And a powerful motive for murder," Delta added. She cast Jonas a worried look. "I don't like at all where this is heading. I thought we were trying to gather evidence to *clear* her."

"We're looking into her case. In principle to clear her, yes, but that doesn't mean we shouldn't look at all angles. We can't be one hundred percent sure she's innocent. We hardly know her."

Delta's mouth went dry at the idea that Tilly might be guilty. That she had invited a killer to town and that the woman had worked in their shop shortly before stabbing someone at the nearby motel. The shopkeepers would have every reason to be angry at her and want to take her title back. If they publicly turned against her, customers might follow suit and shun the store. They could go bankrupt.

Also, she'd be letting Gran down, right when she moved to town. Gran had given Delta the money to buy into Wanted. If it failed, it would be a major blow to them both.

Jonas's hand came under her chin, and he gently lifted her face to him. "Not so glum. Tilly may still be innocent. It's not over yet."

Delta stared into his blue eyes and wished that he would hold her for a few minutes to absorb his confidence.

Her phone beeped. Jonas pulled away his hand. "Who can that be?"

Delta looked at the screen. "Hazel. She wants to know if everything is all right. I guess she's nervous." She quickly typed a reply.

Jonas said, "Yes, well, we'd better get back to the cars. I have a lot to do today."

"Where's Spud, anyway?" Delta asked to defuse tension by raising an innocent topic.

"With Paula."

Or maybe not so innocent. She could feel her muscles tense.

Jonas smiled. "Spud loves spending time with her dogs."

"And with her?" Delta couldn't resist asking. "She is good with animals, right? He must sense that."

"Yeah, he thinks she's pretty great."

"Did you once work together or...I mean, how coincidental she also ended up around here."

"It's just a good place to be." It was a rather vague answer. What connected Paula and Jonas? Had they been involved before, maybe? Paula being Jonas's ex, now coming back into his life?

Jonas stretched his arms up to the sky that was a little clearer for a change. "I'll try and find out where that gold rush talk by Major Buckmore is and let you know. We can go there together to hear him speak and see what he's up to."

"Go there together?" Delta echoed.

"Yes, unless you'd rather have me go alone. Maybe you have something else to do?"

"Of course not, it's my gran we're trying to protect. You let me know when, and I will be ready."

"Okay. If it's farther away, you know, because she said that they'd be taking a few days, it might be helpful if you could uh...bring along some clothes and stuff. If we can't drive back that same evening, we could stay."

"Oh, yes, of course." Delta's heart fluttered.

They reached the cars, and Jonas waved goodbye, climbed in, and started the engine. He waited until she was inside and had her engine running before driving off. His concern for her safety made her feel warm inside, but mostly confusion reigned. Was he in love with her? If they had some time to spend together, could she find out? Jonas did mean enough to her to take some risk, right?

Delta nodded to herself firmly as she drove away from the parking lot. She'd do something about the uncertain situation with Jonas, one way or the other. For now she should focus on the odd meeting in the forest and try to figure out what it might mean for Tilly's case.

At the store she found Hazel talking to an unknown man. He wore an expensive dark-blue woolen overcoat and carried a newspaper under his arm. As Delta entered, he turned to her and Hazel introduced them. "This is Mr. VanderHurst, the husband of Tilly Tay's sister Tabitha. Mr. VanderHurst, my business partner and co-owner of Wanted, Delta Douglas."

"Pleasure to meet you." VanderHurst reached out and shook Delta's hand. "I wish it was under different circumstances, though," he said in a deep baritone. "You've become embroiled in a murder case, I understand, because of Tilly." He made a tsking sound and showed her the newspaper he carried, unfurling a bold headline. *Local store involved in pyramid scheme cover-up?* and below that, in smaller print, *Did shopkeeper of the season shield a thief and killer?*

Delta's eyes widened as she read the first few lines about a group of pyramid scheme victims having shown up at the Tundish police station clamoring for their money now that Weatherspoon was murdered, potentially by the person who had hidden his profits during his imprisonment.

"They can't seriously think that Tilly hid the profits?" She said it without conviction. The man in the forest had claimed Weatherspoon had been harassing Tilly, and why else would he come to Tundish to see her, unless she could provide him with something he needed? More than just a bit of cash to live off of. His score, the loot. It all made sense in a terrible way. And, with the *Tundish Trader* writing about it, treating it as fact sooner than mere speculation, she began to feel like Wanted's fate was sealed.

VanderHurst said, "I'm very sorry you got into trouble because of Tilly. Her relationship with Weatherspoon should have been ended ages ago, but she's just too wishy-washy to cut him out of her life completely. Too kindhearted also, I guess. She never understood how the victims of his pyramid scheme suffered. People lost their savings, pensions, money needed to pay the mortgage. Consequently, some lost their homes, or their marriage ended in divorce because of arguments over the missing money."

VanderHurst gestured with his hand. His wedding ring caught the light. He continued, "Weatherspoon caused terrible heartache for too many people. But Tilly lives in a world of her own, with her miniatures..." He cast a quick look at the display, a mixture of disbelief and resignation in his features. "Her van and her dog. However, you need not worry about it anymore. I told the lawyer, Miss Brenning, that we will pay for Tilly's defense from here on. You need not invest another dime in it or have your name associated with it. Miss Brenning will tell me everything the police have discovered so far, and I'm sure that we can find some way to unravel their tenuous evidence and clear Tilly. Leave that to us."

Delta blinked. This was going a bit fast. "Umm, we didn't hire the lawyer," she faltered. "Mrs. Cassidy did. You might want to talk to her."

"I think you can persuade her that our plan makes sense." VanderHurst smiled at her. "Your reputation is on the line. Public opinion is turning against you"—he held up the paper—"mentioning your business in the same breath as the pyramid scheme that ruined innocent people's lives. You should distance yourself from the case immediately."

Hazel said, "If you put it like that..." She glanced at Delta nervously.

"Don't worry." VanderHurst leaned over to her. "Tilly will be well taken care of. You're not abandoning her." He looked at the display again, assessing it with a speculative gaze. "I can imagine you'd want to end the exhibition prematurely. It hasn't exactly become the tourist magnet you hoped it would. Understandable after the commotion surrounding Weatherspoon's untimely demise. I can arrange for it to be removed, if you want."

"Removed?" Hazel looked at Delta again. "We haven't really considered that."

"We entered into an agreement with Tilly," Delta said. VanderHurst acted like the typical self-assured businessman, taking charge and telling others what to do. But the decision wasn't his to make. "These are her things."

"She's in no position to make such decisions right now. She will understand that others have to step in. Let me know." He extracted a business card from his inner pocket and put it on the counter. He laid the newspaper with the incriminating headline beside it and patted it with his hand. "This sort of thing is hugely harmful. Especially if you live in a small town. Let Miss Brenning know that you want me to take care of things from here. That's better for all parties involved."

When he noticed he didn't get an enthusiastic response,

he added with a forced smile, "My wife and I really have everyone's best interests at heart. You don't want to lose your business. Good day." He nodded and left, pulling the door shut softly behind him.

"A gentleman in every way," Delta observed, grimacing. "But a little too pushy for my liking. No wonder Tilly didn't want him and Tabitha involved. I wonder if Tabitha asked him to do this. She told me at the police station she wants Tilly to give up her wandering lifestyle."

Hazel didn't seem to be listening. She stared at the newspaper and swallowed hard before saying, "I had no idea that this pyramid scheme touched people so deeply. I guess it makes sense when you think about it. Wrong decisions about money impact people for years to come. Divorces, even, because of it... It explains all the anger against Weatherspoon and now Tilly. The victims must assume she killed him to keep the proceeds for herself. They think she has what they are entitled to."

Put like that, Delta also sensed the potential for escalation here. "But we don't know whether Tilly killed Weatherspoon," she pointed out, "and if she ever had access to the proceeds." She ran a finger across the newspaper and the shiny business card beside it. "Having met this man in the forest, I feel like chances are that Tilly did know something about her husband's schemes or else it would have made no sense for Weatherspoon to come to Tundish to see her." She updated Hazel on what she had learned.

"I don't like it at all." Hazel raked back her hair. "This can only become messier for Tilly, and, by association, for us. Why don't we tell Mrs. Cassidy to accept Mr. VanderHurst's offer and let him deal with everything from here? Then we won't be involved with any more unsavory details that may come to light."

"I don't know…"

"We have no idea what Tilly knew about the pyramid scheme. We only invited her to display her miniatures at our shop. She's not a close friend, like Jane or Bessie, and we need not go out of our way to protect her." Hazel waved a hand. "Besides, she will still have a proper defense. To be honest, the VanderHursts probably have a lot more money to pump into this case than Mrs. Cassidy. That's actually good for Tilly, right?"

"True, but why would VanderHurst be so eager to get involved?"

"So he can control things?" Hazel tilted her head. "He looks like a man who's used to getting things his way. He probably thinks he can steer what gets out, handle the media coverage in a way that least damages Tilly and, consequently, her sister. The VanderHursts are merely protective of their good name. People with money like them always hire someone to clean up any mess they encounter. And VanderHurst wants to have Marjorie Brenning do it for him."

Delta admitted that rich people did tend to solve their problems by throwing money at them and hoping it would go away, but something niggled in the back of her mind. "He mentioned that the police will have to share the evidence in the case with him once he pays the lawyer. Does he want that information for a selfish reason? I saw Tabitha in the videos Jane's husband took on the day of the opening. She looked into the shop and left. There was someone with her. I couldn't see who it was, but it could have been her husband. What if they were making sure Tilly was inside, busy, so they could look at her van?"

"What would the rich VanderHursts want with Tilly's old van? They seem like they probably mean well and have Tilly's best interests at heart." Hazel pointed at the paper with a fearful expression as if it were a scorpion ready to sting her. "I don't want angry victims descending on the shop."

"You're right." Delta sighed. "I'll ask Mrs. Cassidy what she thinks. She pays for the lawyer, after all."

Hazel's advice was sound, of course, but something inside of Delta resisted merely handing everything over to the VanderHursts, who had obviously been waiting for Tilly to mess up her life so they could step in and save the day. She had to find out via Jonas if the victims of the pyramid scheme who had appeared at the police station had already been in town *before* Weatherspoon had died.

After all, what better motive for murder than revenge on the person who had ruined their lives?

Chapter Fifteen

MRS. CASSIDY WAS VERY SURPRISED TO HEAR OF THE VanderHursts' offer. "I haven't met them personally," she said, "But, the way you tell it, it feels like both of them are a little smug about how much better their lives have turned out compared to Tilly's."

"Yes, but, even if they are social snobs, they could be genuinely concerned for her, and they can certainly afford the best possible defense." Delta felt obliged to voice Hazel's views as well and make Mrs. Cassidy see all sides. "Stepping back makes sense as emotions are running high, and we all have our position in Tundish to think of. What if Tilly turns out to be guilty? Not of murder, maybe, but of involvement in this pyramid scheme and hiding the proceedings from the authorities? With a committee of victims in town, the missing money will certainly be news for days to come. We'd hate for you and the Paper Posse to be named in the same breath with something like that, because you arranged for the lawyer to defend Tilly, and the Paper Posse ladies supported Wanted, through it all. You all have businesses to think of: Jane's family's bakery, Bessie's boutique." Her gut clenched considering the situation. Would they all suffer from her mistake if Tilly Tay turned out to be someone completely different from what she had believed? It would be safer to transfer the burden to the VanderHursts.

Mrs. Cassidy sighed. "I do understand your reasoning. The sheriff told Marjorie that there is DNA found under the nails of the victim, which could stem from the killer. Assuming Weatherspoon saw the knife attack coming and defended himself against it."

"But he was stabbed in the back," Delta protested.

"I know." There was a rustle as if Mrs. Cassidy was transferring the phone to her other ear. "Anyway, the DNA is being compared with Tilly's. If it's hers, the sheriff feels he has enough to charge her."

This news hit Delta like a bucket of ice-cold water down her back. She said, with difficulty, "When Tilly arrived at Wanted the morning of the opening, she had a nasty scratch on her hand. I even offered to bandage it for her. Tilly claimed it came from a nail. But what if she lied? What if it happened in an altercation with Weatherspoon? If West gets his DNA match, Tilly will certainly be in hot water."

Mrs. Cassidy whistled softly. "I didn't know about the scratch. I have to discuss with Marjorie and see what she thinks. Whether it's best if I let the VanderHursts take over or not."

"Keep me posted. Thanks for everything you're doing."

"That's what friends are for."

Around three, Jonas dropped by the store with Spud in tow. "Hello, boy," Delta said, leaning down to rub his head, "How are you?"

Spud barked and tilted his head as if asking her the same question. As animals were highly sensitive to emotion, Delta wondered if he caught on to her insecurity as soon as Jonas was around.

He extracted his phone and showed her something on the screen. A wooden building in nineteenth-century style. "The Seasoned Saloon in Timbercreek. That's where our friend the major is holding his lecture on gold rush gangs tonight. I called the saloon, and there are still seats available, so I got us two tickets to the event." Jonas looked around him as if scanning for people who might potentially overhear and added, "Did you read in the paper that some of the pyramid scheme victims stopped by the station this morning to demand access to Tilly?"

"Yes. I wondered if they arrived on the scene after the murder hit the news or were already here earlier, on the trail of Bob Weatherspoon."

"Good thinking. I had the same questions, so I called Sven LeDuc at the paper and learned they weren't merely random victims but part of a group that has been hunting the missing money for years. I looked up the contact information for this group online and sent an email asking for a meeting with the members who are here in the area, ahead of the lecture in Timbercreek tonight. I told them I'm an ex-cop interested in their case. Not a lie in that, and it did the trick. They responded within half an hour, setting a meeting for six-thirty. The lecture starts at seven-thirty, so we should have plenty of time. We could get a bite on the way over."

"What a great idea." While bubbling with excitement, Delta's mind started sorting through her packing list and how she could arrange for travel on short notice. It was great that Jonas had arranged for a meeting with these victims of the pyramid scheme so the trip was actually part of the investigation. She would otherwise have felt rather guilty for leaving town for a day or two just as things were so tense with the murder case and the shopkeepers eyeing them.

"I'll pick you up around five," Jonas said. "At the cottage?"

"Fine." Delta waved him off.

"Did I hear the doorbell?" Hazel came from one of the cells where she had been changing the washi tape display. It had been a very quiet day, and Delta wasn't sure if it was just a lack of tourists during the slow season or a conscious choice of people to avoid the shop because of the way it had hit the news. "Thief" and "killer" were ugly words splashed across the front page of the *Tundish Trader*. The idea that they were being ostracized made her heart sink.

Hazel looked around, saw no one was there inside the shop, and said with a sigh, "I can't believe it's only three. I was sure it was almost closing time already." She went to the door and peeked into the street. "I do see a few people going into Mine Forever."

"Might not be paper-crafting fans." Delta twisted her bracelet. "Listen, Hazel. Jonas was here just now. He found out where Gran is going tonight to hear Buckmore speak. He wants to drive over and attend to see what the major is up to. He also arranged for a meeting with some people who might be able to shed light on the pyramid scheme and Tilly's alleged part in it. So I will be throwing a few clothes in an overnight bag and going with Jonas. I won't be away long. Just until tomorrow."

Hazel turned to her. Her expression was puzzled for a moment. Delta watched it carefully waiting to see any irritation or worry. It would hurt if her friend thought she was letting her down.

But Hazel's mouth tilted up in a grin. "Finally. He's taking you out, in a big way. I'd wondered when he'd do that."

A rush of hot blood came up to Delta's face. "He's helping me keep an eye on Gran and investigate the murder case. Nothing more to it."

"Sure." Hazel winked. "I totally get it. Have fun." She checked her watch again. "Shouldn't you be rushing? Maybe you have to get your hair done or something?"

"Why?"

"To show him you cared enough to look especially pretty."

"It's more business than personal," Delta emphasized.

"Whatever." Hazel waved a hand. "But you're going to Bessie's Boutique right now to buy a nice dress for tonight. Off you go." She grabbed her by the shoulders and tried to shove her to the door. Delta broke into laughter. "Let me at least get my purse or I can't even pay for the dress."

Moments later she was walking down the street ducking into her collar against the chilly wind that breathed past the store fronts. At Bessie's she took a moment to study the mannequins in the window and then walked into the welcome warmth inside. Bessie was just saying goodbye to a customer carrying two full bags. She smiled when she saw Delta. "Hello there. If you're after scarves, I'm pretty much sold out. That customer bought twenty of them to hand out to friends as goodbye gifts. She's leaving the area to go work in Boston. Told me all about her new apartment and job. Sounds like a lot of fun if you want city life." Bessie shivered. "It's not my thing. What can I do for you?"

"I'm going to a lecture on gold rush history. Gran is a history fan and... I want to look good." No lies there, and she could avoid mentioning Jonas's part in it to avoid speculation among the Paper Posse.

"Dress? Skirt and blouse? Cardigan? I got it all." Bessie quickly collected a few items. "I think dark blue would suit you."

"I was thinking of something bolder, maybe," Delta said. "Red? Orange?"

"Sure." Bessie got even more items off the rack. "You go to the changing room, and I'll grab a few options."

An hour later Delta had purchased two new pairs of pants, a cardigan, two blouses, the last scarf left, and what she had actually come for: a knee-length dress with long sleeves and a waterfall neck. She had the perfect boots to go with it at home. Bessie cheerfully rang up the total and remarked she hadn't had such a good afternoon in weeks. "Oh, by the way," she said packing the clothes into a large canvas bag with her shop's logo emblazoned on it, "when I was at the Lodge to deliver the dresses Mrs. Tay VanderHurst ordered earlier, she was talking to a representative of a big museum in Helena about putting up a permanent exhibition of Tilly Tay's work there."

"Really?" Delta's mind tried to make sense of this news. "But the VanderHursts have no control over Tilly's creative work, do they?"

"She certainly acted like she was in a position to decide things." Bessie handed over the bag. "Anyway, forget about the case for tonight and have fun."

"I will." Delta took her purchases home in a rush and

changed, combing her hair until it was totally smooth and shiny, and slipping in some long earrings. Despite Bessie's warning to forget about the case, her mind was processing what she had learned. Tabitha Tay VanderHurst seemed like the sort of person who enjoyed being in the public eye. Was she eager to become keeper of her sister's creative legacy? Would there even be money in it for her?

Not that she needed any, probably. She had a superrich husband.

Delta almost forgot she had to pack and, as it was close to five already, threw everything she saw into her overnight bag.

She had meant to get ready at leisure and even write a note for Hazel thanking her for taking care of things while she was away, but she had no time for that. Jonas already drove up to the cottage, and she picked a banana out of the fruit bowl and rushed to open the front door for him.

Jonas stared at her. His eyes drifted down from her face across the dress and boots, back up. His mouth curved in a slow smile. "Wow."

"I want to show Gran how important her new beau's lecture is to me," Delta said quickly.

"Of course. Can I carry your bag?" Jonas took it from her hand. As his fingers touched hers, she held her breath a moment. Despite what she was trying to tell herself about this trip, it did feel like a date. An extended date, a very special occasion. Time to be together. Just them.

Jonas put the bag in the back of the Jeep beside Spud's bench. "I hope you don't mind I brought him along? I didn't want to impose on Paula."

Or had he not wanted to tell Paula he was going away with Delta?

If they were exes, it could be painful. She really had to try and find out more about that.

"When I was on the phone with the Saloon," Jonas said, "I asked whether we could bring Spud to the lecture, and that was okay. I heard more people will be bringing their dogs. Timbercreek is almost more rural than Tundish, so people don't stand on formality."

Uh-oh. Delta glanced down her clothes. "Am I overdressed?"

"I don't know." Jonas leaned over, his eyes sparkling. "But I'm not letting you change out of that for anything in the world."

Delta's heart grew lighter, and suddenly she made an impulsive promise to herself: *during this trip I'm going to tell Jonas how I feel.*

They decided to park beside a takeout restaurant, and Jonas ran in for some food while Delta waited with Spud. It was just like a picnic inside the car. They talked about picnics and the Fourth of July when they were kids, and Delta couldn't remember why she had been worried about tonight. Jonas was just so easy to talk to, and she felt completely comfortable in his company.

Completely? Hmmm. The promise she had made to herself really put on the pressure. How was she going to do it? When?

"Oh, I've got an update for your case file," Jonas said.

"Wait a sec. I'll get it." Delta pulled out her sketchbook and opened it to the right page. "Spill."

"I took a closer look at the VanderHursts, and it seems that they are in therapy because their marriage is on the edge of total breakdown. Mr. VanderHurst already hired a lawyer to start divorce proceedings, but apparently they wanted to try this relationship therapy before making a final decision."

"Interesting." Delta drew a broken heart between the spouses and added "divorce imminent." "Maybe the therapy was her idea? If they do split up, will she get any money?"

"That's the interesting bit. When they married, she signed a prenup. She will be left with virtually nothing."

"So it's in her interest to keep the marriage alive?" Delta bit her lip as she added below "divorce imminent" "leaving Tabitha with nothing." "Or make sure she has another source of income in case it does fall through? That could explain her sudden need to interfere with Tilly's life and get her a permanent exhibition in Helena." She told Jonas what Bessie had shared in the boutique. "If Tabitha thinks she can make money off her sister's miniatures..."

"I assume that if someone really tried to monetize it, there would be a good income in it," Jonas mused. "Tilly didn't strike me as very commercial. Maybe her sister believed she could do better?"

Delta frowned. "Did Weatherspoon know Tilly was under pressure from her sister to change her ways or hand over her legacy? Did he want to offer her an alternative?"

"Financed by his illegal gains?" Jonas suggested.

"It would pit Weatherspoon against the sister. Maybe when he got nowhere with Tilly, he approached her sister?"

"We believe he got nowhere with Tilly because the guy in the forest told us. But what if he lied?"

She stared pensively at the black silhouette she had drawn

with the note "knew Weatherspoon and Tilly, after missing money, what for? Accomplice?" Had the guy been involved in the pyramid scheme at the time or learned about it later? In prison, maybe? Had they been cellmates, and had the mystery man connected with Weatherspoon after his release to get the money? "What if Weatherspoon did have access to the old loot and that guy stabbed him to steal everything from him?"

"If he killed Weatherspoon and has access to what he wanted, why stick around Tundish?" Jonas shook his head. "That doesn't fit."

"And he told me on the phone that he wanted to help clear Tilly. Why would he want that if he's the killer? Then he would be happy with another suspect." Delta sighed. "Nothing makes sense. We can only hope those victims of the pyramid scheme can reveal something relevant."

———————————

The Seasoned Saloon sat on the edge of Timbercreek. The parking lot was full of SUVs and Jeeps with even the occasional truck. Jonas found a space and let out Spud while Delta smoothed her dress after the long time sitting and swept back her hair. "I agreed to meet the victims in the dining area," Jonas said. "That's to the right while the room for the lecture is to the left."

They walked through the sliding doors and turned right into a spacious area with lots of booths. Only a few were taken by diners sitting over large steaks and beers.

Jonas gestured to the last booth in the corner. "They said they'd prefer to have some privacy."

They walked over. A tall man unfolded from the booth and extended his hand. "Adam Baker. This is Cheryl Remington. We represent the Justice group."

A woman of about sixty with artificially platinum blond hair reached out a languid hand. "Hello. Our full name is Justice for Victims of Pyramid Schemes. We got together after we fell for Weatherspoon's lies. Unfortunately, he's not the only one running such cons, and, over the years, victims from other schemes joined us. We fight for the return of missing money."

Adam Baker gestured for them to sit opposite Cheryl and said, slipping back in place beside Cheryl, "Unfortunately, not a lot of money is recovered usually. Those criminals are clever hiding it away abroad in numbered accounts. They serve a few years, get out, and live in luxury off their illegally obtained riches."

"While we can barely pay our bills." Red patches blotted Cheryl's cheeks. "It's so unfair. When we heard Weatherspoon was being released, we decided to make sure he wouldn't enjoy his profits."

"That sounds quite ominous considering he is dead," Jonas observed.

Cheryl laughed uncomfortably. "A former cop, hey." She glanced at Adam, who seemed to signal her with his eyes not to push it. But she said anyway, "I should have known. You always want to do it by the book, stick to the legal channels. But sometimes that just doesn't work."

Jonas looked her in the eye. "Did you manage to talk to Weatherspoon before he died?"

"No." Adam Baker said it quickly. "He traveled under an alias. We weren't able to find him. We read in the local paper that he had died."

"But his ex knows more than she lets on," Cheryl said, her cheeks turning even redder. "He came to her to get the access to his numbered account abroad. Now he's dead, and she has the money. It never ends." She swallowed down the contents of her glass. Judging by the scent wafting toward Delta, it held hard liquor.

"Did you have a look inside her van?" Jonas asked quietly. "For information about the money?"

Cheryl glanced at Adam. "We're not under investigation.

I thought you wanted to help us. You wrote you were interested in our case."

Before Jonas could say something, she added, "But I see whose side you're on. You want to protect that woman. Tilly Tay, the famous artist." Her voice dripped with venom. "You think someone special like her can't be involved in crime. You're blinded to what these people really are. They seem kind and reliable. That's why their victims trust them in the first place."

She put her glass down with a bang and rose. Leaning on the table, she hissed to Jonas, "If the police had done their job at the time, we wouldn't be penniless now." She stood up straight and stalked away. After a few paces she swayed and almost collided with an incoming guest. He caught her arm and asked if she was all right. She shook him off and left the building.

"The fresh air outside might sober her up," Jonas said. "But I hope she doesn't intend to drive?"

Adam Baker reached in his pocket and pulled out a car key. "She won't violate any laws, Officer." It sounded cynical. He leaned back and gave Jonas a provocative stare. "She's right, you know. If the police had tried harder, they could have recovered the money. But they didn't. And we suffer from it. Every single day."

"I feel sorry for you," Delta said. "I honestly do. And there is a chance now to find the money. Whoever killed Weatherspoon must be after the money. If we catch the killer..." She let the silence linger for a few moments before adding, "You might be able to help us. You were in Tundish before Weatherspoon died."

It was a bluff, as Baker had just denied having known where Weatherspoon was and having learned of his death from the local paper. But she wasn't sure he was telling them the truth.

Adam Baker looked away. His mouth twitched nervously.

Jonas said, "Or do you think your high-strung fellow victim killed Weatherspoon?"

"I told you he used an alias, and we couldn't find him." His high-pitched voice carried no conviction. Without his fellow victim by his side, he seemed to unravel.

Jonas leaned closer to him. "Lying to the police is a serious thing."

"You're not with the police anymore. Or did you lie about that?"

"No, but I can ask Sheriff West to interrogate you."

"I had nothing to do with it. Cheryl arranged for the PI who tracked Weatherspoon. I had no idea she wanted to come here because she had actually found him. She drank too much that night, as usual, and she went to bed early. I tell you she can't have killed him. How would she have gotten to his motel? She doesn't drive."

"She could have taken a taxi, a bus. She could have walked if she was determined enough." Jonas's voice was insistent. "Maybe she even faked being drunk to get rid of you."

Adam Baker shook his head. "Cheryl is bitter, but she's no killer."

Jonas glanced at Delta. She bet he was thinking the same thing as she was. Baker was defending the woman, but, deep inside of him, he wasn't sure what to believe. *Or does he act like this to divert suspicion from himself?*

Adam Baker rose. "I have to go and make sure Cheryl is all right. You can't help me. You only want to blame us for a death we had nothing to do with." He added, staring at Delta intently, "Do you think we enjoy knowing he's dead? This means we will probably never see our money again. Everything we hoped for, five long years while he was inside, is gone up in smoke." He huffed as if he couldn't believe it still, and walked away.

Delta asked Jonas hurriedly, "Shouldn't we go after him? Try and talk to that woman? She seemed very upset. Maybe she will let something slip."

"They could be covering for each other." Jonas stared ahead with a look of concentration. "Baker can be much smarter than we give him credit for, knowing his unfortunately alcoholic friend will draw attention to herself, letting him go unnoticed. I will ask West to look into both of them and, if possible, bring them in for questioning and fingerprinting."

"DNA!" Delta put her hand on his arm. "There was DNA under Weatherspoon's fingernails. If West can compare it with theirs..."

"He won't be able to get their DNA unless he can connect them with the crime. Considering how they feel about the police, they won't cooperate of their own free will. No, this case won't be solved the easy way." Jonas gestured to a waitress. "We'd better have a coffee to pass the time before we go into the lecture."

When they entered the room at a quarter past seven, chairs were already filling up quickly. Delta was just deciding where to turn to for a good seat when a voice said, "Delta? Is that you?"

She swung round and saw Gran peering at her with astonishment. She went over and pecked her on the cheek. "Hello.

How are you? I wanted to surprise you. I bought this dress especially for tonight. How do you like it?"

"It looks great on you, darling." Gran kissed her back. "I had no idea you'd pop on over. And not alone either..." She waved at Jonas, who was gesturing to indicate that he would go and find seats before they were all taken.

Delta signaled her okay.

Gran said confidentially, "I can imagine you thought up this excuse to get him to be your driver for tonight. He's wonderful."

Delta flushed. It was good Gran had no idea they were here to check on Buckmore, but she also didn't want Gran dropping hints to Jonas later. "I really want to hear the lecture. You have been telling me all about Major Buckmore's abilities as a storyteller."

"No, no, no." Gran shook her head. "I know you, Delta. I partially raised you. You're far too excited to just be here for a dull lecture. You're up to something."

Delta grew even hotter. Gran knew her too well. But she didn't want to mention the meeting they just had with all of the people buzzing about them. "I needed a break from the murder case." A little white lie couldn't hurt. "Sheriff West is closing the net on Tilly."

Gran didn't look perturbed. "If she has been part of that horrible pyramid scheme, swindling people out of their savings, she should be punished for it," she said with such vigor it took Delta by surprise. Her grandmother usually refrained from judging people harshly, especially if their case was far from clear.

Gran continued in that same passionate tone, "George told me how friends of his lost everything they owned. Their B&B, which was their home and their source of income. The husband of the couple even had a heart attack because of the stress. So sad." She looked away a moment, her lively expression sad. Then she touched Delta's arm. "But George made me swear I wouldn't mention it to anyone. You will keep it to yourself, won't you, darling?" Before Delta could respond, she continued, "Now, murder case or not, you didn't buy that dress for me. It's nothing to be ashamed of. Take a break from it all and fall in love. I can recommend it." Gran winked.

The floorboards shifted under Delta's feet. Was Gran doing that as well—taking a break and falling in love? With a man who might have some ulterior motive for befriending her? How coincidental that Buckmore had friends who were victims of the pyramid scheme Tilly Tay had been possibly embroiled in. The scheme set up by Weatherspoon, who had been murdered.

Her mouth went dry. Was it possible that Buckmore was somehow tied up in the murder?

"I have to go and find my seat," Gran said briskly. "George arranged one up front. I don't like to be the center of attention, but it was so sweet of him I didn't want to tell him no. Have fun."

Delta watched her grandmother walk away with a straight back and a vitality she hadn't displayed since before her house sold. Delta was happy for her and at the same time tense with fear this would go horribly wrong. It had been stressful thinking Buckmore wasn't sincere, but this new revelation really had her blood pounding.

She looked about her, spotted Jonas, and went to sit with him. "Is something the matter?" he asked. "You're all flustered."

"I'm not sure," Delta whispered in his ear. "Gran let it slip Buckmore had friends who fell victim to Weatherspoon's pyramid scheme. They lost everything they owned, and the man had a heart attack. That's serious damage caused by Weatherspoon's greed. What if Buckmore knew he'd be released from prison and coming here?" She didn't want to put the ultimate conclusion into words. That Buckmore might be Weatherspoon's killer.

Jonas put his hand over hers. "We'll sort it out. That's what we're here for."

The warmth of his touch reassured her, and she focused on the platform where Buckmore was taking his place. He welcomed everyone and then dove into a tale of gold rush greed and mishaps. Laughter resounded through the room, and even Delta and all her skepticism found herself joining in. When she glanced at Jonas from time to time, she found him quietly observing Buckmore and the audience, and she wondered what he, with his police training, was making of all of this.

At the end of the lecture, Buckmore said interested parties could buy his book, and he took a seat behind a table with stacks of books piled up. People flocked to buy a copy and have it autographed by the author, and to Delta's surprise, Jonas joined the line. He bought a book and let Buckmore write a dedication in it with his signature underneath.

She didn't dare ask him what it meant while they were inside. She hugged Gran and told her that it had been a great evening. Jonas joined them and said it would be nice to have coffee the next morning, all four of them. Gran seemed surprised but agreed to meet up at the hotel where she and Buckmore were staying. Jonas took down the address in his phone. "Where are you staying?" Gran asked.

"At a resort," Jonas said. "I got us a cabin there. More convenient with my dog and all."

"I see," Gran said in a tone that suggested she had her own thoughts about the arrangement.

Delta flushed again and took her leave before Gran could say more that made her feel like melting into a puddle. Outside, they crossed to the Jeep, and Jonas said he wanted to sit there for a bit and watch the Seasoned Saloon. "When they leave together, I want to see how they are around each other when they're not in a large company."

"And assuming they are unobserved," Delta added.

"Exactly."

She studied Jonas's profile. "What are you thinking? You were so focused all night."

"I tried to decide whether he has the characteristics of a con man. Or even a narcissistic personality. Loves attention, manipulates people, that sort of thing. But I can't really tell. He looks like a genuinely history-loving, funny person who likes to share what he knows. No crime in that. However, if he does know victims of Weatherspoon's crimes, it opens up a whole new perspective. He might have befriended your grandmother to get close to you and the investigation."

Delta hadn't quite thought that far. "I don't think..." she protested.

But Jonas asked, "When exactly did he first contact your grandmother?"

"On the afternoon Tilly came to town and had the altercation with Weatherspoon on Mattock Street," Delta admitted.

"See. Either he was keeping tabs on Weatherspoon or he already knew about the connection with Tilly. When he realized she was exhibiting at your shop, he contacted your grandmother to find out more via her. Have you shared inside details with your gran?"

"A few," Delta admitted. She shifted weight uncomfortably.

Jonas said, "Buckmore might have an ulterior motive that has nothing to do with your grandmother. He doesn't want to trick her out of her savings but could be after information about Weatherspoon and the missing money from the pyramid scheme."

"For the sake of his friends?" Delta asked doubtfully.

"If there are such friends. He could have made up that story to gain your gran's sympathy and get more information from her."

"What do you mean?"

Jonas eyed her with a serious expression. "If we combine what we learned, Buckmore could be a con man who just happens to be in the area where another con man died..."

"Do you think *he* could have been Weatherspoon's accomplice in the pyramid scheme?" Delta's head spun with this possibility. Her grandmother could be in more danger than she had assumed. If there were millions at stake...

"Or they could have been in jail together," Jonas suggested, "and Buckmore learned about the missing money there. Either way he could believe he has a chance of unearthing it and keeping it all to himself. But, with Weatherspoon dead, he is obviously none the wiser as to where the money is. Or he needn't have ransacked Tilly's van." He glanced at her. "Do you think it's too much speculation? I thought you wanted my professional opinion on Buckmore."

"I do. If any of this is true, I'll need you more than ever to keep Gran safe."

And she also needed him to support her, be there for her. She needed to know that what they had was something special. Unique, precious. But how could she tell him? He was completely engaged in working a case, and she was sitting here in a brand-new dress hoping he would lean in and kiss her. Suddenly Delta felt rather awkward. "Maybe we better leave. The parked cars are thinning out, and we don't want Gran and Buckmore to spot us and wonder what we are still doing here. If he's up to no good, we shouldn't make him suspicious. Besides, we're going to have coffee with them in the morning. Smart way to get the address of their hotel."

Jonas waved it off. "It was just an idea. I want to see more of him." He turned the engine on. "Time to get to our cabin on the resort. I hope you don't mind I got one? Hotels can be fussy about allowing dogs in and… Well, it seemed more convenient."

"Fine with me."

Delta sat quietly watching the darkness with the moon above as they drove. Jonas had turned the radio on, and it softly played classical music. An alluring piano, a melancholy violin. The perfect accompaniment to this evening.

They parked beside a wooden house with a porch. In summer the hanging baskets had to look gorgeous. Now there were a few standing pots with heather and mosses. Jonas let Spud out of the Jeep and carried in the bags. Spud sniffed the new surroundings while Delta turned on a lamp here and there. The living room had a big fireplace with a sheepskin in front of it and cozy pillows to lounge against, but it was probably too late to turn on.

"There." Jonas closed the door.

Suddenly they were here together, in this little house, like it was their house. Just the two of them and Spud who had already settled in front of the unlit fireplace. Jonas gestured at him. "Seems like he feels right at home." He eyed her. "Want a drink?"

"I doubt there's anything in the fridge."

"I brought our own bottle of mulled wine and a saucepan to warm it in."

"You really think of everything," Delta said with a grin. Jonas disappeared into the kitchen area with the bottle and pan. Delta found some scented candles and lit them with a lighter from the mantelpiece. The scent of vanilla from the candles mixed with cinnamon and orange from the stovetop as Jonas carried glasses with the mulled wine into the room. "Smells delicious." Delta sat down on the leather sofa and he came to sit beside her. He handed her a glass, and they toasted.

"To…" Jonas left it open, eyeing her with his blue gaze.

This would be the perfect moment to say it. One little word. Us.

To friendship that had become so much more.

"To…a great evening." Delta smiled. "I wouldn't have wanted to do it without you." It didn't come out exactly the way she wanted to say it, but the intention was clear.

Jonas kept looking at her, taking in all her features, it seemed. She waited for him to lean over to her and put his lips to hers. But he sipped his mulled wine and said, "You try."

She tried, letting the spicy aroma roll over her tongue. "Very nice."

Jonas put his glass on the low table and stretched his legs. "Basic but comfy."

"I'm fine with that." *You know, there's something I've been meaning to tell you for some time. It's that...*

"There's indeed nothing in the fridge, but luckily, I brought a few things to make us breakfast in the morning."

"Great." *Isn't it nice to be here together? You and I. We. I mean...*

Spud made a low sound as he settled better on the floor. Jonas leaned down to him and patted his back. "Sleep tight, big boy." Then he looked at Delta again. There was no sound from the outside, not even the splatter of rain. It was so quiet, as if everything was holding its breath, waiting for either of them to make a move.

He'd have to do it. She didn't have the guts for it. She had promised herself, but her mouth didn't want to say the words her head was coming up with.

"It said in the email there is bedding in the bedrooms,"

Jonas said. "You do have to make your own bed. I hope you don't mind at this hour."

"Not at all." Delta emptied her glass. "As a matter of fact, I might try and make it right now. I'm not too tired yet. I'll be back soon." She got up and went to her bedroom. Jonas had put her things beside the bed. She found the duvet and pillows in the cupboard and made the bed. Her heart was fluttering. If she didn't take advantage of this situation to get a kiss, she'd be a total fool.

Okay. I'm going back in, sit down beside him, and then I'll lean into him. If he puts his arm around me, I'll take it from there.

She snuck back to the living room to watch him as he sat there with his dog. To gather courage to go over and do it. For real.

But Jonas wasn't merely sitting there. He was on his phone. Smiling down at it.

It couldn't be anything work-related so late at night. It had to be Paula texting him.

Delta cleared her throat. Jonas looked up. She said, "I'm really tired, so I'm turning in. Thanks for a wonderful evening."

"Sure," Jonas said. There was a moment's confusion in

his face, hesitation as if he wasn't certain what to do next: ask her not to turn in right away yet, chat a bit...be together?

She turned away. "Good night."

"Good night."

Walking into her bedroom, she could just slap herself that she let this chance pass. But, if she made a move, and he didn't share her feelings, it would mean more than just hurt pride. She'd lose their friendship, which meant the world to her. She didn't want to wake up and realize that she no longer had Jonas to rely on, all because she had kissed him while he didn't want her to.

No, it was better this way.

Safer.

Chapter Sixteen

THE NEXT MORNING, DELTA WOKE WITH A FLEETING
sensation something was not quite as it normally was. It took
her a few moments to realize she was not in her bed at Hazel's
cottage but in a strange place. Staring up at the ceiling with
the light creeping over the curtains she recalled, bit by bit,
what had happened the previous day. When she got to the
part where she had walked out on Jonas texting Paula, she
groaned. She could only hope the atmosphere was relaxed this
morning and she could forget about her silly expectations.
And focus on meeting Gran and her possibly dishonest beau.
If Buckmore was after the gains from the pyramid scheme, he
would be a serious adversary. They'd have to watch their step
to lure him into coming clean, somehow.

Delta bit her lip. Gran was still unsuspecting, and here was

Delta, betraying her by keeping silent about her real reasons for being here, about her suspicions and her fears. She was doing that out of respect for Gran, she told herself, and because she had so few facts, but she knew she was mostly afraid that the grandmother she loved so much wouldn't believe her, and Buckmore would come between them. That Gran would choose to side with someone she barely knew, against her own granddaughter.

Delta sat on the edge of the bed and rubbed her face. She wasn't looking forward to today, or, rather, to how this was all going to pan out. Perhaps she had better not interfere at all. But, if you loved someone, you didn't let them walk into danger, right?

She got up, showered and dressed, and then followed the scent of something baking. In the kitchen area, Jonas was busy making orange juice, coffee, and whatever he had in the oven. She went over for a peek, but Jonas stopped her midway. "Uh-uh, no snooping."

His aftershave whirled around her. Spud was sitting at the sink, glancing up with not much hope of a snack. Delta knew Jonas was very strict when it came to never feeding the dog people food, so she gave him a big hug instead. "We've already been out for a run," Jonas told her. "I thought you'd like to sleep a little longer."

"Yeah, sure." She bit back the disappointment of having

missed the early morning forest mist and the companionship with him. "I hope you didn't feel like I bailed out too early last night?"

"Nah." The half-hearted denial made her perk up and study him. "Had you wanted to chat about Buckmore?"

"It might have helped to have a strategy."

"I see. What strategy?" She gave Spud another pat on the head and seated herself at the table. Jonas put a glass of juice and a mug with freshly brewed coffee before her. Then he turned to the oven and extracted the tray. "Ta-da!"

"Croissants!" Delta beamed at him. "I love those, especially when they're warm."

"Right now, they are piping hot, so mind your fingers." He pointed at the dishes on the table. "Butter, jam, cheese."

"You prepped this to perfection."

"I like to be thorough." Jonas picked up his own coffee and took a sip. "If Buckmore is an innocent old man with a penchant for history, I don't want to ruin the friendship he built with your grandmother. But, if he's a smart fraudster who's possibly tied up in Weatherspoon's murder, I want him exposed ASAP before he can do any harm. You don't happen to know who those friends are that allegedly lost money to Weatherspoon?"

"No, Gran let it slip and then told me to keep it to myself. I shouldn't have shared it with you at all."

"So we can't start a conversation about it and try to get more details about them." Jonas pensively tapped a spoon on the edge of the sink. "I'd love to know if they really exist or are just his excuse for being interested in Weatherspoon's fate."

"I see. Why did you buy his book?" Delta asked.

"To get him to write something in it. I wanted his handwriting for analysis. I have a friend who can deduce a lot from handwriting. Not to mention, he knows the hand of well-known fraudsters."

"So you're now actively checking on the major?" Delta asked.

"Yes, I thought that was the plan. Especially now that he could be involved in the murder case as well. Am I wrong?"

He might have been messaging about that, last night, she thought. It wasn't Paula at all. *Silly me.*

"Am I?" Jonas pressed.

"Well, to be honest, I'm not sure myself. I mean, I want to know what he is about, but, at the same time, I feel like checking on him is violating Gran's life. I mean, she made friends with him. He's her acquaintance, not mine. Do I have a right to do this? I feel like I should be protecting her, but what if she finds out and is mad about it? I would feel terrible."

"You would feel terrible if she chose his side. Against you."

As Jonas put it into words, Delta's heart clenched. "Yes. It would feel like...I lost her. And I love her so much."

Jonas put his glass on the table, came over, and hugged her. Delta leaned against him, feeling so safe and certain for just a few precious moments. He was there for her. He'd never let her down.

Jonas released her and smiled down on her. "I can't stop your grandmother from getting mad at you if she does find out. But I will do my very best to make sure she doesn't find out. And you do get to know whether Buckmore can be trusted or not."

"Thanks."

Jonas checked his watch. "We have to mind the time."

Delta looked as well. "I overslept."

"Just have a croissant. I didn't make them for nothing." He kept standing as if he was suddenly restless. Spud circled him looking up with a whine. "Yes, I'd better, uh...get the car ready." Jonas left the kitchen. Spud stared after him as if he couldn't quite place his mood.

How odd that he made all these breakfast preparations for me, and now it's like he doesn't want to sit down to breakfast with me at all. Delta put generous jam on the croissant. It was deliciously light, almost perfect.

Too bad the meeting with Gran and Buckmore hung like a shadow over their day. Delta feared to see them together and sense how much her grandmother really liked this man. The thrill of falling in love was so special. Something she wanted her gran to have. But not with someone unreliable. Someone who might have befriended her for reasons that connected with criminal money and potentially murder.

Having left Spud at the cottage, they arrived at the Lakeview Hotel around ten and heard from a waiter that Major Buckmore and Mrs. Douglas were sitting on the terrace with their after-breakfast coffee. The waiter asked if they'd like coffee as well and went to get it for them.

The terrace was covered and had red lamps on the beams casting a warmth over the hotel guests seated there. "Clever, hey?" Buckmore said, pointing them out. "November, and, still, we are breathing the outside air."

He shook their hands and enjoyed playing host, giving

them seats. "Well, well," he said as they were all around the table. "How did you like my lecture last night?"

"I heard a few things I've never heard before," Jonas said, "and I know the local history pretty well."

Buckmore studied him as if he wasn't quite sure whether it was a compliment or not. Delta wondered if Jonas wanted to provoke the major into showing some more emotion than just this pleasant air he seemed to exude permanently.

"How did you dig up all this interesting information?" Jonas asked.

"I can't tell. Professional secret."

Gran touched his arm. "Jonas is a wildlife guide, so maybe he wants to liven up his tours with some gold rush facts? You could..."

"He bought my book, so he can read it all in there. If he has the time to read it." Buckmore said it jokingly, but Delta had the impression there was a cold flash in his eyes. Did he suspect them of an ulterior motive in buying his book?

The waiter brought their coffee, and Buckmore turned charming again, telling an anecdote that hadn't been in his lecture the previous evening. Gran couldn't keep her eyes off him, smiling the entire time. Delta was glad for her but also slightly put off that Buckmore didn't allow anyone any space to talk. He was completely centering the conversation on himself.

Then, as he was finishing talking, he said, "A wildlife guide, hey? A sort of ranger?"

"No, just telling people about deer," Jonas said casually.

But Gran said, "Jonas did work for the police before he came to live in Tundish."

Maybe Delta only imagined it, but Buckmore seemed to stiffen when he heard the word "police."

Jonas said quickly, "I was a dog handler. I really love working with dogs."

"Yes, you had a dog with you last night," Buckmore said.

"That's Spud, the dog Jonas uses for his current work." Gran kept talking, not aware that this topic had been best avoided. "He helps K9s adjust to civilian life."

"An important task," Buckmore said and finished his coffee. He said to Gran, "We should be getting ready to leave for the museum."

"Oh, yes, of course." Gran shot Delta an apologetic look. "I hope you don't mind this was rather short, but we have so many plans for our stay here."

"Not at all, I'm happy you're enjoying yourself." Delta hugged and kissed her. Gran went up to her room to change, and Buckmore accompanied Jonas and Delta to their car. In the parking lot he said, "I appreciate that you came to see your grandmother, Delta. But remember one thing: she's a grown woman who doesn't need a chaperone."

Delta felt her cheeks catch fire. She struggled for something to say.

Jonas raised an eyebrow. "We were just interested in your lecture and…"

"Really?" Buckmore eyed him without blinking. "Or was there some other reason for turning up there, Officer? I'm telling you one thing. If you think you can smear my reputation, you'll soon discover that you had better not."

Although he didn't use any harsh words, Delta sensed the implied malice in his phrasing. She shivered as she watched Buckmore walk away.

"He didn't seem to respond very well to the revelation that I worked for the police." Jonas spoke quietly. "That could be telling. Why mind it if he's a law-abiding citizen?"

"I'd like to go inside and get Gran and take her away from this man." Delta bit her lip. "But she sees no bad in him and won't listen to me if I try to tell her."

"You should try to tell her," Jonas said. "But not now. Come." He ushered her to the car door. "We're leaving."

While they drove back to Tundish, Delta's head was so full of thoughts she didn't know how to feel. Coming on this trip, she had only wanted to know if she was losing Gran to a con man. Now she wondered what the smart and observant Buckmore was really about. Had he taken it upon himself to look into Weatherspoon upon his release? Had the two of them ever met?

To divert attention, she pulled up her phone. "Oh, I forgot to turn it on this morning." She studied the screen. "Hazel tried to call me several times. I hope there's no bad news." Her heart pounded fast as she pushed the callback button to contact her friend. "What if something happened to Wanted?"

When Hazel answered, however, she sounded cheerful. "I didn't want to disturb your time away, but I have some good news. Excellent news, in fact. Tilly has been released by the police. I'm not sure whether it means they're no longer suspecting her or if it was just because they had no more reason to hold her right now, but she's out and about. Mrs. Cassidy picked her up and took her home to be reunited with Buddy. I bet they are both ecstatic to see each other."

"How sweet," Delta said. "Maybe we can drop by to see Tilly."

"Don't rush home. You ought to make the most of your stay." Hazel sounded a little suggestive.

Delta said, "We're already on our way to Tundish. We had a chance to hear Buckmore speak, and we had coffee with Gran and him. Everything looked rather uh...normal." She could tell Hazel in person about Jonas's suggestion Buckmore might be involved in the murder case.

"Oh." Hazel sounded overtaken. "Does that mean you suddenly trust him?"

"Not exactly, but there's little we can do right now. Does the fact that Tilly was released mean that the DNA found under the victim's fingernails wasn't hers?"

"No, not hers. They don't know whose it is, but the deputy mentioned it was male DNA."

Delta couldn't help thinking of Buckmore. "We're coming over to Mrs. Cassidy's. I can't wait to see Buddy and Tilly, of course."

As she lowered the phone Jonas said, "So Tilly has been released. Only logical when you consider what West has against her."

"The DNA found under the victim's fingernails is male. So the killer could have been male."

"With an emphasis on *could have been*. We don't know

if the DNA got there during the murder. Remember that the victim was stabbed in the back? That doesn't feel like a fight to me."

"Maybe there was a fight, and then Weatherspoon turned and walked away and the killer lashed out at him with the knife." Delta took a deep breath. "It could have been Buckmore."

"Just because your grandmother shared that he knew victims of the fraud? There were hundreds of victims, so there must be thousands of people who are friends or relations of them. Still, it was strange, his hostile reaction there at the end... I'll try my best to get more on Buckmore, and on the pyramid scheme victims—most of all, Adam Baker and Cheryl Remington."

Yes, of course the male DNA could also be Baker's, Delta supposed. She added the two victims to her case file, making notes of what they had told them last night. The fact that Cheryl Remington's PI had traced Weatherspoon to Tundish could be super relevant. They had known Weatherspoon was here before he had died. They could have met him and gotten into an argument with him. *An argument gone wrong?*

Delta let her gaze wander the case file's many suspects and events that still didn't form a logical sequence.

She focused on the shadowy figure she had drawn to represent the man they had met in the forest. If he was Weatherspoon's accomplice, then how did Buckmore fit in? Had the pyramid scheme been run by several people? After all, Weatherspoon's cons had never been very successful, so it made sense to assume that, for the pyramid scheme, he had joined forces with someone with more criminal savvy than he had.

As they arrived at Mrs. Cassidy's home, they found Calamity Jane there, wearing one of her trademark bold-patterned dresses with an array of sweet treats to celebrate Tilly's release. The table was full of plates with cupcakes in several flavors, and Delta accepted a raspberry white-chocolate one. Even Jonas, who eyed all the icing on top with reserve, accepted a blueberry one to try. Jane lifted hers to Tilly, who sat on the sofa with Buddy in her lap. "To your release. Long may your freedom continue."

Delta wasn't sure the exuberant mood was fitting. Tilly may have been released for the moment, but she wasn't off the hook completely. And she had been dishonest with them about several things. Why do that if she was innocent?

Tilly smiled reluctantly. Her hand stroking Buddy trembled. "I doubt it's really that easy."

There you have it. Delta looked at her with trepidation. "Why do you say that?"

Tilly swallowed hard.

Mrs. Cassidy said, "Tilly wasn't happy to learn that her brother-in-law is eager to engage the lawyer and influence her case."

"I hardly ever see my sister," Tilly explained, scooting to the edge of the seat. "And I never liked her husband. I have no idea what Tabby saw in him. Virgil is so smug and focused on status. No one is quite in his league." She grimaced as she added, "Of course Tabby would point out now that I did much worse marrying a criminal."

"You mustn't feel bad about a choice you made so long ago. People change." Mrs. Cassidy handed her a mug. "This hot chocolate will make you feel better."

Tilly accepted it with a grateful smile and sipped carefully. Buddy pushed his head against her, happy to have her back.

Jonas said, "This blueberry muffin isn't half bad."

"It's a cupcake," Jane corrected drily. "And thanks for the compliment. If it even was one."

Jonas had the decency to grow red under his collar. Delta grinned. "It was a compliment, Jane."

Jane lifted a hand in an apologetic gesture. "Fine. Touch

my creations, touch me." She looked at Tilly. "I guess you feel the same way about what you make. All those hours going into it."

"I enjoy it, so it never feels like a chore. I do hope that the ransacking of the van didn't destroy too much stuff. And then the police going over everything." Tilly stared into her hot chocolate.

"Yes," Jane said, "I wondered about that. Do you have any idea what they were looking for? I mean, they must have been looking for something. You don't destroy other people's belongings for fun."

"It was a warning." Tilly said it in a low, almost inaudible voice.

"Excuse me?" Mrs. Cassidy leaned over to her. "Did you say warning?"

Tilly nodded, her shoulders slumped. She looked like a small dog huddling in a corner, afraid of the outside world. "I knew it when I saw the prospector with the mattock in his back in my display. That it was a warning."

"A warning about what?" Jane asked. She came to sit on the sofa beside Tilly and eyed her encouragingly.

"That I was next to die." Tilly looked up, very pale. "I wasn't eager to get out of that police station at all. I mean,

I do appreciate you worked hard to get me released, but I would have been safer in there. There they can't get to me."

"Who?"

"The people who killed my ex. I keep calling him ex, as I never considered us married anymore."

"You think your husband's killer wants to murder you as well? But what for?" Jane gave Tilly a wide-eyed look.

"I can only think of one reason." Tilly brushed Buddy's head. "With his pyramid scheme, he hurt a lot of people. Their savings were gone, some people ended up having to sell their houses and belongings. It caused so much damage. I can only imagine that some of the victims thought he didn't pay enough by going to jail. That he was released too soon or... They came after him to kill him and also warn me."

Delta thought of the people they had met in Timbercreek: bitter and alcohol-infused Cheryl Remington and quiet but clever Adam Baker. Had one of them committed the murder and placed the clue to Tilly in the display as an act of revenge? Or had they even done it together? Cheryl seemed more of a hothead, Adam the thinker. Maybe she had killed Weatherspoon on impulse, and Adam had decided to cover up her tracks by changing the display and maybe also sending the key to Marc to muddy the water?

"Why you?" Jane asked Tilly with a puzzled expression. "You were never part of his crimes."

Delta held her breath for Tilly's answer. This was the moment of truth.

If they could expect Tilly to be honest with them...

"No. But who believes that? Most of the money was never recovered. It was always believed that an accomplice had it. They must assume it's me." Tilly looked up. "I never saw any of that money, I can assure you. I had no idea my ex was doing anything illegal that delivered big money. He didn't seem to have much. Not more than was usual in his profession. I never had any suspicions during our relationship or after. He did pull some small scams, but nothing major. His arrest for a pyramid scheme that had allegedly swindled away millions came out of the blue. I've always believed he could never have pulled it off alone. Bob wasn't smart enough for it."

Delta looked at Jonas. This would be the perfect moment to feel out Tilly about possible accomplices. Jonas seemed to hesitate before he said, "And, once you thought he had done it with someone, did you have a particular person in mind?"

Delta bet Jonas was thinking of the man they had met at the wildlife observation point. He had told them about Bob harassing Tilly and how he had tried to keep him from it. That suggested they had been close.

Tilly shook her head. "I had no idea. I didn't think any of his usual buddies were smart enough either. They had always been caught out before, so they should have known better than try their hand at something major. But, this time, the money vanished and never turned up." She laughed cynically. "Now people think it was me hiding it away. So, apparently, I'm the sort of person who can hide millions, escape capture while my ex goes to prison, and keep the money stashed all those years he's inside. Now is that a compliment or not?"

Jane patted her arm. "We'll figure it out, Don't you worry. You have a good lawyer. And Mrs. Cassidy won't let her go. Not even to your brother-in-law who pays more, right?"

"Right," Mrs. Cassidy said firmly.

She got up and went to the kitchen to get more coffee and hot chocolate for those who wanted it. Suddenly she came back in, on tiptoe, and gestured to Jonas. "He's here again," she whispered.

"Who?" Jonas asked.

"The prowler. I caught a glimpse of him just now through the kitchen window. He's dressed all in black."

Jonas shot to his feet and followed her into the kitchen.

Delta slunk after them, curious to learn what was up. Jonas peeked out. "Don't let him see you," Mrs. Cassidy warned. "He's in the back of the garden, behind my apple tree."

"I think I see him," Jonas said. "I'll get out through the front door and track around back to get behind him. I want to know who it is and what he wants here. Especially now that Tilly has just been released. I don't know if she could be in danger, but she told us that she considers the addition to her display a direct warning of her life being under threat. I can't disregard that."

"Good thinking," Mrs. Cassidy said, and Delta added, "Be careful."

While Jonas left, Delta and Mrs. Cassidy kept watching the shadow outside. Delta said, "They must be after something. First they thought it was in the van, then maybe here with Buddy, and now they think Tilly has it on her?"

"Or they think Tilly can tell them where it is and they want to get to her, one-on-one. Maybe even forcibly take her along to help them." Mrs. Cassidy sounded tense. "Poor woman, she's up to her eyebrows in something bigger than she is."

Delta kept staring outside. Her breathing came in rapid gulps. If Jonas caught whoever was out there, they might learn more. But what if they got into a struggle? The person could be armed. Jonas could get hurt. Why hadn't he taken Spud along?

Probably because he was worried the dog would get injured. Jonas loved his canine buddy over anything else.

"There he goes," Mrs. Cassidy shouted. The shadow appeared from under the tree and dashed toward the house, apparently intending to round it and get to the front. Jonas was a few feet behind him. Mrs. Cassidy threw open the back door and dashed onto the porch, grabbing a broom on her way. She threw it in the fleeing man's path and he stumbled across it, falling into the grass on hands and knees.

Jonas leaned down over him. "Let's do this without hurting one another, okay?" he said, pulling the man's arm behind his back. "I want to know what you're doing here, trespassing on private property and spying on innocent civilians."

The man breathed heavily. Delta, who had come out after Mrs. Cassidy, took a good look at his face with the worried brown eyes and said, "I think it's him. The guy we talked to earlier."

Jonas pulled the intruder to his feet. "You better tell us what kind of game you're playing. Before we call the police."

"I only wanted to see if Tilly was all right," he stammered. "Because she has been locked up and all."

"Why would you care for Tilly?" Jonas asked. "First you pretended to be so worried about the man who died. Now Tilly?"

He sounded disbelieving.

The man took a deep breath and looked at Delta. "Can't I be worried about my own parents?"

Chapter Seventeen

"Parents?" Delta and Mrs. Cassidy echoed in unison.

Jonas said, "The murder victim, Bob Weatherspoon, and Tilly Tay are your parents?"

"Yes."

"Tilly never mentioned she had a son," Delta pointed out, her mind going back across everything she had read about the artist.

"That's because she's not exactly proud of me. She thinks I followed in my father's footsteps. But I haven't. I built a decent life for myself. I wanted her to know, that's why I came out here. Also to keep an eye on Dad. I knew he wanted to contact Mom, and it seemed like such a bad idea."

"You could say that again," Jonas said. He released his grip on the arm a little. "Tilly has no idea you're here?"

"No, and I doubt she'll want to see me. Not if she knows I stayed at the same motel as Dad. She probably thinks we were in it together, to harass her."

"Do you know what your father wanted of Tilly?" Mrs. Cassidy asked. "I mean, others might think she had the money from the pyramid scheme, but surely the man who conducted the scheme can't have thought that. He knew the truth."

"Dad was the only one who knew. And now he's dead." The man hung his head. "I never was close to him, but I never wanted him to die. Certainly not like this. Stabbed in the back and left out to die. Like he was garbage."

Jonas put a hand on the man's shoulder. "I think you can use a cup of coffee. Why don't you come inside?"

The man looked up with a jerk. "And face Mom? She'll be livid."

"Or she'll be happy to know you're all right and not involved in the case." Delta wasn't sure they could trust this story, but they couldn't let him walk again either. He knew things that might be useful to them. In any case, he had to talk to Tilly's lawyer.

"Do come in," Mrs. Cassidy said. "You're very welcome. That is..." She eyed him. "You didn't prowl around this house at night when Buddy was first taken here?"

The man tilted his head. "Was Buddy here then? I didn't know who took care of him while Mom was at the police station."

Mrs. Cassidy stared at him. "If you didn't come to my house that night, then who did, and why?"

"That's something we must figure out by adding up what we all know." Jonas waved them along to the house. "Let's go inside."

When they came into the room with the man, Delta wondered if Tilly would recognize him at all. Apparently, she hadn't seen her son in years.

Everyone present looked at them expectantly, including the miniature artist. The mug in her hand slipped and almost spilled chocolate on her dress as she stared and gasped, "Noel!"

He stood dangling his hands, looking as uncomfortable as a sixteen-year-old caught out past curfew. "Hi, Mom."

Tilly sat up straighter. "If you're here to join in the family pressure to give up my life as I know it, you can go away again."

He shook his head. "I'm here to see if you're all right after being locked up." He looked down. "I knew Dad was after you again. I should have warned you."

"You were here with Bob?" Tilly turned pale. "I told you

not to fall in with him. He wasn't a truly bad man at heart, but he always took the easy way out."

"I wasn't a part of his cons. I tried to keep him from it. I told him to leave you be and…"

"Bob can't have come here for me." Tilly sounded shrill. "He knew, better than anyone, that I don't have a dime to give him. And I never knew where his money was. So what did he want from me?"

"Didn't he tell you when you met him on Mattock Street?" Delta asked quietly. "He did say something to you then."

Tilly seemed flustered. "No, not really…" It didn't sound convincing.

Jonas said, "You might as well tell us. We can't help you if we don't know the truth."

Tilly wet her lips.

Her son said, "Tell him, Mom. Whatever you know, tell them. Please let them help you."

Tilly patted Buddy. She looked into the distance as if seeing the scene again. "I was shocked to see Bob in the street. I thought he was still in jail. But I knew right away that he was after something. He always was." She sighed sadly. "This time he wanted to make me an offer."

"What offer?" Jonas asked.

"He needed me to help him with something. Something big that could set him up for life. He needed me as a decoy, he said. It wouldn't hurt me, wouldn't be risky at all." She laughed. "I knew Bob's definition of 'not risky.' I told him no. He always had these wild plans, and they always went wrong. They hurt people and left him behind bars. I told him to find a decent job for once and make something of his life. He got angry, saying no one wanted to hire a convict, and asked me if I wanted him to rot in the gutter. He had done his time; he deserved his share now. I was to help him get it."

"Share?" Jonas pounced. "In the pyramid scheme proceeds? So he thought you could get to it."

"No. I never had access to it or knew where it was hidden. But someone else apparently did. Someone he was in touch with. That person would give him access to his share."

"In exchange for what?" Jonas asked. "I can't see someone who has access to millions giving away part of it for free."

"I don't know. Bob didn't say. The meeting would go down the next day. He needed my help to make the exchange safer for him."

"Safer?" Jonas frowned. "How? Because you would be a witness?"

"I don't know that either. I didn't want to hear his story at all. I kept repeating he had to go away. He did say he would pay me generously for his help. Or so he claimed. I doubt he would have been good for his word."

"Safer…" Jonas still pondered the deceased's word choice. "So Weatherspoon knew there was risk involved? Because the other party wasn't happy he was out of jail and eager for his share?"

"I didn't ask. I didn't want anything to do with it." Tilly wrung her hands. "I told him no, and that was the end of it. I only wished I would never see him again."

"And, after that, did you see him again?" Delta asked. They had to make sure Tilly had told them the truth about that.

"No. I was restless and asked for the key to work in the shop. I left there and dropped the key off at the cottage. Then I found a place for the van to stay overnight. Bob didn't come to me. That was all."

Jonas looked at Noel. "When we met earlier, you told us you thought your father had gone to see your mother the night he died."

Noel said. "I told you I thought so, but I didn't know for sure that they had actually met. I thought he wanted money off her because he kept saying she was his ticket to a new life.

I had no idea he meant that she had to help him get the money from the pyramid scheme."

"And you have no idea what he meant, exactly?" Jonas asked. "What his plan was, who was involved?"

"No. He only told me that he needed Mom to make it work." Noel hung his head. "I wish I had known a way to stop him. Then he would still be alive."

"It's not your fault, Noel." Tilly looked at her son with pain in her features. "Nobody could make your father stop. That was the way he was wired. Easy money drew him like a moth to a flame."

Jonas asked her, "And he didn't say anything to you that can give us a clue? Please go over his exact words one more time…"

"Don't you think I already have? Countless times. While I was at the Lodge recovering from shock and at the police station." Tilly gestured violently. "I can't tell you anymore. I didn't ask him for details. I didn't want to hear anything about it. I didn't want to know something that might make me complicit in any way. I was certain he was going to commit another crime. If I knew something, I'd feel obliged to go and tell the police about it, and I didn't want that. I wanted to have nothing to do with him and his idiotic plans anymore."

Noel sat down beside Tilly. "He just wanted a better life, Mom. He told me he had done his time and now it was payday. He even said it had been promised to him."

"Promised?" Jonas asked sharply.

"Yes." Noel looked at him. "I asked how he meant that, but he wouldn't say."

Delta stared ahead. "When we piece together what he said to Tilly and to Noel, what does that tell us? He was going to meet someone, it was risky, he needed help or backup doing it. It had to do with the missing money and a promise made to him that he would get his share."

"Only the other party wasn't too eager to share..." Jonas spoke slowly. "They lured him outside the motel, to discuss the deal, perhaps, and then stabbed him."

"But why take the trouble to get the key to go into Wanted and add the murdered prospector to the scene?" Delta asked.

Tilly said, "To strike fear in me. Or make me look suspect. I don't know. But I do know that someone wanted it to look like I was involved. Why else kill him in the town where I'm exhibiting?"

"Yes." Jonas pointed a finger at her. "That is a very good question. Why here? Was Tundish somehow related to his crimes? I heard he was here years ago, with you."

"He did run a con here in the past. He claimed to be the owner of a luxury cottage in the mountains and got several people to give him a down payment for a stay there. By the time they found out the cottage wasn't his and the website advertising it was offline, he was long gone. It was always that sort of thing. Amateurish and embarrassing. It had nothing to do with the pyramid scheme. Once he was caught for that, I couldn't believe he had set it up. It wasn't his style at all." Tilly's forehead scrunched up as she thought hard. "I can't think of any connection to Tundish. You?" She looked at Noel.

He also shook his head and said, "Dad never told me much about the scheme, but the victims were all well-to-do people from the East Coast. I don't see a direct link with this town or even Montana in general."

"So why here?" Jonas paced the room. "Could a clue to the money's whereabouts be hidden around here? West has been asking at banks about safety deposit boxes. Do you own one? Or did your ex have one?"

Tilly shook her head. "I always had the impression the money was transferred abroad into a numbered account. I thought Bob knew how to get into it once he'd be free. I had no idea he needed someone else for it."

"But someone did ransack your van," Mrs. Cassidy

pointed out. "That suggests you have something related to Weatherspoon's murder and the missing money."

"Yes," Jonas said slowly, "but what if the ransacking happened for another reason?" He stood and spread his arms as if he was encompassing a theory. Everyone looked at him expectantly. "Tilly's ex Bob Weatherspoon was asked to come here to Tundish, allegedly to get his share in the fortune he had been to jail for. The killer knew that Tilly was exhibiting here and hoped that her name would be connected to the murder and she would be the most likely suspect. Indeed, her ex contacted her, and they argued in the street. The killer stabbed Bob outside the motel and placed the prospector with the tiny mattock in his back in the display at Wanted. So far so good. But then the killer became antsy about the brief contact between Bob and Tilly. He feared that his victim might have told Tilly something that could connect him to it. That Bob might have handed her something, for safekeeping, that could prove his involvement. To be sure, he searched the van and came to this house to look at Buddy's dog bed."

"But, because I hadn't gone to bridge as I usually do, he didn't get near the bed." Mrs. Cassidy nodded. "It all makes sense. If the killer invited Bob Weatherspoon here, it must have been someone staying at the motel during the same time."

Jonas shook his head. "No, it is far more logical to assume the killer was not staying there. That would be a lot safer. Come in, stab, get out. Quickly."

"So we're looking for someone staying in a place other than the motel." Jane waved around her. "That means a dozen places. Hotels, cottages, B&Bs. At a tourist hot spot like Tundish, you have too many places to take into account. Even in November, most places are at least partially booked. How can you determine who might have been involved?"

Jonas stood with his head down, thinking hard, judging by the frown on his face. Spud came over and pressed his head against his leg, whining low. Jonas rubbed him absentmindedly.

Mrs. Cassidy said to Noel, "You must want some coffee."

"And a cupcake," Jane added.

As they fussed to give the new arrival some treats, Delta took Jonas aside. "Noel just said that the pyramid scheme mainly involved rich people from the East Coast. That it had no direct link to Montana. But Buckmore is a specialist on Montana gold rush history. Is it likely he has friends touched by the pyramid scheme? Does this new information strengthen our suspicions that he's lying and wants to know more about Weatherspoon for another reason? Could he have been involved with him?" She took a deep breath. "Is it even possible that Weatherspoon came here to meet Buckmore and get his share from him?"

Jonas held her gaze. "And that Buckmore killed him to keep everything to himself?"

Delta's stomach churned. Buckmore had befriended Gran on the very day Tilly Tay had come to town for the exhibition. Had it all been carefully planned, to implicate Tilly in the murder and then be close to a source of information about the investigation?

How natural it was for Buckmore to pretend he had heard about the murder and the link with Wanted and get Gran to share what she knew about the case. About what the police had against Tilly. That way Buckmore could ensure he was first to know relevant developments and could even act on them if he had to. For instance, by coming to Mrs. Cassidy's house to look at Buddy's dog bed.

It all fit.

And it chilled Delta to the bone.

At first she had been worried her grandmother had fallen in with a con man. Now she wondered if he might be a cold-blooded killer as well.

Chapter Eighteen

HAZEL WAS AS WORRIED AS DELTA WHEN SHE HEARD ABOUT Gran and Major Buckmore, especially the latter's none-too-friendly words when he had accompanied Jonas and Delta to the car. "I tried to convince myself he wasn't a bad person after all, but this threat of his can't be ignored." Hazel wrapped an arm around Delta's shoulders and added, "You have to talk to your grandmother as soon as she's back in town. Go and spend the night at her cottage and then have a chat. Tell her you're afraid she's being used. You need not tell her that you suspect him of involvement in the murder. She won't believe that, I'd guess. But his behavior to you and Jonas was really odd, she will have to admit."

"I wouldn't count on it. She adores him." Delta swallowed. "To be honest, I'm worried she'll defend him against me, and I'll feel like she's choosing his side. She practically raised me, and I love her as much as I love Mom and Dad. I don't want to lose my connection to her."

"I understand that. But, if your bond is that strong, it won't be broken by one conversation you have. You need not outright accuse him either. Just say it's going fast and you wonder how well she knows him. Raise some doubts in her mind. Let's be fair: if you were dating a guy and moving quickly, your gran would have questions about that as well."

"I guess so." Delta felt relief seeping through her. "Thanks, Hazel. You always cheer me up."

Hazel smiled at her. "That's what friends are for, right?"

The shop's bell jangled, and customers came in looking for scrapbooking materials. Hazel pointed out the new patterned papers and ribbons they had in stock while Delta demonstrated a gel pen to two sisters who wanted to do a scrapbooking workshop at one of their daughters' birthday party. Outside, rain splattered on the sidewalk, and, every now and then, thunder growled in the distance. Delta wondered briefly if Jonas was out with a group, and, imagining the businesspeople's disgruntled looks as they trudged through the mud for what was supposed to be relaxation, she had to laugh.

"If you take these pens…" She pointed at the five different

colors she had shown them. "I can offer you a packet of blank cards and some sticker sheets for a special price."

"That would be fabulous. Can we maybe choose the stickers, or did you have something in mind already?"

"Oh, no, you can choose any stickers you like from that basket over there. Two sheets. Or, if you choose the smaller sheets, three." Delta glanced at Hazel to see if she perked up as she was making this offer, but her friend was busy and didn't seem to listen at all. Delta still didn't feel completely confident when she proposed business transactions, although she had discovered that Hazel usually agreed with them. She needed to feel more self-assured. But that was hard with her doubts about Gran's relationship with the major and her own relationship with Jonas gnawing at her. Why hadn't she had the nerve to tell him how she felt? The moments at the cabin with the mulled wine had been perfect for it.

The door opened, and someone stepped in, shaking the water off a red umbrella before closing it and turning into the shop. It was Ray, dressed casually in denim and a leather jacket. He waved at her. "Real downpour out there."

As her customers were busy with the sticker sheet selection, Delta went over to Ray for a moment. "What brings you here?"

He patted his breast pocket. "I've got tickets to an antique fair. And Hazel can protest all she wants, but, this time, I'm taking her."

Delta smiled at his firm tone. "That would be lovely. She has been working so hard, staying at the store while I'm sleuthing to find out who killed the man at the motel, to clear Tilly Tay's name. Her visit here hasn't exactly provided the good press I was after when I invited her."

"I can imagine. But that's over soon." Ray nodded at the miniature display. "You'll be rid of it in no time."

"Rid of it? How come?" Delta frowned in puzzlement. "Tilly agreed to have it on display here for two weeks."

"That might have been the intention, but I heard plans have changed. At least, that's what Rosalyn told me. She agreed to it with Mrs. VanderHurst. Having heard of all the high-society events she and her investment banker husband go to, Rosalyn was deeply impressed, and, when Mrs. VanderHurst asked her, she agreed at once."

"Agreed to what?" Delta still didn't fully understand.

"To have the display transferred to the Lodge. It will be set up in the boardroom, and our hotel guests can look at it."

"What? But why?" Delta was shocked. Mr. VanderHurst had asked them if they intended to keep the display at the store, but she hadn't guessed he or his wife were actually going to take steps to take over. She looked for a way to express, in a friendly manner, that she felt boxed out of this decision, when she realized something else. "Does Tilly even know about this? She has only recently been released from the police station."

"I don't know. I guess so. I mean, her sister wouldn't make such decisions over her head."

Ray said it confidently, but Delta had her doubts. "I think she might. She does seem to feel like she knows everything better." She sighed. "Her husband also contacted the lawyer Mrs. Cassidy got for Tilly and offered to pay her fee to take charge of how the case is handled. They seem to be quite domineering."

"I'm sorry to hear that. I had no idea. Rosalyn must have thought it was their decision to make or she would not have agreed. And she also assumed it would take a hassle off your hands. After what happened…"

Delta fought a sense of embarrassment at the idea Rosalyn knew that the shopkeepers wanted her to give back her honorary title, but then the incongruity of it all struck her. She tilted her head. "Rosalyn always minds the Lodge's good name so much. Isn't she worried about taking in this display connected to a murder?"

"Oh, Rosalyn knows all about it." Ray rolled his eyes. "That's why I mentioned the investment-banker husband. Rosalyn is duly impressed with all the influential people he knows and confident they will now all flock to the Lodge to train their horses in our beautiful countryside. The sinister sides to the display mean nothing to her if she can attract wealthier clientele."

"Yes, Tabitha VanderHurst did mention to me she came here especially for her horse," Delta said. "I assume they are regulars at your hotel?"

Ray shook his head. "This is their first time out here, I gathered."

"How odd. I thought they came here because they knew the area."

"They could have stayed somewhere else before. But Rosalyn is determined to make them fans of the Lodge now. Them and all of their friends and acquaintances."

Delta frowned. Jonas had told her that the VanderHursts were getting divorced. But Tabitha was acting like there was no such thing as a breach impending, using her husband's status to secure transfer of Tilly's display to the hotel.

Then again, the VanderHursts were in therapy, Jonas had said, so maybe Tabitha was confident their marriage would survive?

Ray said apologetically, "You know how Rosalyn gets when status is concerned. I do hope you're not angry. She has arranged for some van to pull up in front of Wanted and transfer the whole thing tomorrow morning."

"Tomorrow morning?! Like I said, I don't know if Tilly even knows about it." Delta noticed that her customers had selected the sticker sheets they wanted and had come to the cash register. "Sorry, have to help them first."

She gave them a special price, chatted about what they had in mind for the workshop, and then saw them off. As she shut the door, her mind focused again on what Ray had told her. She said to him, "I'll give Rosalyn a call to ask what she agreed to exactly. I'm afraid I'll have to explain to her that it wasn't Mrs. VanderHurst's decision to make after all."

"Fine, but don't mention that I told you. She'll think I ran here to complain or something." He leaned over closer and whispered, "She's not a fan of Hazel as it is. You know she wasn't happy, either, with Finn dating Isabel."

Isabel was Ray and Rosalyn's younger sister. Rosalyn had never supported Isabel's relationship with Hazel's brother Finn.

Ray confided, "Now that he's out of town, she's trying to get Isabel to break it off with him."

"Explicitly?" Delta asked.

"No, more subtly. She points out that Finn could call or email more often. She introduces Isabel to nice men whom she thinks more suitable. That sort of thing." Ray shrugged. "Anyway, she's eager to erase Finn from the family, and I don't think she'd be happy if his sister got into it now."

"But you are determined that you want to know Hazel better?" Delta asked.

Ray held her gaze. "I don't know exactly what I feel for Hazel. Maybe it's just that she keeps turning me down. It intrigues me."

Delta knew Ray usually pretended to take life easy, and he was deeper than he showed. "So it's the thrill of the hunt?" she said with a raised eyebrow.

Ray laughed softly. "You know it's more than that, Delta. Especially now with this trouble in town, the shop being maligned and all, I want to protect Hazel, offer her a shoulder to lean on. But she's so independent she doesn't seem to need it at all. Maybe I'm wasting my time. I want to have tried." He looked past her. "I think she's almost done with those customers."

"Good. Then I'm going into the back to call Rosalyn." Delta winked at him and disappeared. She took a deep breath while selecting the phone number. She and Rosalyn had never gotten along very well, and, although Rosalyn wasn't the type to be openly hostile, she never missed an opportunity to let Delta feel she had come to Tundish recently and wasn't really a part of the community yet. That she still had to earn her place.

"Lodge Hotel, the manager speaking."

"Hi, Rosalyn, it's me, Delta. I heard a rumor that you're sending someone over to collect the display in the morning?"

"Yes. I wanted to call you about it. It's better for all parties. With the display in town people will keep talking about it. If it's here, the tension can evaporate. That's how the VanderHursts feel, and I want to respect their opinion."

"The VanderHursts?" Delta feigned confusion. "How would they be entitled to make this decision?"

"Tabitha is Tilly's sister, and she always fought hard to give her a decent life. She can't help it that Tilly is so eccentric. She only wants what is best for her."

It sounded like words straight from Tabitha's own mouth.

Delta countered, "The display belongs to Tilly. She's entitled to decide where it is and who takes care of it. She agreed with me to have it on display here for two weeks."

Rosalyn sighed. "Delta, you have to see the truth." She

didn't say it in a harsh tone, more like a teacher explaining something to the kid in class who's always last to catch on. "Wanted is under fire. People aren't happy you got shop-keeper of the season and then were embroiled in murder."

"You make it sound like I personally killed someone," Delta protested, but Rosalyn kept talking as if she hadn't even heard.

"They're clamoring for you to return the title. That would be a tremendous loss of face. It would harm your business beyond belief. I don't want you to go through that. I'm taking the thing off your hands. Also, for Hazel's sake." She sniffed. "After all, she's the sister of the man my sister might marry."

"I thought you never were in favor of the marriage between Finn and Isabel." Delta couldn't resist saying.

"People misunderstand my meaning. I'm not an emotional person. I tend to see things rationally and think about the long-term consequences. It's very important to me that people I care for don't make rash decisions and harm themselves. I'm only asking Isabel to test the depth of her feelings for Finn. To protect her from an impromptu alliance she will later regret. You don't have sisters, Delta, so you don't understand how that is."

Delta felt attacked a moment and blinded by a need to

retaliate, but then her mind refocused on the issue at hand. "I appreciate your concern for us, Rosalyn, but you never asked whether we wanted you to take the display off our hands. Worse than that, you didn't ask Tilly what she wanted. I can't imagine her walking in here to see her display and find out it was taken somewhere else without her knowledge."

"The Lodge is a high-class venue. It's not like her display is taken to a garbage dump." Rosalyn's voice trembled with anger. "I'm only trying to do you and her a favor."

"Or do the VanderHursts a favor? Hoping their friends will then come stay at the Lodge?" Delta was tempted to burst Rosalyn's bubble by revealing the strain the marriage was under and the real possibility she'd never get to entertain the high-profile guests she was now hoping for.

But sensitive information like that, collected to help the case, shouldn't be shared, especially not out of spite.

Rosalyn would probably not even believe me.

"They're decent people," Rosalyn said, "unfortunately caught up in a very stressful situation. They want to avoid any form of association with the lowly criminal their sister married."

"Then why would they push for the display to be brought to the Lodge? Doesn't that strengthen the connection?"

"Look, Delta, this discussion is pointless, we obviously don't see eye to eye. The transport is paid for, and the display will be moved tomorrow morning. With or without your consent. Good day." And Rosalyn disconnected.

Delta lowered her phone. This was so not going to happen. She had to talk to Tilly. She dialed Mrs. Cassidy's number and soon heard a friendly, "Hello?"

"It's me, Delta. I just heard the oddest thing." She told her friend what had happened when Ray came to the store. Mrs. Cassidy listened without comment to the entire story, including Rosalyn's infuriating conviction. Delta ended with, "We must ask Tilly to stop them. This is too much."

"I wonder." Mrs. Cassidy sounded thoughtful.

"Whether they are doing the right thing? Do you think they know better?" Delta was taken aback a moment. Mrs. Cassidy was now housing Tilly, so maybe she had seen a side to her that convinced her Tilly was better off listening to her well-meaning relatives.

"I wonder why the VanderHursts want to have that display nearby. If it's at the Lodge, all the hotel guests can come and look at it. Meaning *they* can come and look at it."

"They can look at it right here," Delta retorted automatically.

"Yes, in full view. During opening hours. If the display is at the hotel, they can get to it in the middle of the night."

"In the middle of the... Why on earth would they want that?"

"I don't know. But remember how the van was ransacked? And we thought someone was looking for something? What if the VanderHursts are looking for something? And they think it's hidden in the display?"

Delta's jaw sagged. "Why would they want to search for something hidden in the display their eccentric sister made?"

"I don't know. It's just a thought." Mrs. Cassidy sounded apologetic. "Maybe I watched too many murder mysteries on TV."

Delta grinned. "No, you could be right, of course. The van was ransacked. And the police don't know why. It could all be connected."

Mrs. Cassidy said, "Maybe you should just let them have the display and then make a plan with Ray to have Jonas keep watch at the hotel, and, once they come into the boardroom in the dead of night to search the display, he can arrest them."

"Jonas can't arrest anyone, as he's no longer with the police." Delta clutched the phone. "And just coming into a room where a miniature town is on display isn't a crime.

Besides, Rosalyn will never agree to setting up some...trap at the Lodge."

"Rosalyn need not know about it, if you go through Ray."

Delta bit her lip. Rosalyn already disliked her and Hazel. If they did something that Rosalyn would consider a violation of her position at the Lodge, they'd certainly make a lasting enemy of her. And Hazel might have a future ahead of her with Ray. Wasn't her personal happiness more important than the off chance of solving the murder by catching the VanderHursts red-handed at the display?

Delta said, "I'll think about it. Thanks for sharing with me. Just for the moment don't tell Tilly, okay?"

"Fine with me. Have a nice day."

A nice day? Delta felt like she hadn't had a nice day in ages. It was all so complicated. What to do next? How to make progress?

She peeked into the store. Hazel was at the counter staring down at something. Ray was nowhere in sight. Delta snuck in, tiptoeing up to her friend. The thing she was looking at was a ticket. To that antiques show Ray had mentioned?

Delta said, "Sorry to have kept you waiting. I was on the phone. Are you all right? You look a little out of sorts."

Hazel snatched up the ticket and turned away, slipping

it into her pocket. "I'm fine. I was just…working out a few figures."

Delta felt a little stab that her friend didn't confide in her, but she understood how confusing matters of the heart could be.

Nevertheless, she asked, in an innocent tone, "Did you catch Ray? He dropped by for a minute."

"Yes, we chatted." Hazel turned fiery red. "About the bad weather really having messed up some things they planned at the Lodge. Small stuff."

Delta nodded. "Did he mention Rosalyn making a deal with Tilly's sister about the display?"

Hazel looked bewildered. "What display?"

"This one." Delta stood beside it. She let her gaze wander the small houses and people going about their business. Then she sank to her knees and looked underneath it, studying the construction. Could you hide something in it? Had Tilly put an item there? Something valuable? Or a paper? Connected with her husband's scams?

The killer had been in here that night putting the prospector with the mattock in his back outside the boardinghouse. But why? Had it been about that alleged clue? Or about checking the display for hiding places?

Delta crawled underneath to look better.

Hazel asked, "What are you doing?"

Delta lowered herself so she could turn over and study the display's bottom. "I'm not sure. I wonder if there's something hidden in this thing. I can't see any levers or..."

"You read too many books. Why would it have levers?"

"Tilly might have used it to store something safely. Who would look here?"

"But the guys who build the display for her take it apart. Wouldn't they find something?"

"You're right. It can't be in the construction. It has to be hidden in the models themselves." Delta wormed her way out from underneath with a groan. "But I won't be touching the models. I would be afraid to break something. Tilly put so much time and effort into them."

Hazel leaned back on her heels. "You do have a point that it is odd that the VanderHursts are so eager to move the thing to the Lodge. What for? They don't seem to be fans of Tilly's work, per se. I haven't even seen them in here yet."

"I saw in a video Jane's husband made how Tabitha was at the door the morning of the opening, but she never came in. I wonder why. And Bessie overheard Tabitha at the Lodge talking to the director of a museum in Helena, about putting up a permanent exhibition of Tilly's work. She may be after control of her sister's work. It's worth something."

"But they have enough money."

"Jonas shared with me that the VanderHursts' marriage is in trouble. He wants to divorce her, and she signed a prenup and won't get a thing. I should ask Jonas to check that out further." Delta got her phone from the back. "I'll ask him right away."

She called his cell, tapping her foot impatiently, her head full of thoughts.

"Hello, Paula speaking."

Delta froze. She stammered, "Sorry? What?"

"This is Paula."

The female voice was unmistakable. Paula was answering Jonas's phone.

Delta hesitated. She wanted to say she had a wrong connection and hang up. But that would be the cowardly thing to do. She needed to push through and find out, for better or worse, what was going on here. "Hi, it's Delta. Is Jonas there?"

"Yes, but he's hanging up some paintings, so he can't come to the phone right now."

Paintings? In their home? The place where they were going to live together?

Delta immediately had this mental image of Jonas holding up the painting and asking Paula if it was straight. The tenderness of the scene hit her like a knock against the chin. This wasn't supposed to happen. Jonas was hers.

Hers?

No, of course not, but she did know that he meant a whole lot more to her than just some friend.

"Okay," she said with difficulty, "I'll call back later." Her heart pounded violently under her breastbone. Why hadn't Jonas told her outright Paula was his girlfriend? Why hadn't he introduced her like that when they had met?

Delta pressed a hand against her temple. It need not be like that, she tried to reason with herself. Maybe Paula asked him to hang a painting or two in her own home. To spend time with Jonas? Maybe they weren't an item yet, but was Paula pushing for it?

Then there was still time, however little, for Delta to act. To tell Jonas how she felt and win him for herself.

Her courage sank at the idea, and she wondered if she could ever really do that.

Hazel peeked in. "Did you talk to Jonas? What did he say? Are we suspecting too much? Might be with all that's been going on."

"He didn't answer his phone." Delta wished she didn't sound so squeaky.

Hazel narrowed her eyes as if she had heard and wanted to ask something. But Delta's phone rang. It was Jonas.

So he could call her back. Delta accepted with a shivery "Hello?"

"Hey, Delta. Paula said it was you, and I wanted to know what was up right away. There aren't any problems, are there? With Buckmore or something?"

"No. But I have to talk to you. One-on-one."

"Okay." He paused, sounding a bit reluctant. "I'm up to my eyebrows in work right now, so can it wait until tonight?"

"Sure." Delta's mind whirled, checking off places that weren't suitable. Not at her home where Hazel might catch something, not at Mine Forever where too many locals hung out. It wasn't summer anymore so they couldn't go for a bike ride or walk. Do it casually. No, they had to meet indoors, protect themselves against the ongoing rain.

"I'll pick you up at seven," Jonas said. "I know just the place."

"Okay. I hope Paula doesn't mind."

He paused again. "I'll be done here by then. See you later."

Delta lowered the phone and exhaled slowly.

Hazel grinned at her. "Is it a date? You're so smart, getting a meeting out of it and…"

"It's not funny." Delta walked past her into the shop again. Fortunately, customers had come in and were browsing. She wanted to be very busy so she didn't have time to worry about tonight.

Chapter Nineteen

JONAS PICKED HER UP AROUND SEVEN AS HE HAD PROMISED and drove her along the dark road. The rain hadn't ceased at all and washed in rivulets across the windows. Delta shivered, ducking deeper into her coat. Even indoors you could feel the chill of late fall seeping through.

Jonas glanced at her. "I didn't get far with Buckmore. I've been making a list of known victims of the pyramid scheme, people who went public about their losses during the trial, but I can't establish a direct tie between any of them and Buckmore. I looked especially close at Adam Baker and Cheryl Remington, as they were also here in town when the murder occurred. But no tie I can see. I also couldn't connect Buckmore with Weatherspoon in any way. So I'm not sure what to think. Was he after revenge? Or involved in the scheme and eager to keep Weatherspoon away from the loot? Why did Weatherspoon come to Tundish of all places? For Buckmore or someone else?"

Delta raked a hand through her hair and said, "On one hand, I hope he's not involved, as I'd feel terrible that a criminal came close to Gran, but, on the other hand, if the police picked him up and it would be crystal clear he's bad, I need not tell her and risk my bond with her. I haven't felt so confused in a long time."

Jonas gripped the wheel tighter. "Is that why you wanted to talk one-on-one?"

"It's just that..." *I think you're dating Paula, and I want to date you? No, that is impossible to say.* "How did the paintings come along? This afternoon?"

"No diversions, Delta. What is the matter?" Jonas glanced at her. "I know I should wait until we're at the restaurant, nicely set up with our drinks and waiting for our specials, but..."

Picturing this, him across from her toasting her then focusing on her with his interested eyes, she knew she'd clam up. Now or never. "I thought we were friends."

"We are. Who told you we're not?"

"I just... I feel a little disconnected from you. I'm not sure whether it's the thing with Gran messing with my feelings or..." Delta clenched her hands. "This is probably all very silly to you."

"I never felt before like you were folding under pressure. Why now?"

Delta shrugged. She didn't dare look at him.

Jonas said, "Oh, well, maybe situations do get to people and change them from how they usually are. Paula is having so much wedding stress. I would never have believed it."

Wedding stress. Delta's muscles tightened. "So, she's getting married? When?"

"In two weeks. There is still so much to do it drives me crazy."

Me? He meant her right? Or did he mean me? Was he...

Delta struggled to breathe evenly. "What do you still have to do?"

"Find a ring bearer. Get the right flowers for the venue's decoration. The ones they suggested weren't to Paula's liking." He rolled his eyes. "I have never known she could be such a diva. A real bridezilla."

Delta faked a laugh. "Poor you." Sweat filled her palms. "Of course, I'm happy for her." *You. Come on, say it. You can do it.*

"Yeah, well, when she asked me to be best man, I thought it would be easy. Paula had always been down-to-earth and undemanding, not fussy or anything. I thought it would take me a few hours of my time, and now... She calls me for every little detail. Do this, arrange for that." He waved a hand in the air. "Last week, I felt like telling her to find someone else for the lousy job. But we've been friends for so long, and she once saved my life. I owe her, right?"

"Best man?" Delta repeated. The fog in her brain didn't allow her to fully grasp this.

"Yes." He glanced at her. "And don't ask how she saved my life. I don't want to talk about that tonight."

Jonas was best man. Not groom. He wasn't marrying Paula. Paula was marrying someone else.

"That's great," Delta said with a grin that almost pulled her face apart.

Jonas frowned. "It's great that I don't want to talk about a major life event? I thought you'd be ruffled."

"Not at all. Whatever you want to do. I'm fine with it. Totally fine."

Jonas gave her a suspicious look. "You sound a bit hysterical. Maybe you're closer to the edge than you think. With the murder, Wanted involved and all..."

"I have news to share about that." Delta dared look at him again. "Important stuff you can help me with."

Was it a flash of disappointment she saw in his eyes? She didn't really know, as she was so ridiculously relieved that he wasn't marrying Paula—wasn't even dating her or anything. It was all perfectly fine.

Jonas turned into a parking lot and stopped the Jeep. "I hope you like this place. They serve great turkey specialties. With Thanksgiving coming up…"

Delta smiled at him. "I'm grateful to have a friend like you."

Jonas put his hand on hers a moment. "You can count on me, you know that."

She held his gaze. The relief inside of her wanted out, in a mad moment of throwing herself into his arms. But, as she had just saved their friendship and the potential they had, she wasn't going to risk it now. She gestured at the lit building ahead. "Shall we? I can't wait to see what they have on the menu."

_____

They had finished their turkey roast with mashed potatoes and mixed vegetables from the grill and were into their dessert. Jonas had listened intently to her story about the latest developments and now said, "But if the VanderHursts want access to the display, what could they actually gain by that?"

Delta gestured. "I don't know. I just thought it was odd, considering that they also wanted to pay for the lawyer Mrs. Cassidy hired and then get access to the information that Marjorie Brenning has on the case. It seems they want to be in control of everything."

Jonas nodded slowly. "Maybe it's just damage control? They're worried this case will make a splash in the media, reaching into their circles, over time, and they think that, if they hold all the cards, they can determine the game. As an investment banker, he must be used to making a risk calculation."

"I bet. Well, anyway, I wanted you to know it all. The idea to set a trap at the Lodge might not be totally bad, but I can't see Rosalyn agreeing with it." Delta looked up at Jonas. "After Hazel's suggestion to lure Buckmore into stealing something at our cottage to expose himself, you might think we've gone overboard with our plans to frame people."

"Maybe just a little," Jonas held her gaze. "But I can't blame you for caring."

Delta stared into the warmth radiating from his eyes and wondered why she had ever thought Paula meant anything to him.

Jonas said, "I have a little plan of my own."

Caught up in a fuzzy blur, it took Delta a moment to catch on. "Sorry?"

"A plan. To maybe catch a killer."

Now he had her full attention. "What? A killer? You think you know who the killer is?"

"It's only a guess based on what we know right now. But it's worth a try. We have a chance to do it." Jonas put a bite of crème brûlée ice cream in his mouth.

"Don't stretch the suspense. What is it?"

"The VanderHursts asked for the lawyer to work for them, right? If Marjorie Brenning agreed to that offer, she would have to share some information about the case with them. What if she told them something that they would have to act on?"

"Wait a minute. You think that the VanderHursts are involved in the death of that man at the motel? Bob Weatherspoon, the ex they hadn't been in touch with for years? Why?"

"Remember that the profits from his scams were never recovered? What if the investment banker, Tilly's brother-in-law, found a way to make them disappear? He had control of them while her ex was in jail. Bob kept his mouth shut to protect the money. If he spoke up, the police would confiscate it, and he'd have nothing. Now he counted on coming out of jail and pressuring his brother-in-law into handing over the funds, or part of it. Remember he told his son Noel it was payday?"

"Yes, you're right." Delta sat up. "Go on."

"Bob Weatherspoon comes out of jail and contacts his brother-in-law VanderHurst. The investment banker agrees to a meeting. He chooses Tundish, since Tilly is exhibiting here and the police might suspect her of the murder. He kills Bob, eliminating any danger of ever being exposed and creates a trail leading straight to Tilly."

"But why show his face? Why involve himself in the case, asking for the lawyer to work for him and…"

"He must somehow think there is evidence of his involvement and he wants to find it and destroy it before it lands with the police. That explains the search of the van."

"And the demand to have the display taken to the Lodge."

"Close to him." Jonas nodded. "It all fits. So what I'm thinking of is this. We ask Marjorie, Tilly's lawyer, to pretend she accepts their offer to pay for her representation. Marjorie then gives them false information about the case, perhaps items Tilly has stashed that the police are interested in—something that could clear Tilly's name for good. VanderHurst will have to make sure they are not posing any danger to him, so, when he goes to track them down, we are there to catch him in the act, and voilà. Case solved."

Delta pursed her lips. "Are we going to do it without assistance from the police?"

"I doubt I can interest West in such a scheme. I don't have hard proof of their involvement, and they are reputable people. He won't want to cross them."

"So it's us." Delta nodded slowly. "Do you think Tabitha VanderHurst is involved as well? Do we have to expect two opponents?"

"I don't think so. Remember VanderHurst wants to divorce her? My guess is he plans on divorcing her so he can do what he wants with his illegal gains without her catching on. She tried to prevent the divorce, even taking him to marriage counseling, but I think he never meant for that therapy to be successful. He's going through the motions while working on his own plan."

"Clever. Well, if we have to deal with him alone, I guess it can work. We did it before."

Jonas picked up his glass. "To a gamble that will hopefully pay off."

Chapter Twenty

"I'M NOT TOO SURE ABOUT THIS NOW." DELTA STOOD SHIV-
ering in the wind that breathed from the direction of the
Lodge. It seemed to invite her with its warm lights to forget
about this whole trap and come on in for a nice hot drink.

Jonas said, "You can go inside if you want to. I can do it
alone." Spud by his side made a soft sound as if he wanted to
say, *You're not alone; I'm here.*

Delta smiled. "No, we're in this together." She turned
her head to look at Tilly's van, which had been brought in
by the police earlier that day and parked beside the stable.
It had been carefully combed for evidence and had now
been released to the owner. But, instead of taking it to Mrs.
Cassidy's house, where Tilly was still staying, it had been
brought here. Marjorie, who had been instructed by Jonas,

had informed the VanderHursts that the van was better off under their supervision for the moment, as Tilly had let on to her that something was hidden inside that the police might need to clear her. To ensure its safety, Marjorie had stressed, it had to be kept in a secure place. This was bound to make the VanderHursts believe that they were not considered suspects and would hopefully induce Virgil VanderHurst to act, tonight. The display was also here, in the boardroom, having been transferred that morning.

Delta had felt kind of sad to see it go, but it was all part of the plan to let the VanderHursts have what they wanted, make them feel secure enough so they got careless and betrayed themselves. West wasn't aware of their suspicions or their plans but had just given the important people what they asked for. Jonas had said he couldn't blame him for wanting to avoid commotion, as people with money could sometimes make things very difficult for officers of the law. "And he's not violating any rules by letting them see to some of the suspect's property while the case is still ongoing."

Maybe not, Delta thought, but the VanderHursts weren't treating Tilly very respectfully.

Jonas whispered, "What if I'm wrong about them? They could be sitting over wine now, in the lounge, close to a nice warm fireplace, and we're standing here in the cold wind, getting absolutely nothing for our efforts except maybe an epic head cold."

Delta moved a bit closer to him. "We have to try for Tilly's sake. And to clear Wanted's reputation. This morning, when the men came to take the display away, people in the street were actually applauding. It felt so…awkward. And one woman said, as she walked past Hazel and me, 'You better pack up as well.'"

"Really? I had no idea the atmosphere was so hostile."

"Well, not with everyone, obviously. The Paper Posse supports us all the way, and they have been using their contacts to put in a word for us. But some people are very upset by what happened. They think the tourists might stay away with word of a violent murder at the local motel around." Delta shrugged. "Some businesses are really struggling, so I can't blame them for being afraid that the tourists will avoid Tundish in favor of other towns, and it will be even harder to make a living and survive the winter months."

Jonas leaned down to her. "You're so understanding, it's amazing. You could just think *get off my case*."

Delta looked into his eyes and wished she could just tell him how wonderful she thought he was.

Gravel crunched under a footfall, and Jonas and Delta ducked deeper into the shadows beside the stable. A dark figure moved, stopping every few paces to look over his shoulder. At last, apparently reassured there was no one following him from the Lodge, he halted at the van and pulled out a key to open the door.

Jonas glanced at Delta. They had agreed that, if someone came, they would let them get in and look first, instead of jumping them right away. Because the VanderHursts had kindly taken it upon themselves to care for Tilly's things, as they saw it, they could always claim they were just having a look that everything was secure for the night and laugh off the idea it had anything to do with the murder.

Delta's heart raced. She had been very nervous about whether VanderHurst would see through the ruse and refuse to engage.

However, someone was there now...

They heard shuffling noises inside the van as the figure was busy searching. Jonas held his hand on Spud's collar. The dog was very quiet, but his focus was fully on the van, convincing Delta that he knew exactly what the target of the night was.

They heard something fall over and muttered words. Then

the shuffling resumed. Jonas gestured to Delta to stay put, with Spud, and went a little closer himself. He obviously wanted to see what the intruder was doing inside the van.

As the police had looked at the van's contents, and not found anything, it was natural to assume that Tilly's "evidence" was well hidden and would take some clever searching to unearth. Maybe VanderHurst thought that, because he was family, he understood Tilly's mindset and could uncover her hiding place?

Jonas was at the van and peered in through a window. At that moment, a bang came from the inside. Delta perked up. Spud moved forward, but she stopped him by grabbing the leash tighter. He stopped and stood, his ears forward, staring hard at the van.

Jonas wanted to step away, but he was too late. Already, the intruder appeared from the doorway, pointing something at Jonas. Delta thought it had to be the flashlight he had used to find his way inside the van. But, as she caught better sight of the shape of it, her heart skipped a beat. It was a gun.

Not a flashlight. Not a knife. A gun.

Jonas stood too far away from the intruder to reach him, and, if the man tried to approach, Jonas would defend himself. Delta was convinced he was great at hand-to-hand combat and could disarm someone, especially if that someone was an untrained fifty-something civilian. But the intruder had a gun. Jonas couldn't approach him without running the risk of being shot.

Delta felt Spud move. His neck hairs stood up, but he didn't make a sound.

Delta heard Jonas say, "This is pointless. I know why you are here and what you are looking for. The police released the van on purpose to lure you out into the open."

The man laughed softly. "Nice try, but no dice. The police released the van because we requested it. The sheriff eats out of our hands." It was unmistakably the arrogant tones of Virgil VanderHurst. "So does that little blond lady lawyer. And I heard about you. Sheriff West told me you're a regular pain in the neck. You think you can still play cop about town. But you're not an officer anymore. And you don't carry arms. I, on the other hand, am a very good shot. I wouldn't take any chances if I were you."

Jonas put up his hands, palms out, in a pleading gesture. "I don't want a shoot-out. I underestimated you. I hadn't expected you to come armed. Except, perhaps, with the knife you used to stab poor Bob Weatherspoon."

"Poor? He was a vile little man. A blackmailer." Contempt

dripped from the words. "Do you think I let people pressure me? Not even people who are worth ten times what he was. He was a nobody. It wasn't hard to kill him. He never saw it coming. That was his problem. He always had plans but never any foresight."

"Which was why he went to jail and you enjoyed the profits off his fraudulent scheme."

"You make it sound so despicable. It was simply a very good business deal."

"And Tilly?" Jonas asked. "Did you never think twice about involving that poor woman in your crime? Leaving a clue in her display pointing straight at her?"

"That was a rather nice touch." VanderHurst sounded smug. "Weatherspoon told me that he believed the victims of the pyramid scheme were hot on his trail. I thought that it couldn't hurt to suggest that they were by leaving a threat against Tilly in the display and sending the key to Wanted to that local super-snoop Marc LeDuc. I knew he'd unearth the link to the pyramid scheme in a heartbeat. Then those pathetic whiners Remington and Baker even popped up at the police station demanding access to Tilly. It was perfect. The sheriff didn't know where to turn, who to suspect. Maybe they ransacked the van? Maybe they came after Tilly's dog?"

"But it was you all along," Jonas said. "You sent us all on a wild-goose chase."

Delta assumed the faint note of awe in Jonas's voice was part of an act to reassure VanderHurst and then overpower him.

"In the end, I always get what I want," the banker said. "Money does that for you. It can buy reputation, support, friends. Do you never crave money? I bet you do. You tell yourself you're happy with what you got, your little home, your old car, your time off in the woods." Again, he sounded disparaging. "But you have no idea what real life is. Having yachts, houses in all major cities, being able to buy what you want, whenever you want it. Hop on a plane and see the sunset in Paris. Freedom."

"I have freedom right here," Jonas said. His voice was passionate. "In the forests with the deer and the birds, walking around, listening to the sound of the rain on the leaves."

VanderHurst laughed. "Great. And I will gladly leave you to it. I don't want to hurt you. But you're letting me go." He gestured with the gun to the van's open door. "In there."

Jonas hesitated. Delta could feel his muscles tense as if he got ready to jump his opponent. Her breathing grew shallow. If he did act, VanderHurst would shoot. Jonas would get hurt. He would be injured right in front of her eyes.

Did she have to release Spud? She knew the dog would come to his human's aid. But then VanderHurst might shoot Spud. Could she live with the dog dying because she had made the wrong decision? What did Jonas expect her to do?

Why hadn't they agreed on an emergency plan?

"In there," VanderHurst snapped. Jonas took a step forward. But the man wasn't stupid enough the let him get close and risk a struggle and loss of the gun. He moved back and gestured again. "Get in. *Now*. Before I get impatient and give you an incentive."

"You won't shoot. The sound carries far."

"Nice try, but this gun has a silencer. As you've already seen. Stop bluffing me and get moving."

Jonas stepped up to the van and put his foot inside. He grabbed the doorframe with both hands. Delta was certain he was ready to execute some plan, maybe swing his weight up and attack VanderHurst, but the investment banker wasn't close enough to disarm him in a single movement. No doubt he would fire, and it would be a matter of luck whether Jonas got hit or not.

Delta's hands were slick with sweat. She had to release the dog. But the idea that VanderHurst would shoot Spud... Jonas might never forgive her. Why didn't she know what to do?

Suddenly a dark figure appeared around the side of the van, behind VanderHurst. He yelled, "Down!" to Jonas and, at the same time, hit the gunman with something. A shot popped, faintly, like a cork escaping from a bottle, and VanderHurst sagged to the ground.

At the yell, Jonas had thrown himself into the van. Delta stood there with her eyes wide, not believing what had just happened. Had Jonas gotten someone to help them? A deputy? Why had he not told her? She might have made a move and spoiled the plan.

The figure leaning over the fallen assailant called to Jonas, "Lend me a hand tying him up, will you?"

Jonas appeared from the van and said, "Major Buckmore? What are you doing here?"

Delta couldn't believe her eyes. She rushed over with Spud pulling ahead of her, eager to be reunited with Jonas. "Are you all right?" she asked him breathlessly. "Didn't you get hit?"

"The bullet went wide." Jonas sat on his knees beside Buckmore helping him tie VanderHurst's hands with a length of rope. Beside Buckmore was a piece of wood he had used to strike at the killer.

Jonas took a deep breath before asking again, "What are you doing here?"

Buckmore said, looking up at Delta, "Your gran was worried about you. She thought you might do something silly to find the killer and clear Tilly Tay's name, because the atmosphere in town had turned against Wanted. I promised her I'd keep an eye on you. I've been following you all day. Actually, I've been following this investigation this whole time. I bet you never noticed."

Delta shook her head, still in shock.

Buckmore said, "It might be a while ago that I was in active service, but I still remember how to take down an enemy." He looked at Jonas. "It wasn't very smart of you to assume he'd be unarmed."

Jonas looked annoyed. "I've done this before."

Buckmore rose to his feet. "Of course." He flicked some dirt off his trousers' knees.

"I do want to thank you," Delta said to make up for Jonas's brusque approach. "You came at the exact right moment."

Buckmore smiled at her. "That's the secret of any good military campaign. Timing."

Jonas pulled VanderHurst to his feet. He stood swaying. Jonas said softly, "You love your money because it can buy you what you crave most in life. Freedom. But it's over now.

You will have to give back what you took. And you will never be free again."

The man held his head low and didn't reply. Buckmore picked up the gun, which had fallen from his hand, and put the safety on. "Nice little toy," he observed. "Shall I call the police?"

Chapter Twenty-One

"I still can't believe it was Buckmore who saved the day," Hazel said with a sour expression. "After all the bad things we believed about him…"

"Because one woman told us that he might be a danger to little old ladies." Delta pointed a finger at her. "It goes to prove that you should never believe a single story. I still have no idea why she said that but…" She leaned closer to Hazel and added, "I'm not one hundred percent sure, either, that Buckmore can be trusted. But he saved Jonas's life, so I do owe him for that. I want to give him a chance and see what he is about. Gran likes him so much."

She cast a loving look at her grandmother, who was walking around the display with Buckmore by her side. The light from the lamps above shimmered in the diamond earrings she wore and the glass of champagne in her hand.

The exhibition of Tilly Tay's work had been reopened tonight, festively, at the Lodge, with drinks, snacks, live music, and dancing. Ray had said it was fitting, as Tilly deserved a nice night out after all she had been through. She was allowed to live in her van on the Lodge's grounds and have breakfast at the hotel each morning. She had more color on her cheeks now that her troubles were over, and Buddy was tripping along cheerfully by her side. Every now and then, he dashed off to find Nugget, and they chased each other under the display.

"To think we believed it held a precious secret," Hazel said with an eyeroll.

Delta laughed. "It might have. VanderHurst certainly suggested it by ransacking the van and coming to Mrs. Cassidy's house once Buddy was there. We all believed that Tilly held something valuable and was somehow connected to the pyramid scheme."

She bit her lip a moment, sadness washing over her as she remembered VanderHurst's callous words when he had been caught by Jonas. "He used the pyramid scheme victims all over again by letting the police believe the murder might have been an act of revenge. He knew victims were on Weatherspoon's trail because he had told him so before he died. Poor Cheryl Remington and Adam Baker, playing right into his plan by their appearance at the police station to find out what Tilly knew about the money."

"But at least, with VanderHurst's arrest, they have a real chance of getting their money back," Hazel said optimistically. "That should be some consolation."

"I only hope it doesn't take ages. Bureaucracy can be a real pain," Delta observed. "But, still, the prospect of finally reaping the reward of all their efforts must cheer them up. And Mrs. Cassidy told me that Marjorie Brenning wants to support them, free of charge. I hope that, with the right help, they can put that dark time in their lives behind them."

Sven LeDuc appeared by their sides and toasted them with his half-full glass. "I just had a lovely chat with Tilly Tay," he said. "I'm running her life's story as a special feature for the next three Saturday editions. She has been to so many fascinating places, and she also told me she puts clues in her work. I want to know all about that." Before they could even respond, he walked off to tell his news to someone else.

Ray passed him with a short greeting and extended a hand to Hazel. "Care to dance?"

Hazel flushed and looked at Delta. Delta pulled the glass from her friend's hand and said, "Off you go." She smiled as she watched Ray guide Hazel to where other couples were swaying to the music and put his arms around her. It seemed Hazel was a bit more open to the idea of a relationship.

She checked her watch. It was close to ten-thirty. Jonas had texted her that he was busy with preparations for Paula's wedding and couldn't make the exact opening hour, but he would do his very best to drop in later that night. Now she had a sinking feeling he wasn't coming at all.

"What a wonderful night." Gran stood beside her. "George is off to top up our drinks."

"Champagne goes to your head, you know," Delta said with a smile.

Gran held her gaze. "I know you're thinking, what is this, with a man suddenly stepping in and taking my grandmother away from me? But I will always love you, Delta, no matter what happens with George and me. I do want to find a place for us to live together. I'm not moving in with him. Or marrying him. At least not right now."

Delta's eyes widened. Marrying? Was Gran really thinking about that? She took a deep breath. "I think the major is wonderful after he saved Jonas's life. But he did say something once I found rather peculiar. I mean, we hardly know him. It's best to be a little cautious of who you let into your life." This wasn't coming out the way she had planned it. She had meant to talk to Gran about it in a loving tone and show she understood but was also concerned.

Gran's eyes stayed tender. "I do appreciate your concern, Delta, but I know the full story. George told it to me."

"What full story?"

"Of this woman who spreads rumors about him. Who is convinced he's some trickster, after old ladies. He said it's sad that she believes that and won't be persuaded otherwise, not even after the police told her that she is wrong."

"They didn't tell her she is wrong," Delta corrected. "They told her that they had no evidence of his involvement in anything shady."

"That's the same thing to me," Gran nodded firmly. "I implicitly trust George. He's a good man. Else he would not have risked his own safety to protect you and Jonas. For my sake." Her smile deepened. "He's a wonderful man. And I feel very lucky I met him." She reached out and caressed Delta's cheek. "Enjoy tonight, honey." Then she turned away.

Delta watched her walk off, light on her feet, rushing toward the man, who handed her a fresh drink and offered her his arm. It was nice to see Gran well cared for and happy. But, deep down inside, Delta knew that what her grandmother had said wasn't true. That, even without evidence, people could be criminals. Just think of the decent investment banker Virgil VanderHurst who had been free, living a life of luxury all those years when his brother-in-law had been in prison for the crimes they had committed together.

"Surprise, surprise…" A hand covered her eyes a moment and then pulled away. She turned to face Jonas. He smiled at her and held something up with his other hand. It was a long paper-wrapped parcel. "A present for you."

"For me? Why? It's not my birthday."

"But you got shopkeeper of the season. You got it, and then you earned it again by exposing the real killer and clearing Tilly Tay's name."

"I did that with a lot of help from others. You, foremost."

Jonas put the parcel in her hands. "Open it." He seemed a bit nervous, moving his weight from one foot to the other.

That rubbed off on Delta, and her mouth was dry as she folded the wrapping paper away. It was a long dark box with a jeweler's name on it. She opened it and saw a silver necklace resting on blue cottonwool. On the end was a small pencil with a single clear diamond forming the tip.

"I thought it was very appropriate for the owner of a stationery shop," Jonas said.

Delta looked up with a wide smile. "It's so pretty. Thanks. But you need not have..."

"Shhh, don't say it." Jonas picked the necklace from the box and held it up. "May I?"

Delta collected her hair off her neck, and Jonas put the necklace on her, securing it carefully. As the pencil dropped to her skin, her heart did a little dance. A present from Jonas, something he had picked especially for her.

She touched it a moment and then threw her arms around his neck and hugged him. "Thanks so much. I love it, and I will wear it every day."

As she stepped back, there was a moment of breathless silence between them, as if there was more to be said. More to be done as well?

Jonas leaned down and brushed his lips over hers very gently. He inched back to look her in the eye and wait for her response. Delta reached up to run her hand down his cheek. "I should have done this when we were at the cabin. But I didn't have the nerve. You're amazing." And she kissed him.

Everything around them faded, and it was just the two of them, finally giving in to what they had known much longer.

That they shared a special connection. That they were meant to be together.

Something bumped against Delta's legs, and she woke from a daze, tearing herself away from Jonas with difficulty and looking down. It was Buddy, scratching his paw across her leg, asking for attention. Oh, yes, she was at a party with people around her, laughing and talking and celebrating Tilly Tay's success. Flustered, she scooped up the chihuahua and said to Jonas, "Let's find Tilly. She's the guest of honor, and I have barely spoken to her."

Putting his arm around her waist, Jonas walked beside her, and Delta felt like everyone could see she was wearing his necklace. It wasn't a ring or anything, and it didn't mean that he had...that he would...but, still, it made her very happy.

Standing in a corner, with Noel by her side, Tilly welcomed them, reaching out for Buddy. As she took him in her arms, he rested his head in her neck and licked her. Tilly sighed in satisfaction. "You have made everything right. The display looks perfect here, and I love being able to use some of the hotel facilities. Noel offered to play tennis with me sometime when it doesn't rain for a change."

"And I'd love to show you deer." Jonas winked at her. "Might inspire some miniatures?"

Tilly grinned. "I'm certainly inspired by my stay here." She put her hand in her jacket pocket and pulled out something she handed to Delta. When it rested on the palm of her hand, Delta saw it was a mini version of Wanted's sign. "That's too cute. Thanks so much."

"Thank you for all you did. You helped me come to terms with part of my past I had never fully dealt with. I'm sorry my husband died. I hadn't wanted Bob to be killed, and I don't want to think of his final moments. But it always bothered me the money had never been recovered. Now, with Virgil's arrest, it will be and can be given back to his victims. And people won't whisper anymore that I had anything to do with it. A shadow that hung over me for so many years has been lifted, and I can't thank you enough for that."

"We just did what we had to do," Delta said. "Because we're friends here, and we stand together." She let her gaze wander the crowd, detecting the Paper Posse members and their families. Yes, she had so many friends here, and she felt right in place. She was hopeful about the future, even if it was the dry season for a bit. They would make it through together. They would enjoy life in their little town with the heart of gold.

Last Pen Standing

Chapter One

EVEN THOUGH THE SIGN OF HER DESTINATION WAS ALREADY in sight, calling out a warm welcome to Tundish, Montana, "the town with a heart of gold," Delta Douglas couldn't resist the temptation to stop her car, reach for the sketchbook in the passenger seat, and draw the orange-and-gold trees covering a mountain flank all the way to where the snow-peaked top began. From this exact point, their autumnal glory was reflected in the water of a clear blue lake that stretched without a ripple. Delta could just see this image reproduced on wrapping paper, notebooks, or postcards.

Until today, all her ideas for her own line of stationery

products had lived only in her sketchbook, hidden away in her bag while she worked hard at her regular job as a graphic designer for a large advertising agency. But on Delta's thirtieth birthday, Gran had handed her an envelope. The elderly lady had had a mysterious smile that had made Delta's heart race. Leaning over and pecking her on the cheek, Gran had whispered, "Why wait until I'm dead? You're my only granddaughter, and I'd rather have you spend it now, while I'm still here to see what you do with it."

Inside the envelope had been a check for an amount that to some people might have represented a trip around the world, a boat, or the down payment on an apartment. But for Delta, it had symbolized independence—a way to leave her steady but stressful job with too many tight deadlines and finally do what she had always dreamed of: start her own business.

During summer holidays at Gran's as a little girl, Delta had sat at the kitchen table for hours drawing her own postcards, experimenting with watercolors and crayons, charcoal and felt-tips. Gran had arranged for her to man her own stall at the church fair and sell off her creations. It had been amazing to see her work bring in actual money. Some locals had even placed orders with her for Christmas cards, which she made back home and sent out to Gran to distribute. That sense of accomplishment had always stayed with her, and in her free time, she had continued to draw, cut, and paste with purpose, creating a portfolio of fun ideas that brightened her days. And suddenly, with Gran's gift, her own stationery shop was finally within reach.

It hadn't taken Delta long to take the plunge: she handed in her resignation at the agency in downtown Cheyenne, Wyoming, and crossed off the days until she could clear her desk, clean out her apartment, and drive away from the city she had called home for more than seven years. With every mile of her two-day road trip to the Bitterroot Valley, she had felt more excitement rush through her veins. She was now officially her own woman, ready to take a leap of faith and dive into a brand-new adventure in the small community tucked away at the foot of these glorious mountains.

Delta breathed in the spicy air, which still carried the warmth of summer. The sun was high in the sky, and the wind that had been tugging at her car during the ride had finally died down. She felt almost hot in her thigh-length knit vest, black jeans, and boots. Sneakers would have been better, but they were safely packed up in the trunk with the rest of her limited luggage. Since she had rented a furnished apartment in Cheyenne and donated to a charity shop most of the small stuff she didn't want to lug around, she hadn't had to pack a lot of things for the move. Just clothes, her many sketchbooks, pencils and other drawing materials, and laptop. In Tundish, she'd move in with her best friend from college, Hazel, who ran the stationery shop where Delta was going to be co-owner. Her heart beat faster just thinking about it. Her own shop, and the freedom to design products for it. She couldn't wait to get started. Having put the sketchbook with her brand-new autumnal design back on the passenger seat, she hit the gas and zoomed into town.

Tundish had been developed when settlers migrated to Montana for gold and logging. Most houses were made of wood and built in a sturdy Western style, some with dates carved into the front, placing these builds firmly within the nineteenth century. The word *gold* appeared everywhere: in street names, on signs pointing in the direction of an old mine site or to the gold-mining museum. However, Delta wasn't looking for gold. She was on a hunt for something even more precious: the old sheriff's office that housed the shop of her dreams.

Painted powder blue with black trim, the building sat on Mattock Street like a dependable force. It still had the hitching post in front where riders had tied up their horses before storming in to bring word of a bank or train robbery. The faces of the culprits had soon appeared on wanted posters between the barred windows, and even today, such posters were on display, but they no longer advertised the faces of notorious bandits, instead sporting the latest offering in stationery supplies: collectible erasers, washi tape, notebooks, and planners. A chalkboard on the sidewalk invited everyone to a Glitter Galore workshop on Friday night at the Lodge Hotel with a note at the bottom stating: *All materials included and mocktails to celebrate the results.* Sounded like a ton of fun, and Delta would be there.

Her eagerness to take in everything as she drove past had reduced her speed to about zero, and behind her, a car horn honked impatiently. Waving apologetically at the driver, who probably couldn't even see it, Delta accelerated and passed the neighboring hardware store and grocery shop, spying a parking lot beside the town's whitewashed church. She left her car there, then walked back the short stretch to the stationery shop's invitingly open doors. Over them, a wooden plank carried the name *WANTED* in tall letters burned into the wood, underlining that Western vibe. Delta grinned to herself, anticipating Hazel's expression when she saw Delta amble in. She could have called when she was almost there but had decided a surprise was that much more fun.

When she was a few feet away from the doors, her friend darted out of the entrance with a bright-yellow paper arrow gingerly held between the fingers of her outstretched right hand. Whirling to a stop in front of the wanted poster advertising notebooks, Hazel tilted her head to eye the poster, her blond bob swinging around her ears. She positioned the arrow over the right edge of the paper, moving it up and down as if to determine the perfect spot to stick it on. It read *two for one.*

Delta said, "That probably means I'll buy four. Do co-owners get a discount?"

Hazel swung around and whooped, the arrow still dangling from her finger. "Delta! I hadn't expected you yet."

She rushed to Delta and hugged her, then stepped back and held her by the shoulders, looking her over. "It's been too long. I mean, we did chat and all that, but it's not the same as a real meeting in the flesh. I can't believe you'll be living here now! The guest room at my place isn't all that big, but you can find something for yourself soon enough, once leaf-peeping season is over, and the cottages aren't all rented out to tourists who want to snap pictures of the trees."

"I'm in no rush to find something," Delta assured her. "Rooming together will be just like college." She surveyed

Hazel's deep-orange blouse, chocolate-brown pants, and green ankle boots. "Wow, your outfit is fall to the max! Are there boutiques in town with clothes like that?"

"Sure." Hazel pointed across the street. "Right beside Western World, with all those Stetsons and boots on display, we have Bessie's Boutique. I've got a closet full of their pants. They're the perfect fit, and that's so hard to find. Besides, the owner is a friend of mine, so I get first dibs on all the new stock."

"Sounds great. Can I meet this friend?"

"Soon enough. She'll be attending our first workshop together." Hazel gestured at the chalkboard.

"Glitter and mocktails. Sounds posh." Delta nodded at the cocktail glasses drawn beside the workshop title.

Hazel laughed. "On Friday nights, the Lodge Hotel offers live entertainment for the guests and the locals. A big band for dancing, that sort of thing. This Friday night, it's their gold miners' annual party, a sophisticated affair that's a throwback to the hotel's heydays when tourism was just beginning to boom. It's really fun, and I thought we should have the workshop tie in to that. Of course, we'll be in our separate space, away from all the high-profile guests dancing the night away, but hey, at least we'll be able to breathe the glam atmosphere."

"Sounds fabulous. I'll snap some pictures for Gran to show her what I'm up to."

"Great. Now..." Hazel clapped her hands together and said, "Guided tour of my shop. *Our* shop, I should say. Come on in." She led the way through the entrance's double doors.

Delta followed with a pounding heart. She had seen photos of the shop, but she had never been to Tundish in person. This would be her first real-life view of her new enterprise.

Hazel gestured around her at all the warm woodwork and the authentic hearth where a pair of dusty cowboy boots stood ready, as if the sheriff would appear any moment to jump into them and set out with his posse. "This used to be where the sheriff sat to wait for news about a bank robbery or a gang of cattle thieves. You can see that I kept his desk and used it to display the newest notebooks."

Delta jumped toward the notebooks, eager to pick through the stacks and take Hazel up on the two-for-one offer. But Hazel laughed and pulled her away. "No, no browsing yet. First, you have to see the rest. There, along the wall, I have shelves for crafting packages. You can find anything, from designing your own planner to making a birthday calendar. Then in that old cell..."

Hazel walked through a barred door that led into a small

space with a wooden cot pushed against the wall. Above the cot, replicas of original newspaper pages displayed the faces of the Old West's most notorious gang members, some of them smug, others defiant.

"A few of them spent time in here," Hazel explained, gesturing around her. "And I put up that bit of rope"—she gestured to a rope tied around one of the bars in the narrow window—"to refer to all the escape attempts made. They tied the other end of the rope to a horse and gave it a scare so it would gallop off and tear the bar right from the window. Crude and often not very effective."

"I love it." Delta fingered the rope.

"If you have ideas to give it even more atmosphere, just say so. I'm constantly switching it up to attract people who normally might not walk into a stationery shop but who do want to breathe everything Western. In my experience, once they are sold on the shop's atmosphere, they also buy a little something, if only to show their appreciation for the way in which I preserved it."

"You did a great job," Delta said. "And that's all the washi tape?" She pointed at countless glass jars filled with rolls of tape.

"Yup. I have unique offerings from Japan and Australia

that you can't get anywhere else in the country. You should see me salivate when those parcels come in. I was tempted to keep all the ones with the pandas to myself. And in the other cell, I have all the collectible erasers."

Delta followed her into the second cell, which had a rough table against the wall where small glittery objects were lying beside old-fashioned scales and yellowing papers, folded and unfolded so many times that they were torn along the edges. A plasticized card with information warned visitors not to touch the objects because they were authentic and breakable, while also explaining that mining had often been the seed of crime as people sold fake claims or ended up in fights about gold found.

Hazel gestured across the papers. "Real stake claims donated to me by the gold-mining museum. They have a ton of those and didn't mind me having some. They get attention here instead of sitting in an archive."

"I love the fake gold clumps. At least I assume they are fake?"

"Created by a loving volunteer at the mining museum who also puts these into small wooden mining carts they sell as souvenirs." Hazel gestured to the bunk bed against the wall. "There's our offering of collectible erasers."

Delta wanted to sit on her haunches to study the products closer, especially the miniature makeup replicas, including a blusher box that could be opened to reveal two colors and a little brush inside. But Hazel tapped her on the shoulder and gestured to follow her out of the cell, back into the main space where the sunlight through the windows gave the wooden surfaces an extra-warm glow.

Hazel pointed. "Now, there in the back we have the old umbrella stands with all the wrapping paper. Above, an old clothes rack with gift bags."

Bags in several shapes and sizes were hung by their ribbon handles from the rack. They came in bright colors with glitter or in intricate geometric patterns that created visual depth. Delta closed in and spotted a few Christmassy ones among the offerings. Picking out one with a cute design of cocoa mugs and sweet treats, she held it up to Hazel. "Candy canes already?"

Hazel laughed. "Christmas themes sell well all year round. There's just something quintessentially cozy about them. I've already scheduled some early November workshops we can do to teach people how to make menus and name tags to use on the dinner table, or teach pro-wrapping skills where we turn simple presents into gifts *extraordinaire*. I'll show you my idea list later on. I'm sure you have lots you want to add."

Delta nodded eagerly.

"But first to wrap up our tour: here's the old weapon rack where the sheriff could grab his double-barreled shotgun, now used to hold all my wrapping ribbons, stickers, and tags. The puffy stickers are selling especially well with kids."

Hazel smiled widely as she encompassed the whole shop with a wave of both her outstretched arms. "Now you're free to take a closer look at whatever you want to. And yes, co-owners do get a discount."

Delta made a beeline back to the old sheriff's desk and took the top notebook off a stack. "These dogs are adorable." Her finger traced the rows of small dachshunds, poodles, and Labs that marched across the hard cover. "In the city, I never got around to having a dog, you know. I was away most of the time, and it just seemed sad leaving him or her alone in the apartment all day long. I wonder if I could have a puppy here."

She opened the cover and leafed through the pages. "Wow, every page actually has a different dog. Aw, this border collie puppy is chasing a ball!"

"Remember that it's two for the price of one now! Speaking of, where did I put that arrow?" Hazel checked both hands and then began to look around her. "Maybe I dropped it outside?"

"Then it must be gone. There was a strong wind when I drove over here. Or someone stepped on it and it stuck to their shoe."

Ignoring Delta's predictions, Hazel ambled outside, scanning the pavement for the missing arrow.

Delta was completely engrossed in choosing the four notebooks she planned to purchase. Four initially seemed like a lot for someone who already had more notebooks than she knew what to do with, but in no time, she had selected six and was eyeing two more: one with dancing flamingos and one with letters that formed hidden words. Why not take them all?

Vaguely, she heard a footfall behind her, probably Hazel entering the store.

Suddenly, she felt a slight tug at her hair, and someone said, "Two for one. Yes, please."

Turning around, Delta found herself face-to-face with a grinning man with wild blond curls and brown eyes, a dimple in his cheek. He wore a crisp, white shirt, unbuttoned at the neck, and dark-blue jeans with a silver belt buckle of a running horse. He held up the bright-yellow arrow. "This was stuck to your back, half in your hair."

Delta flushed. "It must have gotten hung up there when

Hazel said hello to me. She's looking for that arrow. I'll take it out to her." She reached out her hand, and the man put the arrow in it. His infuriating grin stayed in place. "I haven't seen you here before. New to town?"

"I'm coming to live here. To run Wanted, with Hazel."

"Really? She didn't mention that to me." The man looked puzzled. Delta couldn't figure out why this man would think Hazel should have told him that Delta was moving to Tundish. Could it be her friend was dating him? Hazel hadn't mentioned anything about it, but then again, over the past few weeks, their conversations had been focused on practical details for Delta's move and the financial arrangements for co-ownership of Wanted, so maybe Hazel had figured she could tell her once she was in town.

Hazel's most recent relationship had ended in heartbreak when she found out the guy had been cheating on her. Delta had assumed her friend wouldn't have been eager to dive into something new, especially not one with a man whose athletic physique and cute dimple probably got a lot of female attention.

"Oh, there it is." Hazel buzzed up to Delta and reached out for the arrow with a smile. "I had no idea where it had disappeared to." Ignoring the man completely, she hurried outside again to put it in place.

To make up for her friend's rather brusque behavior, Delta asked quickly, "Is there anything you need from the shop?"

The man picked up a notebook with peacocks, their large purple-and-turquoise feathers adorned with little sparkly gold foil elements in them. It was the first on top of the stack, and he didn't look inside or check the price, just handed it to Delta as if he couldn't wait to get this chore over with. "Can I have this?"

"Of course, but"—Delta knew men often didn't like shopping, but still, he was entitled to a second notebook, under the deal advertised outside—"it's two for the price of one, so you can pick another for free. I can find you one that matches what you already have. Blue and gold…" She wanted to dig into the stacks, to extract those spines that looked like they might offer a color match, but he waved her off. "I only need one. Can you gift wrap it for me?"

"Certainly." Telling herself that the customer was always right, no matter how illogical their decisions might be, Delta took the notebook from his hand and walked to the cash register, feeling a little giddy at making her first sale. This was awesome, even better than she had imagined. She detected several rolls of wrapping paper stacked under the counter.

Acknowledgments and Author's Note

I'm grateful to all agents, editors, and authors who share online about the writing and publishing process. A special thanks to my amazing agent, Jill Marsal; my wonderful editors, Anna Michels and MJ Johnston; and the entire dedicated Sourcebooks/Poisoned Pen team, especially Katie Stutz and Shauneice Robinson; and Anne Wertheim and Dawn Adams for the adorable cover.

And thank you, reader, for picking up this book. The series as a whole combines two of my loves: stationery and the great outdoors. But in this installment, I could add another of my interests: miniatures. Tiny buildings, furniture for doll houses—I love everything on a small scale and even make some attempts at creating my own. Crafting very small objects is challenging, and at times frustrating, but also very satisfying when the result is lifelike and adorable. I just had to bring a miniature version of gold rush Tundish to Delta's store!

I loved including some new canine characters, Buddy and Prince, also, to underline the important work canines do in search and rescue. Dogs bring a book to life for me, and I love creating their very different personalities as much as I love writing my human characters.

If you're ever near Montana's Bitterroot Valley, you can see the remains of its gold rush past for yourself in the authentic little towns that inspired Tundish. I'm delighted that the Paper Posse's Wild West nicknames keep the stories alive of those remarkable women who were, as Mrs. Cassidy once put it, "seamstress by day, bank robbers by night."

I hope a slice of small-town life brought you a pleasant diversion and you will soon want to escape again into one of my fictional worlds. Happy reading!

About the Author

Always knee-deep in notebooks and pens, multi-published cozy mystery author Vivian Conroy decided to write about any paper crafter's dream: a stationery shop called Wanted. Her other loves, such as sweet treats, history, and hiking, equipped the series' world with a bakery, gold miners' museum, and outdoor activities. Never too far from a keyboard, Vivian loves to connect with readers via Twitter under @VivWrites.